PRAISE FOR IAN HAMILTON AND
THE LOST DECADES OF UNCLE CHOW TUNG SERIES

"I didn't think anything could top Ian Hamilton's Ava Lee novels for originality and style, but his backstory about the rise of Uncle Chow is even better . . . [Foresight] is one of his best." — *Globe and Mail*

"[Ian Hamilton is] a lively writer with an attentive eye for the details of complicated suspense." — *London Free Press*

"Hamilton does a masterly job capturing the sights, smells, and sounds of Hong Kong as he charts Chow's struggle to survive." — *Publishers Weekly*

"[Uncle's] rise through the ranks of the Hong Kong Triads makes for fascinating reading... Those fresh to Hamilton's work or simply looking for something familiar but different, meanwhile, will find much to like in the author's new series." — *Quill & Quire*

"A welcome origin story about the man who helped shape Ava Lee." — *Booklist*

"A magnetic tale of intrigue among rivals and cohorts, the early ascent of 'Uncle' Chow Tung within the Hong Kong Triads is exhilarating and utterly convincing. This is the first in a spin-off series that you'll want to keep spinning forever. Jump on at the start!" — John Farrow, bestselling author of the Émile Cinq-Mars series

"Ian Hamilton's knowledge of the Triads and their operations is fascinating — and slightly unsettling. He unwinds his tale of Uncle's origins with such detail that readers will wonder how he grew so familiar without being a triad himself. A must-read for fans of the Ava Lee novels!" — John Lawrence Reynolds, Arthur Ellis Award–winning author of *Beach Strip*

PRAISE FOR IAN HAMILTON AND THE AVA LEE SERIES

"The only thing scarier than being ripped off for a few million bucks is being the guy who took it and having Ava Lee on your tail. If Hamilton's kick-ass accountant has your number, it's up."
— Linwood Barclay

"Whip smart, kick-butt heroine, mixed into a perfect combination of adventure and exotic location. Can't wait to see where Ava is off to next." — Taylor Stevens, author of the Vanessa Michael Munroe Series

"A heck of a fun series, sharing Ian Fleming's penchant for intrigue and affinity for the finer things in life and featuring Ava Lee — a remarkable hero, a twenty-first-century James Bond with real depth beneath her tough-as-nails exterior. Five stars and first class!"
— Owen Laukkanen, author of *The Professionals*

"Ava Lee, that wily, wonderful hunter of nasty business brutes, is back in her best adventure ever." — *Globe and Mail*

"Slick, fast-moving escapism reminiscent of Ian Fleming." — *Booklist*

"A hugely original creation." — *Irish Independent*

"Crackling with suspense, intrigue, and danger, your fingers will be smoking from turning these pages. Don't ever, ever, mess with Ava Lee. She's not your average accountant." — Terry Fallis, author of *The Best Laid Plans*

FORTUNE

FORTUNE

THE LOST DECADES OF UNCLE CHOW TUNG

IAN HAMILTON

SPIDERLINE

Published in Canada in 2021 and the USA in 2021
by House of Anansi Press Inc.
www.houseofanansi.com

House of Anansi Press is committed to protecting our natural environment.
This book is made of material from well-managed FSC®-certified forests,
recycled materials, and other controlled sources.

House of Anansi Press is a Global Certified Accessible™ (GCA by Benetech)
publisher. The ebook version of this book meets stringent accessibility
standards and is available to students and readers with print disabilities.

25 24 23 22 21   1 2 3 4 5

Library and Archives Canada Cataloguing in Publication
Title: Fortune : the lost decades of Uncle Chow Tung / Ian Hamilton.
Names: Hamilton, Ian, 1946– author.
Identifiers: Canadiana (print) 20200273272 | Canadiana (ebook)
20200280740 | ISBN 9781487004026
(softcover) | ISBN 9781487004033 (EPUB) | ISBN 9781487004040 (Kindle)
Classification: LCC PS8615.A4423 F67 2021 | DDC C813/.6—dc23

Book design: Alysia Shewchuk

*House of Anansi Press respectfully acknowledges that the land on which
we operate is the Traditional Territory of many Nations, including the
Anishinabeg, the Wendat, and the Haudenosaunee. It is also the Treaty
Lands of the Mississaugas of the Credit.*

*We acknowledge for their financial support of our publishing program the Canada
Council for the Arts, the Ontario Arts Council, and the Government of Canada.*

Printed and bound in Canada

For Bruce Westwood,
with sincere thanks for ten years of support.

THE FANLING EXECUTIVE COMMITTEE

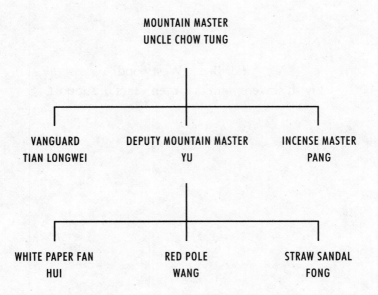

MOUNTAIN MASTER
UNCLE CHOW TUNG

VANGUARD
TIAN LONGWEI

DEPUTY MOUNTAIN MASTER
YU

INCENSE MASTER
PANG

WHITE PAPER FAN
HUI

RED POLE
WANG

STRAW SANDAL
FONG

THE MOUNTAIN MASTERS OF KOWLOON, HONG KONG ISLAND, AND THE NEW TERRITORIES

KOWLOON
Man

Yin

Zhao

Weng

HONG KONG ISLAND
Wanchai — Sammy Wing

Happy Valley — Tse

Causeway Bay — Feng

Central East — Yeung

Central West — Ling

NEW TERRITORIES
Tsuen Wan — Chow

Sai Kung — Ng

Mong Kok — Poon

Sha Tin — He

Mai Po — Tan

Tai Po — Deng

Yuen Long — Ching

Sha Tau Kok — Lee

Tai Wai — Wu Min

Fanling — Uncle Chow Tung

CHAPTER ONE
Macau
Tuesday, February 7, 1995

UNCLE CHOW TUNG SAT IN THE LOBBY OF THE GRAND Hyatt Hotel waiting for his friend Fong to arrive. It was nine o'clock in the evening. Uncle had arrived an hour earlier by jetfoil from Hong Kong to have dinner with Fong. He detested Macau and normally wouldn't have travelled there for any reason. But he was there at Fong's request, and given the nature of this particular invitation, Uncle couldn't say no to a man he loved like a brother.

Fong, a lifelong bachelor, had met a woman he was thinking of marrying. He had asked Uncle to have dinner with the two of them so he could give him a candid assessment of her. Uncle wasn't sure what he would learn about Fanny Wang over a meal, but he had agreed to come. The dinner was scheduled for ten, the lateness of the hour necessitated by Fanny's job as a mama-san, managing a group of sex workers based at the Lisboa Hotel. The nature of her job wouldn't prejudice whatever opinion he might reach about her. Uncle viewed prostitution, properly conducted, as a victimless crime, and he had learned early in his life not to pass judgement on what people did to survive.

Fong had arrived in Macau the day before, and Uncle was sure he had spent more time at the gaming tables than with Fanny. He was a compulsive gambler who had managed to convince himself there had to be a system that would beat the house at the roulette wheel or baccarat table. Fong had tried many; they had all failed, but his conviction didn't wane. He had agreed to meet Uncle in the lobby at nine, but he was obviously running late. Uncle imagined that, as always, Fong was trying to get that one last bet down — that one last bet that turned into twenty.

As Uncle sat contemplating his friend's weakness, he heard what sounded like a fight erupting at the hotel entrance. He stood up and walked in that direction. Whatever was going on had frightened the doorman, who, rather than intervening, was standing inside the lobby looking out through the revolving doors. Uncle went past him to the top of the steps that led into the hotel.

Two groups of men were facing each other. A group of five had a dominant position on the steps and were yelling insults and pointing fingers at a row of four men in front of them. Uncle could see guns tucked into the back waistbands of pants for at least two of the five. The men standing in the row were heavily tattooed and were waving knives in the direction of the quintet. *Triads*, Uncle thought.

"Hey, guys, what's going on here? This isn't the place to settle a dispute," he said.

One of the men on the steps turned to face him.

"I know you. You're Yin's deputy Red Pole," Uncle said.

"And I know you."

"You're a long way from Kowloon," said Uncle.

"We were sent here to help our brothers in Macau, members of Sun Yee On. These creeps have been poaching on their moneylending operations in the casinos."

Uncle knew a lot about Sun Yee On, including its more formal name, the New Righteousness and Peace Commercial and Industrial Guild. He had been approached years before by one of their senior people, and offered an opportunity to join the society and place his independent triad gang under its banner. At the time, Sun Yee On had more than fifty thousand members worldwide, but there were dozens of factions and subgroups within the organization. Men like Yin in Kowloon ran their gangs as they saw fit. Uncle was promised he could maintain his independence, but he still said no, just as he had said no to similar offers from 14K and Wo Shing Wo.

"That may be true, but squabbling in public like this isn't going to benefit anyone," said Uncle.

"We take our orders from Yin, and he said to keep these thieves out of the Hyatt's casino. We'll do whatever's necessary to make sure they don't get in."

The Hyatt fronted a main street, and Uncle saw that the dispute had attracted a crowd of curious onlookers. That wasn't good. He walked down the steps, slipped between two of the Kowloon gangsters, and approached the row of men.

"My name is Uncle. I'm the Mountain Master in Fanling. I'm here to meet a friend, nothing more. I think you should leave now and speak to your Mountain Master. Tell him I suggest he call Yin in Kowloon to settle this."

"He already knows these are Yin's men."

"Then tell him again," Uncle said. "Nothing positive is going to happen if you stay here."

The men looked at each other, and one said, "We should regroup. This isn't going to work." The others nodded and they started walking away from the hotel.

Uncle waited until they had gone down a side street and were out of sight before turning to face the men from Kowloon. "Why don't you vacate those steps now. You are blocking the entrance."

"We'll move off to the sides, but we're not leaving," the deputy Red Pole said.

"Whatever," Uncle said, becoming impatient with their thick-headedness. He stepped forward, the men parted, and he climbed the stairs to re-enter the hotel. There was still no sign of Fong as he sat down once more in the lobby.

He reached into the pocket of his black suit jacket and took out a racing form. Uncle's only hobby was betting on horse races. Twice a week for nine months of the year he could indulge his passion at the Happy Valley and Sha Tin racetracks. Since Happy Valley held its races on Wednesday nights, that was now the focus of his attention. He had bought the form the day before and had already handicapped the races in a cursory fashion, but it was on Tuesday nights that he really went to work. With that objective, he opened the paper.

For Uncle, handicapping horse races was an intellectual exercise that allowed him to escape the stresses that came with heading up a triad gang. The time he spent poring over the form comprised the only hours in the week when his mind wasn't being bombarded by thoughts about the gang's preservation and future. As usual, within a few minutes of opening the form he was immersed in the myriad factors he applied to decide a horse's chances of winning.

The race he was handicapping, though, presented a problem. As a rule, Uncle disliked backing favourites, and since fewer than 25 percent of favourites won at Happy Valley, he rarely bet on one at that track. But in this 1,200-metre race there was only one horse that stood out. In fact, Uncle couldn't imagine him losing and guessed he'd go off at odds of three to five. Frustratingly, there was no clear second choice, only a handful of horses that, with a perfect trip and ride, might challenge him. "I might have to bet on him," Uncle muttered as he drew a star next to the favourite.

There were noises again from outside, and this time Uncle froze. *No, they couldn't have!* he thought as he got to his feet and walked quickly to the entrance.

He was sure he had heard a burst of gunshots, and prayed that he hadn't. The doorman still hadn't ventured outside; he seemed rooted to his spot by the doorway. Uncle pushed past him and walked outside into chaos, overlaid with screams from some of Yin's triads and the frightened onlookers.

The three men who had occupied the left side of the stairs were all bleeding, and one had tumbled onto the street and was lying flat on his face. One of the men on the right had also been hit. The deputy Red Pole didn't appear to have been shot; he was kneeling next to the man on the street. Uncle went to him. "Is he badly hurt?" he asked.

The deputy looked up, a mixture of rage and grief contorting his face. "I think he's dead," he said. "They came in a car — drove by slowly and shot at us through the open windows. The cowards didn't have the balls to take us on man to man."

"Uncle!" a familiar voice called. Uncle looked up to see Fong coming towards him with a horrified expression on his face.

"These men are from Yin's gang. The shooters are local. The idiots decided to have it out in one of the most public places in Macau," Uncle said angrily.

"That's not the worst of it," Fong said, his voice shaky.

"What else has happened?"

Fong pointed to an area partly hidden by the steps, where a group of people had congregated. "A woman and her daughter were shot," said Fong. "It looks like the woman was hit in the arm, but the girl took a bullet to the chest. I don't think she's more than ten years old."

CHAPTER TWO

UNCLE AND FONG REMAINED OUTSIDE THE GRAND
Hyatt behind quickly assembled police cordons, as ambulances took away the wounded triads and the girl. They had avoided any contact with the police, and so had Yin's deputy Red Pole, who slipped away as soon as possible.

"I know this is bad," Fong said, "but I keep thanking god it didn't happen in Hong Kong. We'd have the entire OCTB up our ass."

The Organized Crime and Triad Bureau was a division of the Royal Hong Kong Police established specifically to deal with triads. "It's still bad. The Hong Kong newspapers will have this on every front page tomorrow, and it will be the lead on every TV and radio news program," Uncle said. "Look over there. There are at least three television crews here now, and the cops are giving them full access. And things could get much worse if the girl dies."

"What were Yin's men doing here in the first place?"

"They said they were supporting a fellow Sun Yee On gang that's in a dispute with an independent Macau gang over who controls moneylending in the casinos."

"They had no business being here."

"Maybe not, but there is the Sun Yee On connection," said Uncle.

"I have never heard any of Yin's guys make a big deal about being Sun Yee On."

"They don't when things are going well. But the moment they have problems they can't handle on their own, they turn to their brethren. We're lucky that all our gangs in the Territories are independent. The ones on Hong Kong Island and in Kowloon have complicated connections, which is why we need to keep this mess isolated here in Macau."

"Yin will retaliate," Fong said with complete certainty.

"I pray that he doesn't, but it's out of our hands. If he does, this could really get out of control. He isn't normally a hot-head, but these are stressful times and he might feel that he can't afford to look weak."

"Will you talk to him?" Fong asked.

"I'll call him as soon as I get back to Fanling," Uncle said, checking his watch. "I'm not staying for dinner. I'm going to catch the next jetfoil back to Hong Kong. That's where I need to be tonight. You'll have to explain that to Fanny."

"Don't worry about her. She'll be relieved. She was very nervous about meeting you," said Fong. "Do you want me to come with you?"

"No, I want you to stay here for at least another day. Keep your ear to the ground and let me know if there are any signs of trouble brewing."

"I'll do that."

It was impossible to get a taxi anywhere near the hotel, so Uncle walked to the jetfoil terminal. The boats left hourly, and he arrived just in time to get a first-class ticket on the one leaving at midnight. As soon as he settled into his seat, Uncle took out the racing form, but for once it did not hold his attention. His mind kept drifting back to the young girl and the lunacy of the attack on Yin's men.

There weren't many checks and balances in Macau. The police were notoriously corrupt, so the local gang wouldn't have thought twice about their drive-by shooting. But they should have been more cautious when it came to Yin's men. All the Kowloon-based gangs had a reputation for being tough and vengeful, and those headed by Man and Yin were the most feared.

Uncle hadn't misled Fong when he said he would call Yin, deliberately putting it off until he was home in Fanling. He needed time to think about how best to handle the conversation. He and Yin weren't friends, but they were respectful towards each other. When Uncle had made his first move to invest in China's special economic zones, Yin was one of the first two Mountain Masters who considered joining him. Yin had ultimately backed off, but Tse, from Happy Valley, hadn't, and he had since reaped profits that made his gang the wealthiest on Hong Kong Island.

Yin had never openly regretted his refusal, but once in a while, when there was a price increase for the knock-offs that had made Uncle's gang wealthy, he'd phone Uncle and ask him to withdraw it. "We were almost partners," he would say. "I left that money on the table for you." Sometimes Uncle cancelled the increase and other times he didn't. But he had never once even hinted to Yin that he'd had a chance to get in on the ground floor and had blown it.

Thoughts about Yin and the injured girl dominated Uncle's mind until the jetfoil arrived at the pier in Hong

Kong Central. Half an hour later a taxi dropped him off at his one-bedroom apartment in Fanling, above the Blind Emperor Restaurant.

The apartment was so sparsely furnished that it astonished the few friends who had been there. In the living room, a solitary red leather reclining chair sat facing the window, flanked by two small metal folding tables — on one sat his phone, on the other a large ashtray, a pack of Marlboro cigarettes, and several pencils. Next to the living room was a small kitchen. It had a fridge in which Uncle kept San Miguel beer, bread, butter, and marmalade. And a two-ring burner, which he couldn't remember ever turning on. The bedroom had a double bed, a four-drawer dresser, and a doorless closet in which hung four black suits and a row of white shirts.

Uncle took a San Miguel from the fridge and eased into the leather chair. He took a few sips and then reached for the phone. A woman answered after six rings.

"I am sorry for calling so late, but I need to speak to Yin," he said.

"He's not here," she replied.

"When do you expect him back?"

"I have no idea. He rushed out of here a few hours ago without saying where he was going."

Uncle's spirits sagged as he realized his chances of preventing an escalation of the feud were already diminishing. "When he comes home, or if he calls, could you ask him to call Uncle in Fanling. I don't care what the time is."

"I will."

Uncle sat quietly for a few minutes after ending the call. He thought briefly about reaching out to other Mountain Masters who were closer to Yin, such as Ng in Sai Kung and

Sammy Wing in Wanchai. But it was late, and if Yin wasn't reachable, what was the point? Besides, they had probably heard about what had happened in Macau. Unless he was mistaken, they would be keeping their heads down until things settled. His fervent hope was that there was some chance they would.

CHAPTER THREE

IT WAS TWO A.M. WHEN UNCLE WENT TO BED. YIN HADN'T called, and he hadn't heard from Fong.

He woke at six after a fitful sleep. He made an instant coffee, checked his voicemail in the unlikely case that he'd missed a call, and then sat in his chair with the racing form. He scanned his notes from the night before but again found his mind wandering. He tried to force himself to concentrate. Uncle had been introduced to horse racing by Fong, but unlike his friend he loved the fact that the sport lent itself to analysis and logic, whereas Fong would bet on a horse because he liked its name or the colour of its coat.

If Fong had been in Fanling, he would have gone with Uncle to the track that night. Since he wasn't, Uncle would go alone and most likely meet Tse or Sammy Wing, who were both regulars. His thoughts of them brought the events of the night before back into his mind. Would Yin have the sense not to retaliate against the Macau triads?

Uncle made another coffee and carried it into the bathroom, where he shaved, brushed his teeth, and showered. In the bedroom he put on black pants and a white shirt. His unchanging wardrobe was a habit he'd picked up when he left the ranks of the forty-niners — the gang's street soldiers — for his appointment as assistant White Paper Fan. It was an administrative position primarily responsible for looking after the gang's finances.

Uncle had only been in his early thirties when he took the job, young for a position with that much responsibility. His age and the fact that he wasn't a large man — a shade under five foot six and weighing only 130 pounds — resulted in some people not taking him seriously. He'd decided that the way he dressed and carried himself could partially correct that. From the first week of his new position he had worn only black suits and white shirts buttoned to the collar. Some of the forty-niners had found it amusing and began calling him "Uncle" for dressing like an old man. The nickname stuck, but it didn't take long for it to be used respectfully, as Uncle's competence and commitment immediately became apparent.

Unlike Fong and, indeed, nearly all the other Fanling triad members, Uncle hadn't been born in Hong Kong and his family had no triad ties. He was born in a village near Wuhan in central China and had escaped to Hong Kong in 1959 by swimming four kilometres across Shenzhen Bay. His entire family had died during the previous twelve months from starvation brought on by Mao Zedong's Great Leap Forward, or what Chinese people referred to as "the years of slow death." With him on the swim had been his fiancée, Lin Gui-San, who tragically drowned before she could reach Yuen Long, the town in the New Territories that was their destination. In the thirty-six years since, Uncle had had some business dealings with the Chinese Communists, but the one thing he could never forgive them for was her death.

Tam, one of the men from Uncle's village who had also made the swim with him, was related to Tian Longwei, the Vanguard of the Fanling Triad. Tam's intent was to join the triad as a Blue Lantern — a trainee — and he talked Uncle into joining with him. Tam didn't last three months, but Uncle stayed and grew to regard the gang as his family. It was a feeling that became more intense with each passing year, particularly when he became Mountain Master at the age of thirty-five and accepted responsibility for the health and welfare of 160 brothers and the extended triad family of about 600 people. He was sixty-one now, but his mind was still as sharp as ever. He showed no signs of slowing down and had no intention of retiring anytime soon.

One thing he did notice, Uncle thought as he slipped on his black suit jacket, was that he was beginning to reminisce more. He and Yin, Sammy Wing, and Tse had all been young men together, and when he thought of them, memories of their younger selves would sometimes intrude. Yin had been very violent when he was a forty-niner. Uncle thought he had moderated his behaviour in recent years, but he wondered if that was because circumstances hadn't tested him.

He'll use common sense, Uncle thought as he left the apartment and made his way downstairs. He walked from there to the gang's offices nearly every morning, with two stops in between. The first was at a newsstand to buy the *Oriental Daily News* and *Sing Tao*. He grimaced when he saw that both papers had the Macau shootings at the top of the front page. He put the newspapers under his arm and continued along the street to Jia's, his favourite congee restaurant.

He was early enough that there was no lineup, although

that wouldn't have made any difference, because Jia always seated him at once. He had been going to the restaurant for thirty years and couldn't remember a time when she wasn't there to greet him. She had to be in her seventies, he thought, but despite her age and a body that grew stouter by the year, she showed no signs of slowing down. Neither did her husband, who still manned the kitchen.

"Good morning, Uncle," Jia said as he walked through the entrance. "The table at the rear is yours."

"Thanks."

She pointed to his newspapers. "That was a terrible thing in Macau. How could they shoot that little girl?" she asked, well aware of Uncle's status as a triad.

"I don't know, but it's inexcusable."

She nodded. With her point made, she asked, "What will you have with your congee this morning?"

"Sausage, duck egg, scallions, and youtiao," Uncle said, and then walked to his table.

He looked at the *Oriental Daily News* first. "Young Girl Shot as Triads Battle in Macau" was the headline. He skimmed through a story that relied heavily on information and quotes from the Macau police. It named the four triads who had been shot and said they were residents of Kowloon. One had been badly wounded, but the police thought he'd live. The little girl who had been hit was eight years old and Macanese; she had been walking past the hotel with her mother. Nothing was mentioned about the severity of her injuries.

Sing Tao relegated the girl to a subheading under the main headline, which read "Triad Turf War Breaks Out in Macau." Then underneath, "8-Year-Old Girl Struck by Wayward

Bullet." To Uncle's chagrin the newspaper article included a quote from a senior officer in the OCTB. "We are concerned that this is not an isolated incident," he said. "There has been increasing aggression among various triad gangs in Hong Kong, and we are prepared to act swiftly and decisively if the violence in Macau is a prelude to similar actions in our territories."

Jia came to the table with a pot of tea and a bowl of congee. Uncle knew the add-ons he'd ordered would come in the second wave. Congee, or rice porridge, was bland by itself, so as Jia poured him a cup of tea, Uncle added white pepper and soy sauce to it.

When she left to get his other items, he opened the *Oriental Daily* to the horse-racing section. The paper had a top-notch handicapper, and any pick he made almost automatically lowered the odds on the horse. Uncle read his comments and smiled. Not including the sixth race, the handicapper had matched only two of Uncle's picks. In the sixth he had chosen the three-to-five shot, and Uncle knew that would reduce the odds to two to five or maybe even something as ridiculous as one to five. Whatever the final number, Uncle decided he would take his chances on a long shot.

The rest of his food arrived. Uncle added the egg, scallions, and sausage to the congee and dipped the youtiao fried bread sticks into it. He scanned the *Sing Tao* racing expert's selections as he ate, which distracted him so much that he didn't notice Jia had returned to the table. "Excuse me, Uncle, but Fong is on the phone for you. You can talk to him in our office."

Uncle felt a touch of apprehension as he slid from the booth. The office was not much bigger than three metres square, with space for a desk, chair, and filing cabinet. He closed the door behind him and picked up the phone. "I hope you aren't calling to tell me that things have gone from bad to worse in Macau," he said.

"The little girl died," Fong blurted out.

"How do you know?" Uncle asked, cursing beneath his breath.

"One of the nurses at the hospital works weekends for my mama-san. She just phoned with the news."

"So it isn't public yet?"

"No, but it won't take long for that to change. According to the nurse, there are all kinds of newspaper and television people at the hospital."

"Goddamn it!"

"Did you manage to get hold of Yin last night?"

"No, but I'll try again when I get to the office. I hope I can reach him, because now he really needs to back down. That girl's death will attract more negative attention, and if he attempts any kind of retaliation, he'll only add to it."

Fong hesitated. "There's something else I need to tell you, boss."

"Don't say Yin has retaliated already!" Uncle said.

"Nothing that dramatic, but it's a worry all the same. After you left last night, I went over to the Lisboa to gamble. I was playing roulette when Kan, the Straw Sandal in Tai Po, interrupted my game and said he wanted to speak to me. We went to a bar. I thought he wanted to talk about what had happened at the Hyatt, but as it turned out, he didn't know anything about it. All he wanted to do was ask me a question . . ."

"Please get to the point," Uncle said as Fong paused again.

"Well, he asked me if you've been attending Man's meetings in Kowloon."

"What meetings?"

"He said he didn't know their purpose," Fong said. "He'd just heard that Man has been inviting other Mountain Masters to dinner or lunch, and he wondered if you've been included. When I told him I didn't think so, he seemed to relax. Still, I found the question odd."

"I agree, it is strange. Why didn't Deng come directly to me with the question? The last I heard, he was still Mountain Master in Tai Po."

"Kan said he's incapacitated. He didn't want to go into detail, but he said Deng will be out of the loop for at least a month."

Uncle had known Deng was ill but had been told his cancer was under control. "Assuming that's true, why did Kan speak to you?"

"He and I have always been straight with each other. We've developed a certain trust over the years."

"Are you the only Straw Sandal he's questioned about the meetings?"

"So he claimed."

"He should ask more of them, and you should talk to some as well. Split the job between the two of you," Uncle said.

"Do you suspect that Man is up to something?" Fong asked.

"Not at all, but it would be foolish not to enquire," Uncle said. "Keep it low-key, though."

"Okay, boss."

"And Fong, I've changed my mind about you staying in Macau. The girl's death may alter the way the police here respond. I'd like to have you by my side in Fanling."

"I'll head for the jetfoil terminal as soon as I've had breakfast."

Uncle put down the phone and stood silently in front of a desk littered with invoices and receipts. There was a poster on the wall that showed twelve horses thundering down the stretch at Happy Valley. He looked at it absent-mindedly, his thoughts alternating between the potential impact of the young girl's death and the reflexive uneasiness that Kan's question to Fong had triggered. He sighed heavily, then left the office and returned to his congee.

Twenty minutes later, Uncle said goodbye to Jia and headed for the triad headquarters. It was a sunny, brisk morning, the kind that came too rarely to Hong Kong — the norm was hot, humid summers and damp, dark winters — and walking in such weather usually lifted his spirits. Not this time. Uncle's mind was focused on the phone call he had to make to Yin.

He neared the dress shop that occupied the ground floor of the two-storey building housing the triad office, and nodded at the two forty-niners standing guard on either side of the entrance. They opened the door for him and he climbed the stairs.

Headquarters was a large, open space with a scattering of desks, chairs, and filing cabinets, surrounded by seven enclosed offices, one for each member of the executive committee. Mo, the assistant White Paper Fan, who handled accounting, was the only person already at work. He stood up when Uncle entered the room. "Good morning, boss," he said.

"How did we do last night?" Uncle asked.

"It was a typical Tuesday. Business was slow everywhere."

"There's a good card at Happy Valley tonight. I expect we'll get lots of action in the betting shops."

The betting shops had been their largest source of income until the Hong Kong Jockey Club opened its own off-track operations. The gang's shops were still very profitable, but not close to what they had been. More than 70 percent of the triad's money now came from its Chinese operations; in fact, Uncle could have closed all their Fanling businesses and still have been able to look after the people who depended on him. But the Fanling businesses provided jobs and a sense of purpose, and those had a value that went beyond money.

"I'm going to watch the races at Dong's Kitchen," Mo said. "I like the atmosphere there, and of course you can't beat the food."

"Say hello to Tian for me," Uncle said. His old mentor was still active as the triad's Vanguard and also managed the betting shop at Dong's. "Now, I have some phone calls to make and I don't want to be disturbed."

"I'll tell anyone who arrives," Mo said.

Uncle settled in behind his desk and reached for the phone to call Yin. It rang four times before he heard the voice of the woman he'd spoken to the night before.

"I'd like to speak to Yin," Uncle said.

"He's not here."

"This is Uncle calling. Did you tell him I want to speak to him?"

"He didn't come home last night. I haven't seen or heard from him."

"When you do hear from him, please tell him it's urgent that he contact me."

"I'll do that," she said.

Uncle shook his head as he put down the phone. Was Yin really not at home or was he simply avoiding him? He sat back in his chair and weighed the options. Doing nothing wasn't one of them. He thought again about reaching out to Sammy Wing or Ng, and decided to call the Mountain Master of Sai Kung first.

No one answered Ng's home phone, and when Uncle called his office, he was told that Ng could be reached on his mobile. While more and more of his colleagues were using mobile phones, Uncle had resisted the trend. He embraced change in a lot of ways, but he had been told that the police could monitor calls made on cellphones. Still, it seemed to be the only way to reach Ng, Uncle thought as he dialled the number.

"*Wei*," Ng answered, the sounds of traffic in the background.

"This is Uncle. Can you call me back on a landline? I'm at my office."

"Is this urgent? I'm in my car and I won't be near a land-line for at least half an hour."

"Have you heard about what happened in Macau?" Uncle asked, deciding to forgo caution.

"Who hasn't? Those guys think they're cowboys and Macau is the Wild West," Ng said. "The place can get wild, I grant you that, but there's no reason to start shooting at brothers. I know they'll say they were simply defending their turf, but there's a time and place for everything. In front of the Grand Hyatt Hotel, with all those civilians coming and going, isn't the place."

"You heard about the little girl?"

"The papers are full of it."

"I mean, did you hear that she died this morning?"

Ng went silent and then said, "Fuck. We really didn't need that. How do you know about it?"

"Fong is in Macau, and he has a source who works at the hospital there. I don't think it's been made public yet."

"The publicity will be horrendous when it comes out," Ng said. "How do you think the cops will react?"

"I'm not sure exactly. All I know is that it would be wise for all of us to keep things as quiet as possible for the next few days."

"I agree. I'll pass the word on to my men."

"Has Yin contacted you? He's the one we really need to lie low. I've called his house twice, but I haven't been able to reach him."

"I haven't heard from him."

"Do you know anyone who has?" Uncle asked.

"No, but it's been a week since I talked to another Mountain Master."

"Isn't that unusual?"

"I don't know. I never gave it much thought," said Ng.

"So you haven't been in touch with Man?"

"I've got no business in Kowloon, and besides, I don't like that son of a bitch," Ng said. He hesitated before adding, "Is there a particular reason why you mention Man? Does it have something to do with what Yin's been up to?"

"No. I was told that Man's been meeting with various Mountain Masters. I was wondering if you were one of them."

"Meetings about what?"

"I have no idea."

"If it's true, I'm sure it has nothing to do with the New

Territories. All Man cares about is business in Kowloon and what's going on across the harbour on Hong Kong Island."

"That's what I've always assumed," Uncle said.

"And now you think differently?"

"No, I just heard a rumour about meetings and it made me curious."

"Are you going to talk to anyone else about this?"

"Perhaps."

"I will too. I'm tight with Poon in Mong Kok, and Zhao in Kowloon is married to my wife's cousin. Both of them have always been open with me," Ng said.

"I'm going to Happy Valley tonight. I normally see Sammy Wing and Tse there. If I do, I'll prod them a bit. But Ng, I think we both need to be subtle."

"I know I have a reputation for being blunt, but I can be sneaky when I need to be."

"I said subtle, not sneaky."

"They're the same thing as far as I am concerned."

"If you say so," Uncle said, and then he saw he had an incoming call. "Ng, I have to go. If you track down Yin, let me know, and let's touch base tomorrow morning about Man."

"Talk to you then, if not before," Ng said.

Uncle switched lines. "*Wei.*"

"There's more trouble here," Fong said in a rush.

"What's happened this time?" Uncle asked with a sense of dread.

"Kan just phoned me. He said the Macau gang's Red Pole was gunned down in front of his apartment building about half an hour ago."

"Was it those fools from Kowloon?" Uncle asked, knowing

what kind of chaos another killing would unleash.

"That's what everyone assumes."

"Is the Red Pole dead?" Uncle asked, grasping at a last vestige of hope.

"Uncle, there were four shooters. They weren't leaving anything to chance."

CHAPTER FOUR

THE ONLY POSITIVE THING UNCLE COULD WRING OUT of the news of the Red Pole's death was that it had happened in Macau. The former Portuguese colony was more than sixty kilometres by air or sea from Hong Kong, and more than a hundred by car. And the Macanese police force was less than zealous when it came to going after triads. Uncle could only hope they kept behaving like that. Still, he couldn't take it for granted, he thought, as he reached for the phone.

His first call was to Ng.

"I didn't expect to hear from you so soon," Ng said.

"I wish it wasn't necessary, but I thought you should know that the Macau gang's Red Pole was shot dead this morning outside his apartment," Uncle said. "We have to assume Yin was involved."

"He didn't waste any time, did he."

"No, he did not. What we need to do now is ensure that this is the end of it. We can't let things escalate any further or spill into Hong Kong," Uncle said.

"For that to happen, the guys in Macau will have to accept that their Red Pole's death squares things with Yin's Kowloon gang," Ng said. "I don't want to sound negative, but I don't think that's likely."

"I know. But, though they may not be in a mood to listen, we still need to try to talk sense into them," Uncle said. "Cho is the Mountain Master in Macau. Do you know him?"

"I've met him a few times but we barely spoke. I'm not sure he'd recognize me if we bumped into each other."

"I don't know him either. We have to find someone he knows and trusts who will be willing to talk to him."

"I've been told that your friend Tse helped finance Cho's moneylending business in the casinos."

"Then that's who I'll call," said Uncle.

"Good luck. I'll be in touch later today," Ng said.

This isn't how I planned to spend my morning, Uncle thought as he called Happy Valley. The phone rang five times before going to voicemail. It was the only number Uncle had for Tse. "This is Uncle. I need to talk to you. Call me as soon as you can," he said, and then sighed in frustration.

He got up from his desk and went into the outer office. Hui, his White Paper Fan, was standing at Mo's desk and the two men were talking.

"Do you want to go over the accounts?" Hui asked Uncle.

"Maybe later. For now I'd like to talk to you in my office," Uncle said.

Hui followed him and sat in one of the two chairs in front of Uncle's desk. "Is this about Macau?" he asked.

"Yes. Did you hear the girl died?"

"No. That's really bad news."

Hui had succeeded Xu Bo, Uncle's closest friend, as White

Paper Fan when Xu left Fanling to return to his home city of Shanghai. When Mao Zedong had taken power in China, one of the first things he did was order the People's Liberation Army to eradicate the triads. Xu, like nearly every other gang member, had fled China to go to Hong Kong. His return more than ten years earlier had been negotiated with Deng Xiaoping by Uncle. Since then, Xu had been slowly and carefully building his own gang from scratch in Shanghai, using the strategies Uncle employed in Fanling. Uncle wasn't as close to Hui but respected him for his talents as a money manager, and for an attitude that was low-key and typically unflappable.

"As bad as it is, I'm even more worried about what's going on between Yin and the Macau gang," Uncle said. "Macau's Red Pole was killed this morning, and whether Yin's people did it or not, they're going to be blamed."

"Who else could have done it?"

"No one I can think of."

"You're obviously concerned about the violence spreading," Hui said.

Uncle wasn't surprised by how calmly Hui had processed the situation, and that was one reason why he was discussing it with him. "I want to reach out to the Mountain Master in Macau through Tse, but I haven't had any success. And even if I can get Tse to intervene, there's no guarantee he'll be able to put out the fire," Uncle said. "I'd like to get the executive committee together this afternoon. We need to have a plan in place if this spirals out of control. Call everyone and ask them to be here for two. Don't bother about Fong; he's on his way back from Macau and will come directly to the office."

"Okay, boss."

"One more thing," Uncle said. "I've been told that Man

has been meeting with some of the other Mountain Masters. I don't know the details, but I'd like to find out. Fong and Kan, the Straw Sandal in Tai Po, are making some discreet phone calls. I'd like you to do the same."

"Meetings about what?"

"I don't know, but I'd like you to find out."

Hui pursed his lips. "Things have been quiet. When I mentioned that to Wang last week, he said maybe things are too quiet."

"It's Wang's nature to be paranoid, which is one of the reasons he's such a good Red Pole. Thank god we have him," Uncle said. His pushed aside his newspapers and the racing form. "I'll go over the accounts now. Ask Mo to bring them in."

The paperwork occupied the next three hours, as Uncle didn't just review the accounts but also compared the numbers against those on charts he kept in his desk drawer. The charts were a historical record of the gang's finances from the days when Uncle was White Paper Fan. He had started keeping them during his first year, as a way of providing perspective whenever financial decisions had to be made. Many of his colleagues tended to think in the short term, almost day-to-day, and were always eager to spend money without considering the long-term implications. Uncle had thought it was his responsibility to explain the consequences of their management decisions. When he became Mountain Master, he maintained the charts; even though there weren't many projects the gang couldn't afford to undertake, he liked the financial discipline they imposed.

When he had finished, he tucked the racing form under one arm and carried the account reports into the outer office.

Mo was at his desk, two clerks had arrived, and through a glass window Uncle could see Hui on his office phone. Uncle handed the printed sheets back to Mo. "I'm going to the café across the street for a coffee. I'll be back in an hour," he said.

The café had three tables set up on the sidewalk. There had been a time in Fanling when tables on the sidewalk meant an eviction was in progress, but the town — like the rest of Hong Kong — was becoming more westernized. Shops that served brewed coffee instead of instant were popping up all over town. Uncle still made instant at his apartment, but the café had become a frequent haunt. He sat at the last available table, ordered a plain black coffee, and began to scour the racing form for nuggets of information he might have overlooked. Two coffees and five cigarettes later, he folded the form. Unlike most race days, Uncle now had a firm notion of which horse he was going to bet on in every race, and barring anything dramatic like a late scratch, a jockey change, or a massive shift in the odds, he wasn't likely to change his mind.

Uncle rose from the table. As he started across the street, he saw Fong getting out of a taxi in front of the office. He shouted and Fong waved, then stood waiting for him. He carried an overnight bag that was so small Uncle doubted it could hold more than a toilet kit, a change of underwear, and a clean shirt. Like Uncle, Fong lived a spartan life, except for him it wasn't by choice — gambling consumed most of his money.

"Hey, boss, has anything happened since we talked?" Fong asked.

"No. I reached out to Yin and I called Tse to ask if he'd talk to Cho, the Mountain Master in Macau, but I didn't manage to talk to either of them," he said. "I did speak to Ng, and he's making some phone calls about Man. I've asked Hui to do the same. I figure that between you, Kan, and them we'll get an idea of what's going on."

"I haven't made any calls yet. I'll start when I get upstairs."

"I've called an executive committee meeting for two o'clock, so you don't have much time. Everyone but Yu should be there," said Uncle. His deputy Mountain Master wasn't due back from a holiday in Thailand until the next day.

"Speaking of the committee, here come Wang and Tian," Fong said, looking past Uncle.

Uncle turned to greet his old comrades. The two men walked side by side, Tian holding on to the larger, stronger Wang's arm for support. Tian was in his seventies and had suffered from arthritis for many years. Some days the pain was so bad it crippled him, yet he never complained and never missed a day of work. Wang was in his late sixties, which was old for a man responsible for protecting the gang members and their turf. But he was still fit and adept with knife and gun, projected a fearsome demeanour that accurately reflected his fierce interior, and had the complete loyalty of his foot soldiers.

The four men exchanged handshakes and Uncle hugged Tian gently. "How are you feeling today, my old friend?" he asked.

"I've been better and I've been worse, but it's a long time since I've been this angry," Tian said. "I assume this meeting is to talk about what those fucking idiots in Kowloon and Macau have been doing."

"It is, but let's not start until Pang arrives and we're all settled upstairs."

Tian's progress on the stairs was slow and awkward as he and Wang took one careful step at a time, Uncle and Fong trailing behind. Uncle knew Wang could easily have carried him, but Tian was a proud man and would have considered that humiliating. By the time they reached the top, Pang, the gang's Incense Master, had joined them. The five men went directly to the boardroom, where Hui was waiting. The room was the same size as the executive offices and couldn't accommodate anything more than a large, round table, six chairs, and a side table. Hui had set up an ice bucket full of beers, a pitcher of water, and six glasses on the smaller table.

"Thanks to all of you for coming at such short notice," Uncle said, taking a bottle of San Miguel from the bucket before he sat down. Everyone except Tian followed suit.

"What are you hearing on the street about this mess in Macau?" Uncle asked.

Wang, Tian, and Pang exchanged looks as if they were determining who would go first. Tian was the most senior; when Wang nodded at him, he said, "The men, like me, are angry. There's no excuse for bringing civilians into a turf war. And killing that girl was unpardonable. Whoever fired the bullet that killed her should be thrown out of the brotherhood."

"Or worse," Wang said.

"According to what I was told, there's no way of knowing who fired the actual bullet. It was a drive-by, with four shooters firing at the same time," Fong said.

"Then the brotherhood should deal with whoever gave the order," Wang said.

"I don't think that's going to happen. The order probably came from Cho, the Mountain Master," Tian said.

"Do you know him?" Uncle asked.

"I met him a few times when I was a forty-niner, and then later when we set up our first betting shops. He visited to see how they worked and if he could copy them in Macau," Tian said. "He was a mean prick then and, from what I've heard, he hasn't improved."

"Well, whatever his mood, it could only have gotten worse after what Yin did this morning," Fong said.

"What are you talking about?" Wang asked.

"Cho's Red Pole was shot and killed outside his apartment building this morning," Uncle said.

"What a dumb thing to do," Tian said.

"Yin's gang has to be twice the size of Cho's. Maybe Cho will see reason and not take this any further," Hui said.

"Not a chance," said Tian.

"Cho has a decent working relationship with Tse. I'm hoping Tse will agree to try to talk sense into him," said Uncle.

"You could send the entire United Nations to talk to him, it won't make any difference. If Yin took out his Red Pole, Cho is going to retaliate," Tian said.

"If he does, and he chooses to do it in Kowloon, that's going to bring in the OCTB," Uncle said. "And if they do come in, they won't restrict themselves to Yin's turf in Kowloon. They'll be up everyone's ass."

"What can we do?" Pang asked.

"I won't give up on Tse. Hopefully I'll see him tonight at Happy Valley and convince him to at least try to talk Cho into a truce," Uncle said. "But, given Tian's pessimism, I think we'll have to prepare for some upheaval."

"We assume a low profile?" Wang asked.

"Yes, as low as possible. Let's close the casinos for now.

We'll operate the betting shops tonight, but let's not commit to opening them on Sunday until we know where things stand," Uncle said. "I can't imagine the night market or the massage parlours being a police target, so we'll leave them alone."

"We're going to lose quite a bit of income," Hui said.

"We can afford it. I would rather lose a few days or even weeks of revenue than risk blowing up everything we've spent all these years building," Uncle said. "We also have some official relationships we have to protect. We can't forget about them."

Among the executive committee — and, in fact, among the entire Hong Kong triad community — it was common knowledge that Uncle had a special contact within the Hong Kong police, but the only other person who knew the contact's name was Tian. The contact was Zhang Delun, and he was now Chief Superintendent of the Northern New Territories Division of the Hong Kong Police Force. Tian had been friends with Zhang's father, also a policeman, and had looked after Zhang and his family when the father died. As a mentor to both Uncle and Zhang, Tian had recognized the young men's pragmatism and trustworthiness. He had brought them together, believing that, despite their divergent career aspirations, they could help each other. His judgement had been sound. Over the years, Zhang and Uncle had exchanged information, confidences, and favours that contributed to both the welfare of their organizations and to their own advancement.

"Will you speak to your contact?" Wang asked. "He might know if the OCTB is prepared to strike even if the problem is in Macau."

"It's too soon for that," Uncle said. "I'll wait until I see how Cho reacts."

"If Tian is right about Cho," Hui said, "this could be the start of a war."

CHAPTER FIVE

UNCLE LEFT FANLING IN A TAXI AT FIVE-THIRTY TO make his way to Happy Valley. He had invited Fong to join him but his Straw Sandal had begged off; what with the shootings, gambling, and servicing his mama-san, he hadn't had much rest the night before. "Then use at least part of the evening to make those phone calls about Man to the other Straw Sandals," Uncle had said.

The taxi took Uncle as far as Tsim Sha Tsui in Kowloon. He could have stayed in the car to travel to Hong Kong Island via the Cross-Harbour Tunnel, but out of habit and a bit of superstition he took the Star Ferry across Victoria Harbour to Central and then caught a cab to Happy Valley. The race-track was already packed when he arrived, and he smiled when he heard the familiar buzz of excitement in the air. It didn't seem to matter how often he walked through those gates; every time he did he felt a surge of adrenalin.

He made his way to the grandstand on the third level, settled into his seat, and opened the racing form. His choice for the first race, which had been at four-to-one odds in the morning line, was now five to one. He smiled. It was a good sign when the odds were moving in his favour. He decided to bet on the horse to win and place, and then chose two horses to include in quinellas with it.

He went inside the grandstand to the betting windows. As always, the lineups were long, but they moved quickly, and Uncle got his bet down ten minutes before post time. The horses were on the track when he returned to his seat, and he studied his choice. The three-year-old colt had a spring in his step and looked eager to run. Uncle eyed the inside of the horse's back legs, looking for any sign of sweat that might indicate he was stressed. He saw none and sat back, feeling confident about his chances.

Twenty minutes later Uncle re-entered the grandstand with his winning tickets. He started each visit to the race-track with a budget based on how much he was prepared to lose if all his choices ran out of the money. But the budget was adjustable if he was ahead, and there was no better way to begin an evening than with a big win. He'd double his bet for the next race, and there would be no limit to what he could be betting by the end of the night if he kept winning.

"Uncle, are you in line to bet or to cash?" a familiar voice asked.

Uncle turned and saw Sammy Wing standing in the line next to him. "I won. How did you do?"

"My horse was second, but I had him in the quinella."

"That was shrewd," Uncle said. "I was hoping you'd be here. Is Tse with you?"

"Yeah. He decided to splurge — we're sitting in a box. He knew you'd be here and wants you to join us."

Uncle cashed in and then stood off to one side to wait

for Sammy. He and Uncle were the same age and the same height, but Sammy weighed about double what Uncle did. He had always been heavy-bodied, but now he was just fat. The agility he'd possessed as a younger man was gone, replaced by a waddle.

Sammy had joined the triads when he was eighteen, so he had spent seven more years in the brotherhood than Uncle. They had never been close friends — more friends of convenience. Sammy had always assumed he'd become the Mountain Master in Wanchai, and when Uncle achieved that goal in Fanling five years before him, Sammy responded with a resentment that didn't end until he'd finally made it to the top. Once they were colleagues of equal rank, Sammy had become more amenable, and Uncle was businesslike enough to forget the other man's jealousy.

"How much did you win?" Sammy asked as he approached.

"Nine thousand," Uncle said.

"When you retire, you can make your pocket money here and in Sha Tin."

"I have no intention of retiring."

"Me neither," Sammy said.

"What do you think about the recent events in Macau?" Uncle asked as he followed Sammy to the box.

"A disaster."

"What does Tse think?"

"Ask him yourself."

Tse stood up as they entered the private box. He was five years younger than both of them, six inches taller than either of them, and as thin as Uncle. "So good to see you, Uncle," he said.

The box had six chairs in a row facing the track. In front

of the chairs a ledge ran from wall to wall, providing a rest-ing place for drinks and racing forms. There was a bottle of water and another of San Miguel on the ledge.

"Are you the only occupants?" Uncle asked.

"Yes," Tse said. "I got your message from earlier today. I knew you wanted to talk, so I thought we should have some privacy."

"I'm very concerned about what's going on between Cho and Yin," said Uncle.

"We all are," Tse said. "Take a seat."

"Have you heard anything from your police contact?" Sammy asked.

"Not yet, but my fear is that when I do, it will be too late to stop what those warring idiots have set in motion," Uncle said. He took a seat next to Tse.

"Yin did have a right to support his Sun Yee On brothers in Macau," Sammy said.

"Are you suggesting that Cho didn't have a right to defend his turf?" Tse asked.

"No," Sammy said, after a slight hesitation.

"Let's assume you're both correct," Uncle said. "That still doesn't make it any less of a mess. After killing the Red Pole, Yin will feel that he's evened the score. Tse, I'm told that you know Cho quite well. How do you think he'll respond? Is there any chance he'll decide there's nothing to be gained by retaliating?"

"I've been doing business with him for six years. *Reasonable* is not a word I'd use to describe him. He's hard-headed and he loses his temper more easily than most," Tse said. "Part of the problem is that he feels he has the Macanese police in his pocket and he doesn't have to worry about the ocTB."

He thinks he's insulated from the machinations of the Hong Kong gangs."

"Are you saying he'll extend this war with Yin?" Uncle asked.

"It's more of a skirmish than a war," Sammy said. "Besides, despite my friend Tse's opinions about Cho, I have to think the man is smart enough to realize that taking on Yin's gang is a losing proposition."

"He is smart, but not in the way you suggest," Tse said to Sammy.

"What do you mean?" Uncle asked, noticing Sammy's frown at the rebuke.

"He knows we're apprehensive about the OCTB, while he has nothing to fear from the Macanese cops," Tse said. "He might be willing to gamble that it's Yin who won't risk taking this feud any further."

"Do you really think he'd risk striking back at Yin for the death of his Red Pole?" Uncle asked.

"That's what I expect is in his mind."

"Can you talk to him?" Uncle asked.

"Yes. In fact, I've already made plans to go to Macau tomorrow," Tse said. "He's agreed to meet with me, but I can't promise he'll listen."

"I feel better already, just knowing that you're going," said Uncle.

"I'll do what I can," Tse said, then turned towards the track. "But enough about Cho. Which horse do you like in this race?"

Uncle's success in the first race was duplicated in the second, and both he and Tse cashed in large winning tickets. Sammy went with a different choice, lost, and then grumbled about the jockey who had been riding his horse. Uncle smiled and said nothing. One of the reasons he hadn't bet on that horse was precisely because of the jockey.

Uncle's winning streak ended in the third race, and he also failed to cash in for the fourth and the fifth. All three men were now drinking beer, and their conversation had become less guarded. Sammy openly enjoyed each of Uncle's losses and couldn't resist bragging about his wins. He was betting on the favourites. Uncle was tempted to point out that one of his wins had returned more money than three or more of Sammy's combined, but he resisted.

Tse had been betting on Uncle's choices. "We need to recoup," he said to Uncle as he looked at the sixth-race entries.

"Number five can't lose," Sammy said.

Number five was the favourite that Uncle had put a star next to on his racing form. "I can't bet on a horse that returns two-to-five odds," he said. "I think number three has a shot, and it's at eight to one."

"A small return on a sure thing is better than no return on a long shot," Sammy said.

"There are no sure things in horse racing," Uncle said.

"For a man who has a reputation for being the most cautious of any of us, it always surprises me to see the chances you're willing to take at the racetrack," Sammy said. "I've often wondered, which is the real Uncle?"

Uncle shrugged. "I'm going to bet now," he said to Tse. "Do you want me to place yours or will you do it yourself?"

Tse reached into his pocket. "Put five hundred on the number-three horse to win and place," he said to Uncle.

Uncle placed their bets, and when he returned to the box,

he saw there was a fresh round of beers. He took a deep swig and noticed that his colleagues had already downed half their bottles. "Since you're both here, do you mind if I save myself having to make phone calls to you later?" Uncle asked.

"Phone calls about what?" Sammy asked.

"I've been told that Man has been holding a series of meetings with some of the Mountain Masters. I was going to ask if either of you has been part of them."

Sammy glanced ever so briefly at Tse and then quickly turned to Uncle. "I have no idea what meetings you're referring to," he said.

He's lying to me was Uncle's immediate thought, but he simply nodded and said nothing. He looked at Tse, who was staring very deliberately at the track, where the horses were being assembled at the starting gate.

"Your pick looks ready to run," Tse said to Uncle as the gate opened and the horses hurtled out.

The race was a thousand metres. After five hundred, Uncle's horse was last, more than fifteen lengths behind the favourite. He said, "He may have looked ready, but I'm afraid this isn't his day."

The number-three horse made up a little ground in the stretch, but it still finished ten lengths behind number five.

"See, there *are* sure things," Sammy said.

Ten minutes later Sammy left the box to cash in his ticket. Uncle waited for a minute after the door closed before he said to Tse, "Why is Man having meetings?"

"Don't be paranoid."

"So he is having meetings."

"Yes, but they aren't anything for you to get alarmed about," said Tse. "He's concerned about what's going to happen when the British hand over Hong Kong to the Chinese. That's only two years away, and he believes it's time we started focusing on it."

"Focus on it how?"

"As you know better than most, the Communists don't have much tolerance for triads. I know you negotiated our way back in to China to a small extent, but there's still a fear that when the Communists take over Hong Kong, they will consider us a threat and try to destroy us."

"And how does Man intend to deal with that threat — if it actually materializes?" asked Uncle.

"He believes the triads need to consolidate their bases. The stronger each gang is, the less eager the PLA or the Security Service might be to take us on."

Uncle stared at Tse until his colleague averted his eyes. Tse looked uncomfortable, and that in turn spiked Uncle's discomfort. "I agree it makes sense to discuss the implications of the Chinese takeover," he said slowly. "What I don't understand is why Man is meeting with Mountain Masters on an individual basis, and why no one in the New Territories has been invited."

"Man thinks the greatest threat is to the big-city gangs on Hong Kong Island and in Kowloon. We're the largest and most visible," Tse said. "With all due respect to the New Territories, he doesn't think the Communists will concern themselves with gangs in places like Tai Po."

"Or Fanling."

"Perhaps."

Uncle drained his beer. "Assuming that's true, what does Man mean specifically when he says the city gangs need to consolidate their bases and grow stronger?"

"He says they need to recruit more men."

"Is that all?"

"No," Tse said, then became quiet.

"Don't stop there," said Uncle.

Tse sighed. "I think I've already said too much. I'm worried that anything else I say might be misconstrued."

Uncle started to speak but stopped at the sound of a loud knock on the door.

"Come in," Tse said, sounding relieved.

The door opened and a man Uncle recognized as Tse's Red Pole stood grim-faced in the entrance.

"What's going on?" Tse asked.

"Boss, there's been a shootout in Kowloon."

"Who's involved?"

"Yin's crew and the gang from Macau."

"Are you sure it was them?"

"I'm certain about Yin, and who else would attack them on their home ground than those idiots from Macau?"

"How bad is it?"

"At least two of Yin's men and one of the guys from Macau are dead. More are wounded. The Macau gang burst into a bar where Yin's guys gather."

Tse looked at Uncle. "I guess that means there's no reason for me to go to Macau tomorrow."

CHAPTER SIX

UNCLE LEFT THE HAPPY VALLEY RACETRACK FIFTEEN minutes later, not sure what he should be most worried about — the escalating war between Macau and Kowloon, or what Tse had told him about Man. He was desperate to get to a phone but first had to endure two cab rides and the ferry trip across the harbour before he got to his apartment. The travel time passed so slowly he almost wished he had one of those new mobile phones.

When he reached his apartment, Uncle raced upstairs. His first call was to Wang, at the restaurant he used as his nighttime headquarters. "Those fools from Macau attacked Yin's men in Kowloon tonight. They killed at least two," he said as soon as he heard Wang's voice. "We should prepare for the OCTB to authorize an offensive against all the gangs. Keep our men off the streets. Let's not give them any easy targets."

"Okay, boss."

"I'll touch base later when —" Uncle started to say, then saw he had an incoming call that couldn't be ignored. "I have to go. We'll talk later," he said quickly, and switched lines.

"Uncle, what the hell is going on with you people?" Zhang Delun asked.

"There's a dispute between one of the gangs in Kowloon and one in Macau. It will be resolved."

"Is this a carryover from the shootings in Macau?" Zhang asked.

"Yes."

"We can't tolerate that kind of behaviour in Hong Kong. If there are disputes, they should be settled in private, not in public."

"I know, but the problem is restricted to Kowloon. You know we maintain peace in the New Territories."

"Headquarters doesn't differentiate between triads in the northern sector and triads in Kowloon," Zhang said. "I want you to know that we've been put on alert. If there's any more violence, every division will be expected to take some kind of action. Pass the word to your colleagues."

"Most of them dislike public displays of violence as much as you do, but I will talk to them, and we'll bring whatever influence we have to bear on the Macau-Kowloon situation."

"Do it quickly. As I said, we've already been put on alert, and it won't take much to trigger a reaction."

"Thanks for the call. It's appreciated."

"Keep your head down, Uncle," Zhang said, and ended the conversation.

Uncle felt a sense of relief as he hung up. That the police weren't yet committed to coming after them was good news; the fact that they had been put on alert wasn't. What was important now was to bring an immediate end to the hostilities between Yin and Cho. He thought about who to call next and decided Tse was still the best option. Uncle thought he would have gone home after the racetrack and dialled that number.

"*Wei*," Tse answered.

"This is Uncle."

"I was hoping you'd call," Tse said. "Have you heard from your police contact?"

"He says all the divisions have been put on alert, but they won't do anything drastic unless there's another public display of violence," Uncle said.

"Thank goodness they're holding off."

"We still need to bring an end to this nonsense, and we have to do it as quickly as possible," Uncle said. "I've been thinking about Macau. You should reconsider your decision. Someone has to talk to Cho, and you're the best man for the job. Don't say no to me."

"Cho isn't the immediate problem right now. Surely we have to expect that Yin will raise the stakes again. I can't believe he won't strike back."

"I'll talk to Yin."

"Good luck with that," Tse said.

"This can't continue."

"I agree, but there's no point in my going to Macau. What's done is done," Tse said. "Our best chance to stop this stupidity is for you to convince Yin to declare a truce."

Uncle put down the phone and walked into the kitchen. He took a beer from the fridge and then retreated to the comfort of his chair. He reclined it, took a swig of beer, and thought about how complicated relationships among Mountain Masters could be. Theoretically they were all part of the same organization, but that was like saying they were all members of the same political party. There was still fierce competition, rivalries, conspiracies, backstabbing, and questionable ultimate loyalties. One large difference was that a political party had a leader who could pull together all those different personalities and positions and maintain a semblance of unity. Beyond the rank of Mountain Master there was no senior leadership role, and Uncle knew they all suffered because of it.

His phone rang. Thinking it might be Tse, he leapt for it. "This is Uncle," he said.

"Ng here."

"Are you calling about the shootout in Kowloon?"

"Partially. What are the Hong Kong police going to do?"

"Nothing for now, so we still have a chance to calm things," Uncle replied. "Tse won't go to Macau tomorrow to talk to Cho, but I'm going to try to convince Yin to back off."

"I'm not sure talking to Yin will do any good. That's the other reason I'm calling," Ng said carefully. "From what I've been told, what happened in Macau was planned and deliberate. Yin went there looking for trouble, and he has no intention of stopping until he's taken control of that sector."

"What are you talking about?" Uncle asked. "What I heard was that he went to Macau to support the local Sun Yee On gang."

"He'll support them until he doesn't need them, and then he'll take them over as well."

"Who told you this?" Uncle asked.

"I can't say."

"Zhao?"

"I gave my word that I wouldn't mention my source," Ng said. "Besides, what I heard was an opinion, not something backed by hard facts."

"If it isn't based on facts, what is it based on?"

"Things he heard and the conclusions he drew from them."

Uncle felt his patience slipping and caught himself. "Ng, you and I have been colleagues and friends for a very long time. Have you ever known me to betray a confidence, no matter how large or small?"

"No, Uncle, I haven't."

"Then could we please stop dancing around what's obvious? I know you spoke to Zhao and that everything you're telling me came from him."

"I won't dispute that," Ng said after a slight hesitation.

"That's a good start," Uncle said. "Now please tell me why Zhao thinks Yin's aggression in Macau was planned."

Ng paused again, then said, "You were correct about Man having meetings with various Mountain Masters, but so far it's only been with the ones who control Hong Kong Island and Kowloon — and one from the Territories."

"Who from the Territories?"

"Wu."

It was Uncle's turn to pause. Wu ran Tai Wai New Village and had tried several times to infiltrate Fanling's operations. "What was the purpose of these meetings?" he asked, putting aside for the moment his concerns about Wu.

"Man believes that when the Chinese Communists take over Hong Kong, one of the first things they'll do is go after us. He has been trying to convince the Mountain Masters in Kowloon and Hong Kong Island to form an alliance."

"Tse said something similar. Is Man trying to pull the gangs together?"

"I think it started that way, but the idea fell apart because the Hong Kong Island gangs don't trust the Kowloon gangs,"

Ng said. "So then Man suggested that the Hong Kong Island and Kowloon gangs each form their own alliance but pledge to stay out of each other's way."

"What did Man mean by *forming an alliance*?"

"Zhao was vague."

"Did Zhao commit to join?"

"He said no, but I interpreted that as *not yet*. He may not trust Man, but he's nervous that the other three gangs will get together and come after him."

"Putting three of those gangs together would create a small army," Uncle said. "It would be tempting to use that kind of firepower — and not just for defence."

"Kowloon's main rivals are the Hong Kong Island gangs, who are as strong as they are. I can't imagine they'd risk taking them on directly," Ng said.

"I don't care about Hong Kong Island," Uncle said. "I'm more concerned about the New Territories. Does Man's master plan include us in any way?"

Ng hesitated and then said, "Uncle, this is still in confidence, yes?"

"Absolutely."

"Zhao has heard rumours."

"That alarms me, because Zhao isn't a man who repeats rumours unless he thinks there's validity to them."

"I share that opinion."

Uncle took a deep breath. "Go ahead. Tell me what he had to say."

"Man has been trying to convince the other Kowloon triad leaders that they need to expand their bases, but as it stands, the four gangs are crowded together in a small territory with no room to grow. He's saying that the easiest and most logical way for them to expand is by taking over smaller, more vulnerable gangs."

"And given that the smaller gangs are not in Kowloon or on Hong Kong Island," Uncle said, "it doesn't take much imagination to conclude they'll be looking at the New Territories."

"And Macau," Ng added quickly. "Zhao says that Yin has bought into Man's ideas and is making a play to take control of Macau. The others are watching to see how the other gangs and the police react. If Yin is successful, it might embolden them to try it themselves."

"Try it where, specifically? Including Tai Wai, the New Territories have ten gangs."

"Zhao doesn't know. He was cut out of further conversations after he expressed reservations about the alliance."

Uncle drained his beer and sat forward in the chair. "How concerned are you by all this?"

"I'm trying to stay calm. I keep telling myself that, despite Zhao's usual reliability, these are only rumours and I shouldn't take them to heart."

"Macau isn't a rumour."

"No, but that story hasn't played itself out yet. Maybe Cho will be able to fend off Yin. Maybe the Macau police and the OCTB will get involved and bring it to an end."

Uncle sighed. "I don't share your optimism, or I should say I think it's dangerous to be optimistic," he said. "Can you excuse me for a minute while I get another beer?"

"Sure. I'll do the same thing," Ng said.

Uncle slid from his chair and went to the kitchen. If what Ng had told him was true, the consequences could be devastating. He took a San Miguel from the fridge and returned to the chair. "I'm back," he said into the phone as he sat down.

The other end of the line was silent. A moment later Ng said, "Are you there?"

"Yes."

"You haven't mentioned Wu yet. The moment I spoke his name I expected you to react more strongly," Ng said. "How many years ago was it that Tai Wai New Village and Fanling were going at it?"

"It was ten years ago, and it never got to the point of open war. Wu tried to sell drugs in our territory and made an effort to poach some of our gamblers. We put a stop to it. Now and then he tests us, but our response is always the same and he backs off," Uncle said. "In terms of my reaction to his meeting with Man, I was waiting until I had a better understanding of what Man is up to. But now that you've brought Wu's name into the conversation, I have to say I don't like it being linked with this. I didn't realize Wu and Man are close."

"Man's wife died two years ago. He began going with Wu's sister last year. They were married three weeks ago."

"I didn't know."

"I didn't either, until Zhao told me," Ng said.

"So Wu and Man have family ties. That doesn't sit well with me, if everything you're telling me about Man's intentions is accurate," Uncle said. "Did you ask Zhao about Wu's role in all this?"

"Yes, but he didn't have any detailed knowledge."

"Did he at least guess at it?"

"He thought Man and the others in Kowloon might use Wu to rattle some cages up here, and if one of us overreacts they'll have an excuse to move in and support Wu," Ng said.

"If Wu does start to agitate, the most important thing we can do is not overreact."

"Most of us react in direct proportion to the level of provocation brought against us, but that's all hypothetical right now," Uncle said.

"I'm afraid the possibility of their trying something isn't just hypothetical."

"No, I agree with you. But now we have an idea what Man has been plotting and we have time to come up with a plan to counter it before it actually starts."

"How do you propose we proceed?"

"I need to sleep on this," Uncle said abruptly. "I want to think it through and talk to some of my people. When that's done, I'll get back to you."

"You won't mention Zhao when you talk to your people?"

"No. I also won't talk to any other Mountain Master in the Territories until you and I have had a chance to speak again."

"Uncle, do you have any idea how we can resolve this?"

"Not yet, but one thing I'm certain of is that we won't do it by being passive."

CHAPTER SEVEN

WHEN HIS CONVERSATION WITH NG WAS OVER, UNCLE slumped in his chair and stared out the window at the street below. It was raining, and the street was deserted except for an occasional taxi. He saw a streak of lightning cross the sky, and seconds later heard the rumble of thunder. Given his mood, it sounded particularly ominous.

Uncle knew that sleep wasn't going to come easily. Ng had turned the unease he was feeling about Man's meetings and Yin's foray into Macau into something deep and disturbing — a sense that the world was beginning to shift beneath his feet, and that if he didn't move quickly and decisively, it would tear apart and swallow him. But move how, and against whom?

He looked at the phone, but when he did, the names of everyone he wanted to speak to became a jumble in his mind. *Slow down,* he thought. *I need to gather more facts. Even if everything Ng told me is true, I can't believe that Wu or any of the Kowloon gangs will move against their brothers in the Territories until the issue in Macau is resolved.* Still, there were things he could do, and it was time to act.

Uncle picked up the phone and called Wang again. When the restaurant owner answered, he said, "This is Uncle. I need to speak to Wang."

"Yes, boss?" Wang said a moment later. "Have you heard something about the OCTB?"

"No, but I've been told that Wu has his eye on us again," Uncle said. "Tell all the men to be alert for any kind of intrusion."

"I will. And what are they to do if they encounter Wu's men?"

"I want them removed from Fanling, but with as little disturbance and violence as possible."

"I'll deliver those instructions," said Wang. "How did you hear about Wu?"

"Ng told me, and right now that's all I want to say about it," Uncle said, then paused. "How many forty-niners do we have who are fit for a fight if it comes to that? I don't think it will, but we can't take anything for granted."

"I'd say we have about sixty men."

"How many Blue Lanterns would you feel comfortable adding to that number?"

"Another twenty."

"How well armed are we? If some extra money were available, could you make good use of it?"

"When it comes to weapons, we always need updating, especially if we're going to use Blue Lanterns. Most of them just have basic guns. I'd buy semi-automatics for them."

"I'm going to call another executive committee meeting tomorrow. I'll request the money then. I don't imagine there will be any opposition."

"Boss, we can match Tai Wai man for man. Do you really think Wu is crazy enough to take a run at us?"

"I don't know, but even if it is unlikely, I still want to be prepared," Uncle said. "I'll have Fong call you as soon as I decide on a meeting time."

As he put down the phone, lightning lit the sky again and thunder rolled over Fanling. Uncle shuddered. *What is going on in Kowloon? Is Yin planning revenge? If so, will it be tit-for-tat or a full-out assault designed to take over Macau?* he thought. *Well, why not ask the man himself?*

For a third time, the woman answered.

"This is Uncle. Is Yin there?" he said.

"Just a moment," she replied.

It sounds as if he's at home, Uncle thought, hopeful that Yin would come to the phone.

"Uncle, this is Chang," a man's voice said a moment later. "The boss says he knows why you're calling, but he doesn't want to talk to you."

"Ask him to give me just five minutes," Uncle said to Yin's Straw Sandal.

"It's pointless," Chang said. "But the boss does have a message he wants me to deliver to you."

"Which is?"

"Tend to your business in Fanling. Stay out of his."

"And I have a message for him," said Uncle. "What he's doing is affecting us all. Even if he's successful in Macau, there could be a price to pay that surpasses any gains he makes there."

"That sounds like a threat," Chang said. "My boss respects you. I'd like to see that respect maintained, so I won't pass along that message. It would only damage your relationship."

"Shit," Uncle said as the line went dead. He slid from his

chair, went to the kitchen, and returned with another San Miguel. He sipped the beer while he ran through the list of names in his head. Two were prominent. He picked up the phone.

"This is Fong," a voice answered groggily.

"Were you sleeping?"

"Yes. It takes a good night's sleep to recover from Macau."

"Before you went to bed, did you get a chance to call any of your Straw Sandal colleagues about Man and his meetings?"

"I did. And I talked to Kan. He'd made some calls as well," Fong said. "A few of the guys in the Territories had heard about the meetings, but they knew nothing about their substance."

"Were they concerned that their bosses were being left out?"

"Not particularly," said Fong. "But strangely, Kan and I encountered more concern from the Straw Sandals in Central and Causeway Bay. Although maybe *concern* isn't the right word."

"What is?"

"I talked to Yeung's Straw Sandal in Central East. I've known him forever, and I can't remember a time when he was so skittish and evasive with me. Kan spoke to the Sandal in Causeway Bay and got the same reaction."

Uncle took a swig of beer. "I want to call an executive committee meeting for tomorrow at three. Phone everyone tonight," he said. "I'll explain everything when we're all together."

"In other words, don't ask you now."

"Exactly," said Uncle. "And first thing in the morning, I want you to scout the area for a place where we can hold a meeting of between forty and sixty people. It should be private and secure. I would prefer not to use a hotel, unless we have no other options."

"You do know that's a rather strange request?" Fong said hesitantly.

"I'll explain tomorrow," said Uncle, and ended the conversation.

He checked the time and saw it was past midnight. Beijing and Hong Kong were in the same time zone, and he knew it was late to be calling, but the Fanling gang's well-being was almost as important to his contact in Beijing as it was to him.

When Uncle began investing in the Shenzhen Special Economic Zone more than ten years earlier, he had encountered Colonel Liu Leji, the zone's director of Customs. Whatever hierarchy there was in the Communist Party, Liu's family was firmly ensconced in it. Liu Leji's father had died when he was young and he'd been raised by his uncle, Liu Huning. Huning had been on the Long March and was a close associate of Zhou Enlai and Deng Xiaoping. Liu Huning and Deng were virtually joined at the hip, and Huning's career had fallen and risen in lockstep with Deng's. By the time Uncle had met Liu Leji, Deng was premier and Liu Huning was the sixth-ranked member of the Politburo Standing Committee, which made him one of the most powerful men in China.

Liu Leji had convinced Uncle to go into business with him in Shenzhen. Their arrangement was secret and included Leji's wife and his aunt — Gao Lan, Liu Huning's wife — as active partners. They started with warehouses to which the customs department helpfully directed customers, then added cold storage facilities and eventually formed their own trucking company. The business was enormously profitable, and Uncle was its public face. He also managed the money, and did it so well and discreetly that he had earned the absolute trust of the Liu family.

Liu Leji was no longer in Shenzhen. He had been promoted to the second-highest position in the customs department in Beijing, and there were rumours he might be elected to the Politburo Standing Committee after his uncle died. He went to Shenzhen once or twice a year to make sure his officials understood that Uncle was to have their continuing support, and his wife and aunt were still hands-on involved in running the business. Given all the upheavals in Liu Huning's life, his was a family that valued stability and disliked nothing more than being blindsided by a problem.

Uncle wasn't sure he had a problem or, even if he did, that it would have a negative impact on the businesses in Shenzhen. What he did know was that if it did and he hadn't warned the family, the repercussions would be unpleasant in the extreme.

The phone in Beijing rang five times. Uncle was preparing to leave a short message when Liu Leji finally came on the line.

"I apologize for calling so late, but there's an issue here that I thought you should know about," Uncle said.

"My wife and aunt are in Shenzhen. Has something happened that should cause me to be concerned about them?" Liu asked.

"No, the issue is here on the Hong Kong side. There is restlessness among some of the triad gangs, and it's threatening to turn into a broader and perhaps more violent confrontation."

"That isn't how you operate. Why are you involved in something like that?"

"Nothing has happened yet, but there are signs that it might," Uncle said. "And our involvement won't be voluntary. I have a hunch we've been targeted for an attack. If that happens, we'll have to defend ourselves."

"We can't afford to lose you," Liu said quickly. "Personal feelings aside, it would cause massive disruption to our businesses."

"That's why I'm calling," Uncle said. "My hunch might be wrong, but in case I'm right, I want you to know that the business end of things on our side will continue. If for any reason I'm taken out of circulation, Hui, my White Paper Fan, will take over. And if anything should ever happen to him, John Tin, president of the Kowloon Light Industrial Bank, has delegated authority."

"John manages my aunt's financial affairs."

"That's correct. I introduced him to your aunt and he has performed well for her. I know she has confidence in him."

"Even so, she wouldn't like his direct involvement in our business to become necessary. Like me, she would much prefer the status quo," Liu said. "What's behind this triad restlessness?"

"One of the Mountain Masters from a large Kowloon gang believes the triads could be targeted by the PLA or some other Chinese security force after the handover by the British," Uncle said. "He claims the best way to prevent that is to create larger gangs, and the best way to create larger gangs is to take over smaller ones. All the large gangs are on Hong Kong Island and in Kowloon. The smaller ones are in the New Territories. We could all be targets."

"That's an absurd assumption," Liu said angrily.

"Which part?" asked Uncle.

"The notion that triads would be threatened by the PLA or any other Chinese force," Liu said. "Has no one bothered to read the basic terms and conditions of the handover?"

"I don't know."

"If they did, they would see that under the 'one country, two systems' policy, the Ministry of Public Security of the People's Republic of China will have no enforcement role in Hong Kong. The Hong Kong Police Force will be officially independent from it."

"Maybe there's some skepticism on this side."

"More like foolishness."

"I'm not in a position to argue with you," Uncle said. "All I can tell you is what's being used as motivation. If I had a way of disproving it, I would."

"I'll poke around here," Liu said. "If there's the slightest fact to justify your colleagues' fears, I'll let you know. If there isn't, I'll see what I can come up with that might convince them they're wrong."

"I didn't call to ask you to get involved."

"Uncle, we're partners. Over the years you've shouldered most of the responsibilities that entails. Let me do this for you."

"Okay, and thank you," Uncle said.

"Let's stay in touch," Liu said.

Uncle put down the phone. Maybe Leji could come up with something that would debunk Man's rationale for expansion, but even if he did, would Man listen? Uncle thought not. He had wanted to say that to Leji, but it would have sounded unappreciative.

He rested his head against the back of the chair, closed his eyes, and wondered what things would be like in a week. "Gui-San," he muttered, "I think I'm going to be tested again. The past ten years have been peaceful, and I'm afraid that's about to end. I just hope we're up to meeting whatever challenge is thrown at us. I don't doubt our determination, but the gang hasn't been involved in real conflict since the last time Wu tried to move into Fanling. Now we're all older and we have more to lose. Will that make us hesitant? Have our comfortable lives dulled our instinct to survive? Help me, Gui-San. Help me make the right decisions. Help me keep this family intact."

CHAPTER EIGHT

UNCLE SPENT THE NIGHT IN HIS CHAIR. AFTER TALKING to Liu, he had another beer and smoked half a pack of cigarettes as he thought about Man and Wu and the problems they might present. At some point he fell asleep. When he woke, the sun was up and it was almost eight o'clock. "Damn it," he said, annoyed at the disruption of his normal routine. He made an instant coffee, drank it quickly, and hurried into the bathroom. Twenty minutes later he left his apartment to walk to Jia's Congee.

He stopped at the newsstand to buy his newspapers and flinched when he saw the headlines. Nearly every paper had some variation of *Sing Tao*'s "Triad War Erupts in Kowloon and Young Female Dies in Macau." He wondered if he'd hear from Zhang Delun again. The HKPF and the OCTB were notoriously sensitive to media proclamations about lawlessness. Would these be enough to push the force into action?

"You're late," Jia said when he reached the restaurant. "I was beginning to wonder if you were coming."

"I went to Happy Valley last night and then I had to deal with a few problems when I got back."

She looked at the newspapers, nodded, and said, "According to them, things seem to be getting out of control."

"Sensational headlines sell papers."

"Still, a lot of people have been talking about the little girl."

"That was a tragedy. I'm sure something will be done to help compensate the family."

"That won't bring her back."

"My dear Jia, I come here for my breakfast, not to be lectured about the failings of my colleagues," Uncle said.

She lowered her head. "I apologize, Uncle. That was rude on my part. What would you like with your congee this morning?"

"Today I'll have it plain, with just soy sauce and white pepper. That suits my mood."

At nine-fifteen he left the restaurant and made his way to the office. As he got to the top of the stairs, he saw that Hui, Pang, and Fong were already there.

"Good morning, guys," Uncle said. "Fong, is everyone available for the three o'clock meeting?"

"Yes, boss, and Yu is back, so we'll have the full committee."

"Excellent. And did you have any success finding a meeting venue?"

"Not yet, but I'm working on it."

"Let me know when you come up with something," Uncle said. "In the meantime, I'm going to make some calls from my office. I don't want to be disturbed unless it's an absolute emergency."

Uncle went into his office and settled behind his desk. He took a notepad and a Pelikan fountain pen from a drawer and began to make a list of New Territories Mountain Masters.

Sai Kung — Ng
Mong Kok — Poon
Sha Tin — He
Tai Po — Deng (Kan)
Yuen Long — Ching
Tsuen Wan — Chow
Sha Tau Kok — Lee
Mai Po — Tan

The only name not on the list was Wu.

Uncle's first call was to Ng. "I spent most of the night thinking about what we discussed, and about how the gangs in the Territories should respond to Man," he began. "Do you have time to listen to a few of my ideas?"

"I have all the time you need," Ng said.

Half an hour later, Uncle moved on to the second name on his list. Initially Poon agreed only reluctantly to listen to what Uncle had to say, but the moment he heard what Ng and Uncle had discovered about Man's plans, he became eager to co-operate. Conversations with He, Kan, and Ching took up the rest of the morning. Just after twelve, Uncle left his office to go to the bathroom.

Fong saw him and walked over quickly. "I think I've found a place for your meeting," he said. "The White Jade Restaurant has a private dining room that can accommodate more than a hundred people."

"Reserve it for the entire day tomorrow. I'm not sure yet what time we'll actually need it for, but let's tie it up. Also, ask the owner if he can arrange a lunch for sixty people on short notice," Uncle said.

"Okay, boss."

"And Fong, can you do me a favour? I'd love a coffee from the café across the street. Could you get me one?"

"Sure," said Fong.

When Uncle returned to his office, he called Ng again. "Does the White Jade Restaurant in central Fanling at one o'clock tomorrow afternoon work for you?"

"It does."

"Excellent. I've already spoken to Poon, He, Ching, and Kan, Deng's Straw Sandal, and all of them are prepared to join us. Can you call them for me with the meeting details while I try to reach the other Mountain Masters?"

"I'd be pleased to," Ng said.

At five to three Uncle finished his last call. He had managed to speak to everyone on his list except Lee in Sha Tau Kok, for whom he had left a message stressing that it was important for them to talk. He then walked over to the boardroom, where the six other members of the executive committee were already seated at the table.

"I made the reservation at the White Jade," Fong said as Uncle entered. "The owner says lunch for sixty people is no problem."

"Lunch for sixty people? What's going on?" Tian asked.

Uncle took a San Miguel from the ice bucket and sat down at the table. "I'll talk about the lunch in a few minutes. I want to begin by saying that we are potentially facing the greatest challenge we have had as a gang since the day I took the oath."

"Wang mentioned something about Wu making trouble again," Tian said.

"I wish it were as simple as dealing with that, but Wu's only a small part of the problem," Uncle said. "I believe that Man and at least two other Kowloon gangs have decided that the triads in the New Territories are ripe for the picking. Yin's foray into Macau was the start of a planned expansion. They want more turf. They want more men. They want more money. Man says that only bigger, stronger gangs will be able to fend off the Communists after the handover. Taking us over is his strategy for achieving that growth."

No one spoke. Finally Hui asked, in a voice full of concern, "How do you know this?"

"Is it for certain?" Yu added.

"There are rumours that Ng, Fong, and I have been trying to confirm. Last night Ng spoke to someone close to Man and got what he considers to be confirmation," Uncle said. "But even if it isn't certain, we can't take the risk of ignoring the possibility. We have to prepare for the Kowloon gangs making a move against the Territories."

"I'm the oldest of us, and even I can't remember the last major gang war," Tian said. He stared across the table at Uncle. "You're completely serious about all this?"

"Unfortunately, I am."

"That fucking Man," Tian said.

"I've also been told that Wu has cut some kind of deal with Man," Uncle added. "I imagine he's been promised that his turf will be left alone and that he'll get a piece of our action if he helps take us down."

"I have my men on alert, and Uncle has authorized me to use Blue Lanterns. So we'll have about eighty men on the street if Wu tries anything," Wang said.

"Man's gang has more than two hundred soldiers," Yu said. "If he joins Wu, we'll be hopelessly outnumbered."

Uncle held up his right hand. "Let's not get ahead of ourselves," he said. "After observing what's going on in Macau

and parsing what Ng told me about Wu's possible involvement, I don't believe there's any immediate threat of a direct
attack. I think their strategy will be to trick us into being the
aggressor. Yin's people went to Macau and goaded the local
gang into initiating the violence there. When they did, Yin
used that as an excuse to retaliate by killing their Red Pole.
The Macanese responded by killing a couple of Yin's men
in Kowloon last night. I think Yin will be back in Macau
tonight or tomorrow to take out even more of the Macanese."

"A slow and steady escalation of violence that Yin can
claim is justified," Hui said.

"Exactly, and we should expect them to adopt the same
approach in the Territories. I've been told Man might use
Wu as a stalking horse, which is why I've told Wang to make
sure our men don't overreact if Wu's men make an appearance in Fanling," Uncle said. "But at the same time I want
our men to be equipped to handle anything, so I've asked
Wang to make sure we have the best weapons we can get
our hands on. Do any of you have objections to spending
on weapon upgrades?"

"None whatsoever," Yu said. "Wang should be free to buy
whatever he thinks he needs."

When Uncle saw the other committee members nodding
in agreement, he said, "Hui, make sure Wang has all the
money he needs."

"I won't waste it," Wang said.

"I know you won't . . . and that brings me to the lunch,"
Uncle said, reaching for another beer. He opened it, took
a swig, and leaned forward. "I've invited every Mountain
Master in the New Territories — except for Wu, and Lee, who
I haven't reached yet — to attend a lunch meeting tomorrow

at the White Jade Restaurant. I've already explained to them what Ng and I believe to be Man's plans, and I've told them how I think we should organize ourselves to respond to the threat. A few of them were alarmed, but others don't want to believe there's a threat. However, they've all agreed to come."

"You said lunch for sixty," said Tian.

"I told the Mountain Masters they should bring their Red Poles and as many other members of their executive committee as they see fit," said Uncle. "I would like all of you to be there as well."

"What's the purpose of the meeting, boss?" Pang asked.

"It may be an easy feat to pick off one gang, but it's quite another to take on nine."

"You're going to propose an alliance of all nine gangs?" Yu asked.

"The word *alliance* implies a deeper level of commitment than the other gangs might be willing to make. I prefer to think of it as a mutual defence pact. Attack one of us, you attack us all."

"But Uncle, how can that work? The gangs are all different sizes and have different degrees of strength. How could each one's contribution ever be equitable?" Yu asked.

"We'll have to come up with a formula."

"And some of them hate each other," Tian said. "It's hard to imagine, for example, Tai Po and Sha Tin coming to each other's assistance."

"I know there are concerns we'll have to address, but I'm relying on the fact that whatever problems exist among us are completely dwarfed by the threat the Kowloon gangs represent," Uncle said. "Think of us as a large family. As with any large family there may be issues among the members, but when an outsider threatens, the family closes ranks."

"Uniting this group will not be easy," Tian said, shaking his head. "But if anyone can do it, you can, Uncle. And you know you have our complete support."

"Thank you. Are there any more questions or comments?"

"Yes. If sixty people actually attend the meeting, how do you expect to keep it secret?" Hui asked.

"I don't, and that's one of the reasons I want so many to attend. Word will spread, and if Kowloon knows we're supporting each other, it might give them pause."

"Or it might cause them to attack us before we're able to reach an agreement," Wang said.

"That is something I've considered, but it's a risk we'll have to take," said Uncle.

There was a loud knock on the boardroom door, and everyone's head swung in that direction.

"They know not to disturb a committee meeting," Fong said, irritated. He went to the door and opened it. Lau, Wang's deputy Red Pole, stood in the frame. "What is it?" Fong snapped.

"There's been more trouble in Macau. I thought you should know," Lau said.

"What kind of trouble?" Wang asked.

"There was a gun battle a few hours ago between the local gang and Yin's men."

"In broad daylight?"

"It's worse than that. They went at each other in St. Paul's Square, in front of hundreds of civilians. Luckily, it doesn't seem that any of the civilians were hit."

Uncle knew the square in Macau. It was the historic centre of the city and a public gathering place. Any confrontation between those two gangs was bad news, but having it in front of the Ruins of St. Paul's was foolish to the point of insanity.

"That is absolute craziness!" Tian said, echoing Uncle's thoughts. "When will this stupidity end?"

Wang looked at Uncle. "This may be happening in Macau, but tomorrow the Hong Kong newspapers will be full of triad war stories."

"The OCTB will be all over it, and the cops will have to do something to show they're in control here," added Fong.

"You're most likely correct," Uncle said. "We did not need this, but we do have to deal with it. We have to stay out of sight and out of mind."

"What do you suggest?" Wang asked.

"We've already closed the casinos, so now I think we should temporarily cease operating the rest of our businesses — except for the night market — until things quiet down."

"What about Sunday? Will we open for the racing?"

"We'll decide on Saturday."

"It would upset a lot of our customers if we were closed," Tian said.

"They would be more upset if they got caught up in a police raid."

CHAPTER NINE

AFTER THE MEETING, TIAN INVITED UNCLE TO GO WITH him to Dong's for dinner. "A plate of Dong's chicken feet will remind you that the world isn't completely out of rhythm," he said.

"Thanks, but I'm going back to my apartment," Uncle said. "I hardly slept last night, and I need to be fresh for the meeting tomorrow."

"Don't worry so much about the meeting," Tian said. "You have the respect of the Mountain Masters. I'd be surprised if a majority don't support you."

"I want them all onside. A unified New Territories could beat back anyone."

"That's asking a lot."

"Maybe, but it's still my goal."

"Do you have a detailed plan to present?"

"No. My starting point is to get them to understand and accept that we have a problem we need to deal with together. Once I have that, we can start figuring out how we'll approach it."

Tian smiled. "You've always been able to see the big

picture. The men know that and trust you to take them in the proper direction."

"*Our* men do. I'm not sure about my Mountain Master colleagues," Uncle said as he flagged down a taxi.

"Are you riding with me?" Tian asked.

"No, this is for you. I'm going to walk home. It always helps to clear my mind."

Uncle helped Tian into the taxi. As the car pulled away, he began to walk in the direction of his apartment.

He was pleased with the way the executive meeting had gone, and heartened that all the Mountain Masters in the Territories — except, of course, Wu — had agreed to attend the lunch at the White Jade Restaurant the following day. Lee from Sha Tau Kok had called him at the office an hour earlier and was willing to commit. Uncle had spoken briefly to most of the Mountain Masters after hearing the latest news about Macau, and whatever reservations they might have had about the meeting had been eliminated by the events there. Uncle knew that didn't mean they would agree with him, but it did mean they understood that Man and Yin could be a source of difficulty for all of them.

As he walked along, Uncle started putting together in his mind the case for unification. As sensible as he thought his arguments were, the Territories gangs were defiantly independent. He knew that suggesting they weren't capable of defending their own turf wouldn't sit well with some of them. He had to find a way to say it without making them feel like they weren't in control of their own destiny.

He figured he could count on support from Ng, Tan from Mai Po, and Kan from Tai Po, who would be sitting in for the ailing Deng. He decided he'd call them later and plant some questions and comments with them that would be helpful to the cause.

Uncle checked the time. He'd be home by seven, which was too early to phone Zhang. The two men spoke only over their home lines and rarely met in person. Uncle often thought it remarkable that their arm's-length relationship had survived as long as it had, but maybe that was precisely because it was arm's-length.

As Uncle neared his building he could smell the aromas of fried garlic and ginger wafting from the Blind Emperor. He entered the restaurant and ordered dou miao — snow pea shoots fried in garlic — and barbecued pork. While his food was being prepared, he sipped a San Miguel. When the food was ready, he bought two more San Miguels and carried everything upstairs.

He ate quickly, his chopsticks almost never stopping as he shovelled the food into his mouth. It was a habit he was aware of, but it was also one he couldn't break. The memories of his family having to eat boiled grass to survive were etched into his subconscious. No matter how much money he had or how much food was in front of him, Uncle felt an irrational compulsion to eat it as fast as possible, for fear that it would disappear.

After emptying both containers he settled into his chair. He thought about having a beer, but then he yawned several times and knew that was a bad idea. Instead he reached for the phone and called Zhang.

"Uncle, I've just walked through my front door. Do you have any idea why I'm getting home so late?" Zhang said.

Uncle noted the sarcasm in his tone but tried to down-play the possible reason for it. "I imagine the problems in Kowloon and Macau have everyone on edge."

"We went past the edge today with Macau. I was just at a meeting where we were told to drop the hammer. My men will be out in full force tomorrow, as will the Hong Kong and Kowloon divisions."

"I closed all my businesses tonight, except the night market. They won't reopen until things calm down."

"What are the other gangs in the New Territories doing?"

"I don't know, but since many share our aversion to the types of activities you and I have agreed won't take place in the Territories, I believe it's fair to give them a warning about tomorrow."

"I think that is appropriate, but I don't want you to make any calls to Hong Kong or Kowloon. Let my people and the gangs there sort out their own relationships."

"I agree."

Zhang paused, then said, "When is this stupidity going to end?"

"Some of us are working on it. Hopefully in two or three days there will be a return to normalcy."

"The sooner the better. But in the meantime, I think it's wise to keep your businesses closed until I tell you otherwise."

"You have my word on that."

"Good. Now let me go so I can have my dinner."

Uncle shook his head as he hung up. What did Yin and Man think they could accomplish by riling the OCTB and the Hong Kong police? He reached for the phone to call Fong.

"Yes, boss," Fong answered.

"The police will be raiding tomorrow. Make sure all our

businesses are closed as directed, and that our people maintain a low profile," Uncle said. "I'd also like you to phone our usual friends and give them a heads-up."

"That will be appreciated," Fong said. "It might also persuade them to be more supportive tomorrow."

"That's not why I'm doing it," Uncle said.

"I know, but they might want to express their appreciation all the same."

When is this crisis in Macau going to end? Or, maybe more to the point, what will it take to bring it to an end? Uncle thought as he hung up and then called Tse. He had told Zhang he wouldn't warn any of the Hong Kong gangs, but he was making an exception for Tse. He even thought Zhang would agree with that, if it could contribute to a ceasefire between Macau and Kowloon.

"I thought I'd hear from you," Tse said when he answered.

"It sounds like a mad day in Macau," said Uncle. "I don't have many details. What have you heard?"

"Yin's men tried to corner a group of Cho's near a restaurant in the old part of the city. Cho's men ran into the square, thinking Yin's people wouldn't dare open fire in such a public place. They were wrong."

"What was the outcome?"

"Three of Cho's men are dead, three more are wounded. I don't believe any of Yin's men were hurt."

"Were any civilians hit?"

"No. Given how many people normally congregate in that square, it was a miracle."

"It wasn't enough of a miracle for the Hong Kong police," Uncle said. "There's going to be a crackdown tomorrow."

"Is that the word from your contact?" Tse asked.

"It is. Tse, I promised him I wouldn't alert the gangs in Kowloon and on the Island. I'm making an exception in your case, and I want this warning to end with you."

"I'll keep it to myself."

"I'm closing all our businesses except the night market until this feud ends. I suggest you do something similar."

"Well, I'll close them for at least the next two days. Crackdowns don't usually last longer than that."

"It's your decision," Uncle said. "Tell me, how did you get the information about what happened in Macau?"

"Is that your way of asking if I've been in communication with Cho?"

"Yes."

"You're usually more subtle than that, Uncle," Tse said.

"Let me be even less subtle. Did you speak to him?"

"Yes. He's angry, but he's even more shaken. I think he's beginning to realize he can't win a war against Yin," Tse said. "He asked me if I would support him. I told him I'll give him all the moral support I can, but that Macau and Yin's turf in Kowloon are completely off-limits for my men."

"Can he get support from anywhere else?"

"I don't think so. He's on his own."

"Is he stupid enough to strike back at Yin again?"

"I'm not sure, though if I had to bet, I'd guess it's over," Tse said. "He won't want to acknowledge that for a day or two, so he can save face, but I don't know what other choice he has."

"Then what?"

"He'll probably request a truce. I think he knows it's too late for that, but he'll ask anyway," Tse said.

"I agree, it is too late. Yin will insist that Cho surrender on his terms."

"Which will be?"

"I believe Yin wants complete control in Macau. After what's been going on, I can't see him settling for anything less," Uncle said.

"As things stand, who's to stop him from getting it?"

CHAPTER TEN

UNCLE LEFT HIS APARTMENT AT THE USUAL TIME THE following morning to make his way to Jia's. As he neared the newsstand, he could see that every paper had a variation of "Triad War" in the headline. He considered avoiding the news altogether but then purchased an *Oriental Daily News* and *Sing Tao*. He also bought the racing form for Sunday's races at Sha Tin. He wasn't sure he would be going, but even if he didn't, the handicapping would be a mental distraction.

Jia didn't comment when he entered the restaurant, simply placing a pot of tea on the table as she seated him. He asked for a double order of sausage with his congee and, while he waited for his food, read the stories on the front page of each paper. There was a surprising and not unwelcome lack of detail. Neither gang was named specifically; they were simply identified as Macau and Hong Kong gangs at war over control of moneylending operations in and around the Macau casinos. The stories did confirm that three men had been killed and three wounded; their gang affiliations weren't mentioned.

The spokesperson for the Macau Polícia de Segurança

Pública condemned the shootings in St. Paul's Square and said they were rounding up local suspects. He added that the Macau force was co-operating fully with the OCTB to bring the Hong Kong–based perpetrators to justice. Beneath that pronouncement, the head of the OCTB was quoted as saying: "We are alarmed by the open display of gang violence that took place yesterday afternoon and put innocent lives at risk. We do not tolerate such violence in Hong Kong, and we won't tolerate the Hong Kong triads exporting it outside the colony. The OCTB will be taking appropriate steps to ensure it does not happen again."

If the Hong Kong and Kowloon gangs didn't recognize that those words signalled an imminent major crackdown, they weren't paying attention, Uncle thought.

When Jia arrived with his congee and sausages, Uncle pushed the newspapers to one side. But before he could begin to eat, he saw Fong enter the restaurant. Uncle held up an arm, and Fong nodded and came towards him.

"You're up early," Uncle said.

"It's a big day. I wanted to talk to you before we get caught up in business at the office."

"Has something happened?"

"Nothing in particular, but I want to brief you on the conversations I had last night when I called the other gangs to warn about the crackdown," Fong said. "They were grateful, of course. I think it might have pushed a couple of them who were leaning towards supporting you more firmly into your camp."

"Did you speak to the Mountain Masters?"

"No, they're above my station. I talked to White Paper Fans or Straw Sandals."

"What did they say about my proposal?"

"The guys in Mong Kok and Tsuen Wan said their bosses are worried about losing their independence, but if you guarantee they'll keep total control of their turf, they'll probably sign on."

"I got similar feedback from Ng, Kan, and Tan. So, including ourselves, that already gives us six gangs," said Uncle. "None of us is particularly large in number, but combined we could be formidable."

Fong pointed to the newspapers. "The people I spoke to also talked about Yin and Cho. They're making everyone nervous. The feeling is, the longer they go at each other, the harder the cops will come down on the rest of us."

"I spoke to Tse last night. He thinks the shootout yesterday will end the conflict. He expects that Cho will ask for a truce and then take whatever deal Yin offers him."

"That's good to hear, but Yin making a successful attack on Macau might convince Man or Yeung to try the same tactics in the Territories," said Fong.

"I'm thinking the same way. That's why we need to reach some kind of agreement with the other gangs today."

Jia approached the table. "Are you going to eat?" she asked Fong.

"No, thank you," he said, and turned back to Uncle. "There are a few other things I want to discuss with you."

Uncle looked at his congee. "Do you mind if I eat and listen at the same time?"

"Of course not," Fong said. "I was wondering how you want the dining room set up at the White Jade, and what you want to serve."

"Give each gang a table of their own. They'll feel more

comfortable that way," Uncle said. "We'll serve beer, water, and tea. Let the restaurant owner decide what food to serve, but tell him it isn't a banquet, it's a working lunch."

"Okay," Fong said, and then paused, seeming a bit distracted.

"Was there something else?" Uncle asked.

"Yes. Wang called me late last night. He's worried that Wu may attack us."

Uncle cocked an eyebrow. "We all are, which is why we authorized him to buy more weapons, agreed to augment our fighting force with Blue Lanterns, and are having the meeting later today."

"Sorry, I didn't express his views properly," Fong said. "What I meant to say is he's concerned that you aren't properly protected. There are no impediments to entering your building, and the fact that you walk to and from the office by yourself every day is a worry."

"Does Wang think Wu may target me directly?"

"Every other tactic he's tried in the past has failed. Maybe he thinks we'll cave in if he takes you out."

"Is that Wang's reasoning or yours?"

"It's Wang's, but I have to say I agree with him. You should have protection, Uncle. He's hoping I can convince you of that."

"He wants to place bodyguards at my apartment entrance?"

"Yes."

"And he wants me to be driven back and forth to and from work?"

"Yes."

"I thank both you and him for your concern, but I've survived all these years without a bodyguard," Uncle said.

"That is true, but times are changing. The old codes of honour and conduct aren't followed as much as they used to be."

"If you're referring to the belief that directly targeting a Mountain Master is off-limits, I can tell you that's been fiction for years. I know of at least five who died at the hands of another Mountain Master or unhappy members of their own gang. Most of them had bodyguards, and in some cases the bodyguards died with them. I'd rather put my trust in karma."

"Uncle, please," Fong pleaded.

"No, and that's final."

Fong sighed. "Wang thought you'd react like this, which is why he asked me to make the request."

"The discussion is closed."

Fong slid out of the booth. "I'll tell Wang."

Uncle watched his Straw Sandal leave the restaurant. In some ways, he thought, Fong had a romantic notion of what it meant to be a triad.

He returned to his congee, finished it, asked Jia for a refill, and finished that as well. Given that he'd be speaking rather than eating at the meeting, Uncle figured the congee would carry him through until dinner.

He took his time walking to the office. It was another beautiful day, but he barely noticed; his mind was preoccupied with formulating the message he wanted to deliver to his colleagues. They weren't men prone to panic, and he felt that overstating the threat they faced would be met by skepticism or even resentment. It was better to understate, he thought — keep it simple, truthful, and low-key.

When he reached the office, there were four men rather than the usual two at the entrance. Uncle nodded at them and made his way upstairs. He expected to see some of the executive there, but only Mo and a couple of clerks were at their desks.

"Where is everyone?" Uncle asked.

"Fong went to the restaurant to make sure everything is properly organized for this afternoon," Mo said. "Wang called in; he's visiting all our businesses in town to make sure they're closed. Hui will be here in about fifteen minutes. I don't know about the others."

"Thanks," Uncle said, then went into his office and closed the door behind him. He sat down at the desk, took a notepad from a drawer, and wrote down the thoughts he'd had during his walk. When that was done, he turned to a fresh page and began to compose his opening remarks. Rather than reading them at the meeting, he would memorize them and try to make them sound as spontaneous as possible. It wasn't easy getting the right words and tone; he made several false starts before settling on something satisfactory. He read aloud what he'd written, made a few more changes, and read it again. It still wasn't perfect, but it would do for the time being, he thought.

As he set the notepad aside, his phone rang. "This is Uncle," he said.

"Hey," Ng said, "have you shut everything down yet?"

"We did it last night."

"So did we, thank god. I just got a phone call from my deputy saying the cops are all over us," he said. "Your heads-up has spared a lot of gangs a lot of grief."

"Fong is hoping that will earn me some extra credibility this afternoon."

"People will be grateful, but I'm not sure that will translate into support," Ng said. "I've had calls from three Mountain Masters this morning asking me what I think you're trying to do."

"They have doubts about my motives?" Uncle asked.

"It's in their nature to be suspicious. They're wondering if you have a hidden agenda," Ng said. "I told them no as strongly as I could. I'm not sure they believed me, but no one challenged me."

"I'm very conscious of how territorial we all are. I'll speak to that this afternoon," Uncle said.

"You'll certainly have some support. I just think it will be tough to get everyone onside," Ng said. "There are guys who are friendly with Wu, and some have ties to gangs in Kowloon. They may think that gives them all the protection they need."

"I will present the facts. After that, it's up to them to decide whether they will align with us or not."

"You don't expect them to make a decision today, do you?"

"I would like them to, but I know that's unrealistic. They'll need time to think it through. But we can't let them drag it out," said Uncle.

"I'll commit today, and I think a few others will as well. It will at least be a step in the right direction," Ng said.

Uncle saw he had an incoming call. "Tse is phoning on my other line," he said.

"You should take it. I'll see you at one," Ng said.

Uncle switched lines. "Tse, do you have news for me?"

"First, I want to thank you. We were raided this morning, and thanks to you, our losses were minimal."

"I'm glad it worked out for you."

"You won't be so glad when you hear that Cho and Yin have cut a deal."

"A truce?"

"No. As we suspected, Cho asked for one and was denied. He was forced to put his gang under Yin's control. He'll still be Mountain Master, but Yin will be making all the decisions."

"That didn't take long."

"Cho thought the longer he waited, the worse deal he'd get. I can't say I disagree with him."

"Well, at least I don't have to think about that anymore," Uncle said. "I have enough on my plate here."

"Are you referring to the meeting you're holding this afternoon?" Tse asked.

Uncle paused. Had he told Tse about the meeting? "How did you hear about it?"

"Man called me, after Wu called him. I told him I knew nothing about a meeting, but I'm not sure he believed me. He's rather paranoid right now, and I'm sure Wu is as well."

"There's nothing sinister about the meeting. I simply thought it was time for the Mountain Masters in the Territories to discuss how we can improve our co-operation."

"Was Wu invited?"

"No, and I'm sure you can guess why. But the meeting isn't a secret, so I'm not surprised he knows about it."

"I have a hunch I know what you're doing, but I don't want you to tell me," Tse said.

"That's a clever approach."

"It's the safe approach," said Tse. "Keep safe yourself, Uncle. I don't want to lose you."

CHAPTER ELEVEN

AT TEN AFTER ONE, UNCLE SURVEYED THE NINE CIRCU-
lar tables arranged around the dining room in the White
Jade Restaurant and smiled. Every Mountain Master he had
invited was there, and judging by the number of seats occupied at each table, they had brought most of their senior
people with them.

"Welcome to Fanling, and thank you all for coming," Fong
said loudly. "We will serve food now and then Uncle will
say a few words."

"I'm betting he'll say more than a few," Poon from Mong Kok
yelled. "But as long as the food is good and the beer is cold, I'll
stay for them." There was a ripple of laughter. Uncle joined in,
pleased that Poon had helped break the tension in the room.

It took close to an hour to serve and consume six different
dishes. At one point Uncle turned to Fong. "I thought I told
you this was to be a working lunch, not a banquet."

"It's only six dishes, Uncle. The restaurant owner wanted
to serve more. He really wants to impress us," said Fong.
"Besides, everyone seems to be enjoying the food, and that
can't be a bad thing."

Uncle ate lightly. He left his seat several times to visit the other Mountain Masters and thank them for coming, trying to gauge from their responses what level of support he could expect. They were all friendly, but many were reserved, which he interpreted as not ready to commit.

As the dishes were being cleared, Fong stood up again. "Now is the time to go to the washroom if you need to," he said. "Uncle will speak in ten minutes."

It took longer than ten minutes for the room to settle, but eventually it did and Uncle walked over to the centre. He looked at each table in turn, acknowledging the Mountain Masters with a slight nod. "I can't remember the last time so many of us were in one place. It must have been at a funeral," he said, and noticed some grim smiles. "Thankfully this isn't such a sad occasion, but while we have no reason to mourn, that time could come. If it does, it isn't just lives that could be lost — it's everything we've spent our lives building.

"Before I go any further, I have some news I want to share with you. The good news is that the war between Cho and Yin has ended. So, hopefully, no more newspaper headlines," he said. "The bad news is that Cho has ceded control of his gang to Yin. Kowloon now controls Macau."

"Are you sure of this?" He from Sha Tin asked.

"I was told this morning by someone who was informed directly by Cho. It's over. Yin won. Now the only question is, who's next? I'm convinced it will be one of us gathered here today. If it is, can any of us survive on our own?" Uncle paused and looked at each table in turn. "I think not. In fact, I believe we have only two choices. We either stand together or we fall alone."

"Excuse me, Uncle," Tan from Mai Po said. "I know you

explained most of this on the phone yesterday, but how certain are you that expansion into the New Territories is what Man and the others have in mind?"

"That's an excellent question," Uncle said, pleased that Tan had followed through on the promise he'd made the night before. "The truth is, I'm not certain. I know what I've been told and I trust the people who told me. I also know what happened in Macau, and although Yin will try to attach blame to both parties, I believe the result tells us everything we need to know. Does that mean I can predict when one of us will be attacked? No, I cannot, but if we wait until an attack comes, by then it will be too late. But, although I can't give you any guarantees, I can tell you what I believe."

Uncle then delivered a speech that encompassed the five pages of notes he'd made that morning. He spoke slowly and without hyperbole. He outlined Man's rationale for expansion, described the firepower of the Kowloon gangs, and did it without demonizing them. He spoke to the individual weaknesses of the Territories gangs, then switched to praising the potential of their collective strength.

"Let me finish by stating something I hope is obvious," he said. "We should have formed an alliance — even an informal one — years ago. The fact that we're talking about doing it now, as a way of protecting ourselves, only adds a touch of necessity to what is essentially a very good idea."

"Uncle, I'm not interested in merging with anyone. I run my gang as I see fit. I don't need anyone else to tell me how to do it," Chow from Tsuen Wan said.

"I'm not talking about a merger or any loss of your independence," Uncle said quickly, realizing that his comment about an alliance might have gone too far. "All I'm suggesting is that the nine gangs in this room pledge to stand united against any outside interference."

"My gang is twice the size of most of the others," He said. "If trouble starts, will we be expected to throw more men than anyone else into a fight?"

"We need to determine a formula that's fair," said Uncle. "If the most one gang can provide is twenty men, then no one else should be expected to provide more. And twenty times nine is a hundred and eighty men, a formidable force when added to the men of the gang that's being threatened."

"And there isn't a gang here that can't provide twenty men," Ng chimed in.

"I have men," Lee from Sha Tau Kok said. "But I only have old weapons, and not enough of them."

"Fanling will help you buy weapons," Uncle said. "I suggest that Wang, my Red Pole, meet with the other Red Poles to figure out what everyone needs. Within reason, we'll put up the money."

"I don't want my Red Pole meeting with anyone until we've decided what we want to do," He said. "I won't be rushed into a decision."

"I understand," Uncle said. "I have made a proposal, but I don't expect an answer from you today. I know you all need to talk it over with your executive committees. The only thing I ask is for you not to take too long. Time is not on our side. Can I suggest that we meet again in a week? Those who have decided not to join needn't come. Those who are in or are still trying to make a decision can gather here. By then I'm sure you'll have more questions and suggestions."

"I like that idea," Tan said.

"Does anyone disagree with it?" Uncle asked.

The room became silent. Uncle waited, giving anyone an opportunity to speak. When no one did, he said, "Thank you for coming today. Hopefully I'll see all of you again next week."

CHAPTER TWELVE

THE FANLING TRIADS REMAINED SEATED AT THEIR TABLE until everyone had left. When they were finally alone, Uncle said, "I want to apologize to all of you for volunteering to finance weapons purchases for some of the gangs. I should have cleared it with you in advance."

"It isn't a problem," Yu said. "It was the right thing to suggest, and your timing was perfect."

"I agree," Hui said to Uncle. "I also have to say I think the case you made for us banding together was very persuasive."

"Let's hope it was persuasive enough," Uncle said.

"How do you want us to follow up?" Fong asked.

"I don't want you to do anything," said Uncle. "I laid out the facts and told them where we stand. It's now up to them to decide if they want to join with us or not. So let's not harass them."

"You know we have all kinds of interactions with these gangs. You don't want that to stop, do you?"

"Of course not. And if one of their members raises the subject with you and wants to discuss it, then do it. I just don't want us to initiate anything. I don't want them to feel we're pressuring them."

"They'll talk among themselves," Tian said.

"I know, and we have advocates in Ng and Tan, who will keep pushing our proposal. We need to let that happen without being perceived as the instigator."

Wang started to speak, then looked towards the door. "What are you guys doing here?" he asked two men Uncle recognized as Fanling forty-niners.

"We were waiting outside for the meeting to end. You told us to inform you as soon as the cops started leaning on us," one said.

"What have they done?"

"They went after our businesses, but since most of them are closed they weren't able to do much damage," he said. "They did break into the mini-casinos, though, and took away the roulette wheels and baccarat tables."

"Those are easily replaced," Yu said. "Did they take anything from the massage parlours?"

"No," the man said.

"Good. Those footbaths and massage tables are expensive."

"Do you still want to operate the night market tonight?" Wang asked Uncle.

"That was the plan. Do you have a reason why we shouldn't?"

"No, but it might be wise not to display our most expensive products," Wang said. "If they do raid us, let them cart off the cheap stuff."

"I'll leave that decision to you and Hui," said Uncle, rising from his chair. "I'm suddenly tired. I think I'll head back to my apartment. You can reach me there if anything needs my attention."

"There are three cars outside," Wang said. "You take one and we'll share the other two."

"I'll take Tian with me. His place is on the way to mine," Uncle said.

Uncle and Tian didn't speak as they walked to the car or during the ride, but when they reached Tian's apartment block, Uncle got out with him and instructed the forty-niner to wait. Tian grabbed Uncle's arm for support as they walked towards the entrance.

"Tell me how you really think the meeting went," Uncle said.

"I agree with Yu and Hui. You couldn't have done better."

"How many of them do you think will come to our side?"

"At the minimum, I think you'll get five. At the most, you might get them all. It will depend on how deeply they believe Kowloon is a threat."

"I won't be happy with five, but I will be satisfied. That will give us numbers."

"It will give you numbers if only Man and Wu combine to attack any of us. But if you add another Kowloon gang to the mix, you'll still be outgunned," Tian said.

"Maybe outgunned, but not overwhelmed. I'm counting on the fact that if they know they can't just steamroll over us, they'll think twice before attacking."

Tian stopped when they reached the building entrance. "I don't like to hear you counting guns, Uncle, but I know why you think it's necessary," he said. "I have some old friends in other gangs. Although some of them aren't active, they still have influence. Despite your admonition that we not lobby other gangs to support us, I would like to call those friends. Do I have your permission?"

"Of course you do," said Uncle.

"I will be discreet."

"I trust you completely, Tian. You know that."

Tian nodded and smiled. "When you were speaking today, I couldn't help thinking about the young man from Changzhai that my nephew brought to meet me so long ago. Your clothes weren't much more than rags, you were scrawny, and you looked younger than your years. But there was a sense of purpose about you that caught my attention. I remember thinking, *This is a young man to be taken seriously.* You proved that correct many years ago, and you know I thought you'd make a great Mountain Master before you attained the position. But Uncle, what you are trying to do right now is beyond any of my expectations. If you can even loosely unite the gangs in the Territories, you will have accomplished something for the ages."

Uncle shook his head. "Any success I've had is because of the support and friendship of men like you. If some of the gangs do come together, it will be because of your efforts, and those of men like Ng and Tan. I may have had the idea, but I can't make it a reality without you."

"As always, you can't accept a compliment, but that modesty is another reason you are so respected," Tian said. "Now go home and rest. You've earned it. Let the rest of us contribute what we can."

Uncle waited until Tian had entered the lobby before making his way back to the car. "Thanks for the ride, but I don't need you now. I'll walk the rest of the way," he said to the driver.

The forty-niner looked hesitant, and Uncle guessed that Wang had instructed him to make sure Uncle got home. "It's a short walk from here and I need some fresh air," he said, and then started off without waiting for a reply.

As he walked along, Uncle thought about what Tian had said about their first meeting. Most of it was true. He had been so scrawny that his ribs were almost sticking through his skin, the result of a year of near starvation. His clothes were indeed raggedy, but the shirt and trousers were all he had brought with him, and they hadn't fared well during the swim across Shenzhen Bay. As for his demeanour, he had been so stricken with grief after the death of Gui-San that he had felt numb; maybe Tian had confused that grief with something else.

Tian had always been one of his strongest supporters. Uncle was intensely grateful to him, but his old mentor saw virtues in Uncle that he didn't believe he possessed, such as modesty. While it was true he had difficulty accepting compliments, modesty had nothing to do with it. His view of compliments was that they were standards other people were setting for him, and he didn't want such obligations. Moreover, he didn't think he was modest. He knew he was intelligent and possessed the discipline to make good use of his cleverness. He also considered himself an excellent leader of men and a superior Mountain Master. No one had ever voluntarily left his gang, and why would they? Uncle had made the Fanling Triad the wealthiest in the New Territories without incurring the wrath of the authorities. And he had created a path forward that promised more of the same — assuming, of course, that he would be able to blunt the plans of Man and Wu. He thought the meeting at the White Jade had been an important first step in doing that.

Uncle replayed the meeting in his head, trying to recapture the reaction of each Mountain Master as he presented his proposal. He thought Tian correct in his assessment that he could already count on five leaders, but he wanted them all. The fact that he might not achieve that ambition nagged at him. A united front of all nine gangs would be truly formidable. Any less than that would just make them weaker, and also create the possibility that those who didn't join would align themselves elsewhere. Having one gang in your territory you didn't trust was bad enough, but two or three more would create the potential for enemies on all sides.

Uncle was pleased that Tian had offered to contact some of his old colleagues. His mentor had credibility and a reputation for being wise that the younger men, despite their competence, hadn't yet earned. Ng and Tan likewise had great reputations and their own webs of trusted allies. Uncle knew they would make calls on behalf of the proposal if he asked them, and that was exactly what he intended to do when he got to his apartment.

It was late afternoon when Uncle reached his building. He had been too tense to eat much at the lunch, and now his appetite kicked in. He went into the Blind Emperor and ordered steamed bok choy with oyster sauce, a double order of beef short ribs, and six beers. He drank one beer while he waited for his food.

When he entered the apartment, he saw that the message light on his phone was blinking. He thought briefly about checking his calls but didn't want the food to cool. Fifteen minutes later he put the empty food containers in the garbage can, took a beer from the fridge, and settled into his chair. He picked up the phone and accessed the messaging system.

"This is Poon. My men and I have just finished talking over your idea. We're in," the Mountain Master from Mong Kok said.

Uncle hadn't been sure which way Poon would go, but he wasn't entirely surprised that he was onside. Mong Kok was close enough to Kowloon to make things uncomfortable — uncomfortable enough, in fact, that Poon had decided not to wait a week. That was prudent on his part, Uncle thought as he phoned Wang.

"Good news," he said when Wang answered. "Poon left me a message saying that he's joining the coalition."

"I'm not surprised about Poon. He's shrewd, and his Red Pole is forward-thinking. They're a good combination," Wang said. "I have news as well. I've heard from my counterparts in Wanchai and Central. They tell me Man is trying to convince their Mountain Masters that the meeting today was your attempt to organize the gangs in the Territories to attack them. But they also told me no one is buying what he's selling."

"I'm glad to hear that."

"Still, I'm worried that if he keeps spinning those lies, someone will eventually believe him," Wang said. "Have you thought about approaching Man directly? He might back off."

"Or he might think I'm calling because I'm either worried or afraid. I'd rather have him guessing about our real feelings," Uncle said. "So let's forget Man for now. Tell me how things are on the street."

"It's quiet. The cops did what they usually do and then left. Our men stayed out of their way, and the fact that the businesses weren't up and running made it quick and relatively painless."

"Things should start to get back to normal now that Cho and Yin have made peace, but we'll keep the casinos closed until we can replace the roulette wheels and baccarat tables. If it's still quiet tomorrow afternoon we should open the massage parlours. Saturday night is their busiest time of the week."

"How about the betting shops on Sunday?"

"If Saturday goes well, then let's open them too," said Uncle. "And Wang, I know I might be sounding overly cautious, but I want you to increase the number of men we normally have on the street, starting with tonight's market."

"We usually have six men at the market. I'll double that," Wang said.

"Good. And I'm staying in tonight, so if you need me I'll be here."

"Hopefully you won't hear from me," said Wang.

Uncle put down the phone and rested his head against the back of the chair. He thought about calling Poon and Tse, but the day had taken its toll and he wasn't sure how much more conversation he could handle. He reached for his pen and the racing form.

He handicapped for several hours, drank two more beers, dozed off, then woke up and worked for a few hours more. Again, atypically, his attention wandered. He had started the day full of assurance that the meeting was logical and necessary. He had felt the same when it was over, but Wang's news about Man struck a different chord. Now Uncle wondered if he had gone too far, been too ambitious. Had he unwittingly forced Man's hand? Had the meeting turned a possibility into a certainty?

Uncle thought about having another beer but decided he'd sleep well enough without it. He rose from his chair and started towards the bedroom. The ringing of the phone stopped him before he got there. *Another late-night call,* he thought. *What is it this time?*

"This is Uncle," he answered.

"Sorry to call so late, but there's been trouble at the night market," Wang said.

"The police?"

"No, I wish it was. Some of Wu's men arrived early in the evening. They just hung around at first, pretending to be customers, but then they began hassling our vendors and driving away business. Threats were made and the vendors came to us for help. Our men moved in. There was a bit of a scuffle at first — nothing serious — and then our lead man, Yan, thought it was over. But one of Wu's men flashed a knife in Ren's face and Sonny Kwok went after him."

"Is Kwok the forty-niner who almost killed one of Wu's men the last time they tried to drag us into a confrontation?"

"Yes. That was a long time ago; I'm surprised you remember."

"I hope Kwok showed more control this time."

"He didn't," Wang said, and paused. "Ren thinks he killed the guy. Then Kwok took out two more of Wu's men when they tried to help the knifeman. They're not dead — at least, they weren't when Wu's men left the market."

"We didn't need this," Uncle said angrily.

"I know, but the good thing is they went at each other in an alleyway. Not many people saw it and there was no gunplay. So far there's been no sign of the police."

"That's all well and good, but didn't I make it clear that I thought Tai Wai would try something like this, and that we should have a measured response?"

"You did, and I passed the message along. Ren apologized five times to me in a five-minute conversation. He said Kwok lost his head and there was nothing he could do to stop him," Wang said. "Uncle, that guy might be the best streetfighter I've ever seen."

"What use is that to us if he creates problems that are greater than his value?"

"What do you want me to do with him?"

Uncle sighed. "We might have to cut him loose. If I call Wu and tell him that we've dealt with Kwok, it might buy us a little time," he said. "And Wang, this next week is all about buying time. We need to give the other Mountain Masters a chance to make the right decision. Come next Friday, I hope I won't have to care anymore about how Wu reacts. But right now, I do."

"Do you want me to deal with Kwok?"

"No. Tell him to come to the office tomorrow morning at nine. I'll talk to him. Putting someone out of the gang is a serious step. I should deal with it myself."

"Shall I warn him what you're thinking of doing?"

"No. I want to sleep on it."

CHAPTER THIRTEEN

UNCLE DIDN'T SLEEP WELL; IN FACT HE HARDLY SLEPT at all. Several times he contemplated phoning Wu, but he eventually decided the negatives strongly outweighed the positives. Among other things, he wanted to know the status of the men Kwok had attacked, because that might have a bearing on what he would have to say to him. He also wanted to consult with Ng, Tan, and maybe Tse. Using one of them as an intermediary seemed to be the best way to keep things civil with Wu. But one of them would have to agree to take on that role, and he wasn't sure any of them would.

It was eight-thirty when he reached the office after his breakfast at Jia's. She had mentioned that he looked tired, but thankfully there was nothing in the newspapers about the altercation in the night market for her to comment on. Uncle nodded to the four forty-niners at the office entrance and made his way upstairs. All the executive were already there, huddled in Fong's office. Uncle started to join them but stopped when he saw a man who had to be six foot four leaning against the wall outside his office. He had seen the man before but had never attached a name to him.

"Are you Sonny Kwok?"

The man averted his eyes and lowered his head. "Yes, boss," he mumbled.

"I'll be right back," said Uncle.

He walked over to Fong's office and stuck his head inside. "Has there been any retaliation from Wu?"

"No," Wang said. "But I have all of our men on the street, and we'll keep them there until you decide otherwise."

"There was nothing in the papers about last night and I didn't hear from the police, so we have that to be thankful for. Have the other gangs heard about the fracas?" Uncle asked.

"Wu's people have been spreading the word. Predictably, they're blaming us for starting it," Fong said. "Wang, Yu, and I all got phone calls from our colleagues. They may not believe the tale Wu is spinning, but it's fair to say they wish it hadn't happened. They're nervous."

"I can't fault them," said Uncle. "How are the men that Kwok fought?"

"One is dead, another is in really rough shape, and the third should be okay," Wang said.

"What did he attack them with?" Uncle asked.

"His fists."

"That's all?" Uncle turned to look back at Kwok. "I know he's large, but he looks a bit soft. Taking out three men with just his fists . . ."

"Sonny may look soft, but he's the furthest thing from it. He's strong as hell and incredibly quick, and he's able to strike without giving the slightest warning. The problem is that he doesn't take time to think; he just acts," Wang said.

"In this case he hammered the guy with the knife before he could get close to Ren, and then he turned on the other two guys before they could react. He would have taken on more if Ren hadn't intervened —"

"Uncle, I have to say this," Tian interrupted. "Sonny is a good guy. He comes to Dong's at least twice a week and there's never been the slightest bit of trouble. He's also loyal as hell. I'd hate for us to lose him."

"He was defending a brother. Maybe he went overboard, but you can't doubt his intentions," Yu added.

"There's a lot more at stake here than the future of one forty-niner, but I appreciate your opinions," Uncle said. "I will talk to him before I make a decision."

Kwok was still leaning against the wall with his head lowered when Uncle returned. "Come inside," Uncle said, opening his office door.

Uncle sat down behind his desk. Kwok looked at the chair in front of it but remained standing.

"What do people call you, Sonny or Kwok?" Uncle asked.

"Sonny."

"Okay, Sonny, tell me. Did Ren make it clear to you before you went to the market last night that we needed to keep things low-key?"

"Yes."

"What was low-key about what you did to the three guys from Tai Wai?"

Sonny closed his eyes and hung his head. "Nothing."

"Do you realize that you've created a huge problem for our gang?"

"Ren told me that last night."

"It's such a huge problem that I have to decide what to do with you," Uncle said.

"What do you mean?" Sonny asked, his voice trembling slightly.

"I have to decide if we can risk keeping you on as a brother. You might have to leave the gang."

Uncle saw Sonny's body tense and felt a touch of trepidation. But then the big man's shoulders collapsed, his head drooped so low that his chin was buried in his chest, and tears began to run down his cheeks. Uncle stared, not quite believing such an emotional reaction.

"This is my home. This is all I have," Sonny said, his voice quivering. "The brothers are my family. They're the only family I've known since I was sixteen years old. I have no one else. Please don't take them away from me."

Uncle felt his own emotions surge. The last thing he'd expected was tears, and he found himself fighting back his own as Sonny's words struck a nerve. Regarding the gang as family was something Uncle shared with Sonny. Maybe it was the only thing they had in common, but it was the most important thing in Uncle's life.

"I can't allow you to keep behaving like this," Uncle said.

"I have a temper, I know I do. I work really hard at controlling it, but then I snap. I don't know why. It just happens. I promise I'll work even harder at it."

Uncle sat back in the chair. What should he do with this man? He knew now that he couldn't throw him out of the gang, but neither could he let him return to the street. "Can you drive a car?" he asked.

"Yes," said Sonny.

"Then go and find Wang and tell him I want to talk to him. You wait outside while I do," Uncle said. *I hope this isn't a mistake,* he thought as Sonny left.

Wang entered the office a moment later, closing the door behind him. "Sonny looks crushed," he said.

"I can't let him go back on the street," Uncle said, and saw Wang's face fall. "But what if I take you up on the suggestion that I should have a bodyguard and a driver? Do you think Sonny could fill both positions?"

"I can't think of anyone who would be a better bodyguard, but I don't know if he can drive," Wang said.

"He told me he can."

"Then I think it's a great idea," Wang said, smiling.

Uncle nodded. "I know I'm taking a gamble, but loyalty has to count for something," he said. "Please ask Sonny to come back in. And I'd appreciate it if you stayed while I talk to him."

"Sure thing, boss."

When Wang returned with Sonny, they stood side by side in front of Uncle's desk.

"Wang and I have discussed what should happen to you. We've decided that you shouldn't be working on the street — but before you react, let me say that you will remain in the gang," Uncle said.

Sonny glanced at Wang and then looked at Uncle with a combination of disbelief and relief. "I'll do whatever you want me to do," he said.

"Wang thinks I should have a bodyguard and a driver. Are you up for that?"

"Yes, boss," Sonny said quickly.

"Before we finalize the arrangement there are some things we should make clear," Uncle said. Then he looked at Wang. "How do you see this working?"

"Sonny should drive you back and forth from the office and, naturally, drive you anywhere else you want to go. It will be a seven-day-a-week job and he'll be on call twenty-four hours a day," Wang said. "Given what's going on now with Tai Wai, we also need to start guarding your apartment. You're in the office or elsewhere in Fanling most days, so I'm mainly concerned about the nights. I'll assign a couple of guys on a rotating basis to take care of weekday nights, but I think Sonny should have full responsibility for weekends."

"That means you won't have much time for a life of your own. Are you okay with that?" Uncle asked Sonny.

"Yes, boss."

"I'll leave the scheduling to you and Wang, but there are some other things I want to make clear," said Uncle. "First, this is the last time I want to see you wearing jeans and a T-shirt. I suggest you buy some black slacks and white shirts. We'll give you the money if you need it."

"I don't need money," said Sonny. "I'll buy the clothes as soon as I leave here."

"Good. And next, I don't want you to worry about making decisions. I'll do the thinking for both of us. Will you be able to follow orders without questioning them?" Uncle asked. "I can't have a repeat of what happened last night. If you go against my wishes even once, I will expel you from the gang."

"I won't fail you," Sonny said.

"Then off you go and buy some clothes," Uncle said.

"And Sonny, I'll make arrangements for the car," Wang

said. "You should consider this building your home until this crisis passes."

"I won't let you down either," said Sonny.

Uncle and Wang watched him leave. The reprieve had put a spring in his step, and Uncle noticed an agility he hadn't seen before. "I hope that two weeks from now I'm not regretting this," he said.

CHAPTER FOURTEEN

THE DAY WAS FILLED WITH PHONE CALLS AS UNCLE reached out to his peers in the New Territories with his version of the previous night's events. Most of them had already heard from Wu, who was claiming his men were simply shopping at the market when they were attacked. None of the Mountain Masters said they believed Wu, but despite that, Uncle sensed that the Tai Wai leader had succeeded in planting some seeds of doubt. The question he kept asking himself was, what was Wu's intent? Was he creating a rationale for an immediate attack? Or was he trying to isolate Fanling by sabotaging the coalition before it had a chance to form?

The entire executive committee was in the office for the day, and that resulted in several impromptu meetings. There was tension, almost a sense of foreboding, as they related the gossip they were hearing from other territories. According to one of Yu's sources, Wu was planning to attack them in force, while a Wang source had said Wu had no intention of retaliating. Uncle suspected that the truth lay somewhere in the middle.

At one o'clock Wang came into his office. "The weapons

that I ordered yesterday have been delivered. So whatever Wu wants to do, we'll be ready for him," he said.

"That's good news."

"And there's a Mercedes-Benz for you at the curb downstairs. Sonny is there as well. I've explained the rules and the routine to him. He seems to understand."

"What are the rules?" Uncle asked.

"He drives you wherever you want to go and then waits for you or accompanies you when you get to your destination. If you want to walk somewhere, he'll walk with you. He'll always be outside the office when you're here, and he or one of the other bodyguards will always be outside your apartment building during the night. Regardless of who is at the apartment during the night, he has to be there with the car by seven in the morning."

"Will he be carrying a gun?"

"There will be one in the car if he needs it, but I don't think it's necessary for him to have it on his person. You know how much the police frown on guns being displayed in public."

Uncle shook his head. "I hope this isn't a permanent arrangement."

"Don't we all," Wang said.

Uncle had been drinking instant coffee during the day, but around three o'clock he felt like something a bit more upscale and left the office to go to the café across the street. He saw the grey Mercedes as soon as he exited the building.

Sonny, wearing a white shirt buttoned to the collar and black slacks, was standing off to one side with the other guards. When he saw Uncle, he hurried towards him. "Am I driving you somewhere?"

"No, I'm going to the café for a coffee."

"I'll walk with you," Sonny said.

"That isn't necessary."

"Wang was quite specific about my orders. I don't want to mess up the very first time I should be following them."

Uncle smiled. "Then walk with me, but I like to drink my coffee alone."

"I wouldn't think of sitting with you," Sonny said. "I'll just stay close."

Fifteen minutes later, Uncle returned to the office. Sonny walked a few paces behind, his head swivelling in all directions.

"Tse just phoned," Fong said as Uncle cleared the stairs. "He wants you to call him back."

Tse had been on Uncle's list of people to call, but he had given priority to the Mountain Masters in the New Territories. "I was going to call you," he said when Tse answered the phone. "You've heard about what happened last night?"

"Who hasn't? Man and Wu have been letting everyone know. I'm surprised it hasn't made it into the newspapers."

"Hopefully it never will."

"What happened exactly? Everything I know came from Man. As you can imagine, it was kind of one-sided."

"Wu sent men to our night market. They were harassing some vendors, and Ren, one of our senior men, asked them to move on. One of them pulled a knife on him, and one of our forty-niners took him and two others out."

"They were goading you."

"I know. Our man shouldn't have overreacted, but he did."

"You do realize that you've given Wu an excuse to retaliate."

"I know."

Tse hesitated and then said, "If he does, you should assume that Man is prepared to support him. He hinted as much during our call, and then he tried to feel me out about how much support I'm prepared to give you."

"What did you tell him?"

"That I'm not going to get involved," Tse said. "I did add, though, that I thought a substantial group of Mountain Masters in the Territories would stand with you. He laughed when I said that."

"Why did he think that was funny?"

"He said it's easy to be supportive when the threat is just that — a threat. Contending with the reality of a gang war is a different matter."

"That cuts two ways, which brings me back to Wu. Did Man say what kind of support he's prepared to give him?" Uncle asked.

"He was vague, even when I asked him directly what he has in mind. He said there's no point in discussing it until Wu decides what he's going to do."

"The last time we did this dance with Wu, he backed off as soon as he saw we'd fight. As much as I regret what happened last night, it might have reminded him that we aren't pushovers. We have a great Red Pole and a determined group of men on the ground, and we've just bought the newest weapons we could get our hands on."

"I assume you'd like me to pass on that message to Man."

"It might be helpful if you did."

"Consider it done," Tse said. "On a less serious note, will I see you tomorrow at Sha Tin?"

"If things are quiet overnight, I think you will."

"For all kinds of reasons, I hope you'll be there."

Uncle found Wang sitting in Fong's office. "If there's nothing more for me to do here, I'm going home," he said.

"Are you going to the races tomorrow?" Fong asked.

"Maybe. I'll let you know if I am."

A moment later Uncle started down the stairs to the street, thinking that it would be a pleasant walk home. But then he remembered Sonny Kwok and the Mercedes. He thought briefly about waving Sonny off, then decided that would be setting a bad precedent.

Sonny had moved the car so it was directly in front of the building entrance. He was sitting behind the wheel but leapt out when he saw Uncle.

"I'd like to go home," Uncle said. "Do you know where I live?"

"One of the guards told me you live above the Blind Emperor Restaurant," Sonny said. "I've eaten there."

"The guard was correct. You can take me there."

Sonny opened the back door of the Mercedes. Uncle hesitated, debating whether to sit up front. "I'll feel more like a proper driver if you sit in the back," Sonny said, as if reading his mind. "Besides, those were Wang's orders." Uncle slid into the back seat, quietly impressed with Sonny's manner.

The car pulled into light traffic and headed towards the town centre.

"When I spoke to you this morning, you mentioned that you've had no family except the gang since you were sixteen," Uncle said. "What happened to your birth family? Mine died of starvation in China."

"I've heard the men talk about that," Sonny said, looking warily at Uncle in the rear-view mirror. "But my family didn't die in that sense."

"Then what happened to them?"

"My father threw me out of the house. He told my mother and my five sisters never to speak to me again. They haven't," Sonny said. "I'm dead to them, and they are dead to me."

"I shouldn't have asked that question."

"I don't mind," Sonny said deliberately. "I was one of six kids, born in Kowloon Walled City. When I was thirteen, my father took me out of school and apprenticed me to a stonemason. What little money I made, he took. If I protested, he beat me. Then one day I'd had enough and I hit him back. That was it."

"How did you find your way from there to the brotherhood?"

"I met a triad in jail. He explained the history of the society to me and recited the Thirty-Six Oaths from memory. The oaths struck a chord in me. I was at an age when I wanted to belong to something. He agreed to recommend me to his gang, which was here in Fanling."

"What was his name?"

"Seto. He died six months after I was accepted as a Blue Lantern."

"I remember him. How long was it before you took the oaths?"

"Four years. The day I did was the proudest and happiest day of my life," Sonny said.

"I felt the same way," Uncle said.

The car eased through traffic and stopped in front of the Blind Emperor. His normal twenty-minute walk was less than a five-minute drive.

"I'll be here until eight if you need me," Sonny said.

"I doubt that I will, but I'll see you in the morning, Sonny."

Uncle walked over to the entrance, then, realizing he

hadn't eaten since breakfast, made a detour into the restaurant. He ordered steamed fish with ginger and sticky rice with barbecued pork, asking the owner to bring the food upstairs when it was ready.

When he entered his apartment, he saw there was a message on his phone. He played it and heard Liu Leji's voice. "As promised, I have looked into the matter we discussed, concerning how the Chinese government might deal with triads after the handover. Call me."

There was something in Leji's tone that made Uncle think he would be pleased with what his partner had discovered. With a sense of anticipation, he phoned Leji's home in Beijing.

"You caught me just as I was getting ready to leave the house," Leji said when he answered.

"I can call back later."

"No, we can talk now. It's been an interesting day here, which ended up with my uncle speaking to Deng Xiaoping."

Deng? Uncle thought. *Why would he be involved?* "How is Deng? He must be older than ninety now. Is he enjoying retirement?"

"He's ninety-one, his health is good, and he's hardly retired," Leji said. "Jiang Zemin may be president, but that's in name only. No one takes him seriously. Deng is still running the government from the shadows."

"Then I'm even more curious to know why your uncle spoke with him."

"That's not something I'm permitted to share. It's enough for you to know that they spoke," Leji said. "I have been told, though, that the fearmongering being perpetuated by your triad colleague is complete nonsense. There are no plans to eradicate the triads after the handover."

"I am very pleased to hear that."

"We were as well. We've built a substantial business together, and my uncle is aware of the details. No one wants to see that business threatened or disrupted," Leji said. "And I should add that we're far from being the only family with similar ties to Hong Kong."

"Please thank your uncle for his assistance in getting to the truth. The fact that it comes from Deng eliminates all doubt."

"Uncle, if you decide to tell your colleagues they have nothing to fear, you can't use Deng's name, or my uncle's."

"That's unfortunate but I understand, and you know I'll honour that request," Uncle said. He was disappointed, wondering how seriously the other Mountain Masters would take assurances from an anonymous source.

"You might want to hold off saying anything for now," Leji said. "My uncle is working on something that may be better at allaying fear."

"What are you getting at?" Uncle asked, his interest spiking again.

"I'm going to be in Shenzhen this coming Wednesday. Can you join me there?"

"Of course."

"Bring Fong with you. I'll arrange a dinner with my aunt and wife."

"You aren't going to tell me what this is about?"

"No. There are still some details to be worked out, and I don't want to risk looking foolish if plans change," Leji said. "I'll be in touch about the dinner."

CHAPTER FIFTEEN

DESPITE RECURRING THOUGHTS ABOUT HIS CONVERSA-
tion with Liu Leji, Uncle slept well. It wasn't like Leji to be so
vague, but it was that vagueness that finally convinced Uncle
there was no point in thinking about it anymore. He had
spent most of the evening handicapping the Sha Tin races.
It had been quiet, with only two phone interruptions from
Wang to tell him that the streets were calm. Uncle woke at
six-thirty, made an instant coffee, shaved, showered, and
went downstairs with the racing form in hand. Sonny was
outside, leaning against a wall.

"Good morning, boss," Sonny said.

"Good morning. I'm going to Jia's Congee for breakfast.
It's a short walk, so I don't need the car."

"I'll walk with you," said Sonny.

Uncle started to say that wasn't necessary, but Sonny had
already moved next to him with an air of determination.
It was another beautiful morning and Uncle was beginning to look forward to his day at the Sha Tin track. It had
opened in 1978 and, while it didn't have the long history
of Happy Valley, it was a first-class racing venue, with two

huge grandstands and an audience capacity of 85,000. Uncle normally sat with Tse, who had a permanent table in the Racing Club restaurant, which overlooked the finish line. Entry to the club required a pass, and Uncle knew Sonny wouldn't be allowed in.

"I'm going to Sha Tin for the races today. I'll leave here around eleven-thirty. You should drop me off and come back later to pick me up," Uncle said.

"Okay," said Sonny.

Uncle bought his papers at the newsstand, then continued on to Jia's. "Are you coming inside?" Uncle asked.

"No, I'll stay out here."

After a leisurely breakfast and another hour poring over the selections of the *Sing Tao* and *Oriental Daily News* race handicappers, Uncle left Jia's. When Sonny fell in about half a step behind, Uncle felt a touch of annoyance. He hadn't realized how much having a bodyguard would impinge on his privacy. He decided to talk to Wang about making Sonny less of a constant presence.

It was a typical early Sunday morning in Fanling, with only a few pedestrians and sparse traffic on the street. Activity would pick up by mid-morning, and by dinnertime the place would be bustling. The Blind Emperor was always packed with families on Sunday evenings, so Uncle either ate a late lunch at the racetrack or went to Dong's Kitchen to get the numbers from the day's betting action and a plate of Dong's famous chicken feet. He was trying to decide which option he would prefer when Sonny said, "Boss, slow down."

"Why?" Uncle asked.

"I think I saw someone moving in the doorway to your building. Let me go ahead and check."

"The restaurant cooks always arrive early on Sunday to prep the food for dinner," Uncle said, continuing at the same pace.

Sonny sped up and moved past him. Uncle's annoyance flared and he was about to say something when Sonny stopped and his body stiffened. Uncle looked towards the doorway and saw three men coming towards them, machetes pressed against their sides.

"Run," Sonny said to Uncle.

"No. I have a switchblade in my pocket and I know how to use it," he said, reaching into his jacket.

"Don't come any closer," Sonny said to the men, who were inching nearer.

"Yes, back off. This is a mistake," Uncle said.

One of the men said something indistinct and his colleagues nodded. Then one screamed, "Aiiiiiiiieee!" and they charged.

Sonny stepped towards them, shielding Uncle. The men were about a metre apart, and Uncle guessed their plan was to encircle him. Before they could reach him, though, Sonny leapt at them. Uncle froze, shocked at his protector's audacity.

The three men were also caught off guard. The one to the left managed to swing his machete before Sonny was on top of him. The blade bit into his forearm, but that didn't deter Sonny. He smashed the man in the face, sending him and the machete clattering to the ground. The other two men jumped towards Sonny as he reached down to pick up the weapon. In one seamless motion, the machete in Sonny's hand left the ground and slashed the thigh of the man closest to him. As he reeled back, his partner came to a stop.

"C'mon, try me. I'll cut your throat, you son of a bitch," Sonny growled.

The man stared at him, and Uncle could see his hand shaking. Without saying a word, he turned and ran.

The man on the ground began to stir. Sonny walked over to him and planted a foot on his head. "Don't move," he said, and then looked at the man with the bleeding thigh. He was still upright, machete in his hand. "And if you want to get away from here, I suggest you do it now."

The man nodded, shuffled backwards, and then charged at Sonny, his machete held head-high. Sonny waited until the man was almost on top of him before he took a quick step to the right. The blade missed him by what looked to Uncle like no more than a hair's width. Sonny's machete didn't miss. As the man went past him, Sonny drove the weapon into his shoulder near the neck. Blood spurted and the man collapsed to the ground, grabbing at his neck in an attempt to stem the flow.

"Oh my god," Uncle heard someone say. He looked towards the restaurant and saw two of its cooks standing in the doorway.

"Are you okay, Uncle?" one asked. "We saw the whole thing through the window. We saw them attack you first."

"Call for an ambulance," Uncle said.

"Sure, right away," the other cook said.

Uncle looked at the man with the neck wound. "I don't think he's going to make it," he said to Sonny. Then he turned his attention to the man whose head was being pressed into the ground under Sonny's foot. "Lift your foot, Sonny. I want to talk to this one."

Uncle looked down at the man. That one punch from

Sonny had destroyed his nose, and whatever other damage it had done Uncle could only guess at. Blood covered the entire lower half of his face, and the man's eyes were glazed.

Uncle knelt down so he was close to the man's face. "Do you know where you are and what just happened?" he asked. "Nod if you do."

The man's head moved ever so slightly in the affirmative.

"Good. There's an ambulance on the way for you and your buddy, but before I let you get into it, you need to answer a few questions. Will you do that?"

The man groaned as he nodded.

"Are you from Tai Wai New Village?"

The man hesitated. "Answer," Sonny said, tapping him on the side of the head with his shoe.

"We are," the man mumbled.

"Did Wu send you?"

The man nodded.

"Were your instructions to kill me?"

"Yes."

"What's your name?"

"Kwan."

"And his?" Uncle asked, pointing to the other bleeding man.

"Kwan. He's my brother."

"That's all I want to know," Uncle said.

Sonny pulled back his foot. Uncle sensed that he was about to kick the man in the head. "Don't," he said. "It's over."

"An ambulance will be here in about ten minutes," the cook said from the restaurant doorway.

"My friend and I are going upstairs to my apartment," said Uncle. "When the ambulance gets here, I want you to tell them you have no idea what happened. You heard a commotion, and when you came outside, you found these men in this condition. Tell them and the police, if they get involved, that you don't think these men are from Fanling. Say they've been hanging around the neighbourhood for a few days, and you were concerned about what they were up to."

"We'll do that, Uncle," the cook said.

Uncle looked at Sonny's bloody arm. "How is it? I have iodine and some bandages in the apartment. Will those do until we can get you proper treatment?"

"It looks worse than it is; he didn't hit bone. I've dealt with this kind of injury before."

"Still, we'll get you to a doctor after the ambulance is gone."

"I guess this means we won't be going to Sha Tin," Sonny said.

"Just the opposite. Now I have more reason than ever to go."

CHAPTER SIXTEEN

UNCLE TOOK SONNY INTO HIS BATHROOM, SHOWED him the iodine and bandages, and then went into the living room to make some calls. Before he'd finished dialling the first number he heard a siren. He went to the window and watched attendants load the two men into an ambulance. The one who'd been struck in the neck wasn't moving. When the ambulance left, Uncle picked up the phone and called Wang.

"If you're calling to ask if everything is quiet, it is," Wang answered. "You and Fong can enjoy your day at Sha Tin."

"Except it isn't quiet. In fact, it's the furthest thing from quiet," Uncle said. "Three of Wu's goons just tried to kill me. They ambushed me with machetes in front of my apartment building."

"Oh, fuck. Are you okay? Where are you now?"

"I'm in my apartment and I am okay. They're not — Sonny Kwok took care of them. Two of them are brothers; their family name is Kwan. One may die and the other will need medical attention. The third ran off," Uncle said. "And Wang, about five minutes before it happened, I was beginning to question whether having a bodyguard was worth the trouble. There are no questions now. Kwok was incredible. I'd be dead without him."

"Thank god you weren't hurt," Wang said, and then paused. "What are we going to do? How should we respond to this? Do you want us to go after Wu?"

"No," Uncle said sharply. "And that's an order, so don't give it another thought."

"Then what do you have in mind?"

"I'll phone Fong when you and I are finished. I want the two of you to spend the afternoon calling your peers in the Territories, Kowloon, and Hong Kong Island. They need to know what happened. I want to isolate Wu from the gangs in the Territories and give the others pause if they're thinking of siding with him. After this, even Man might have doubts about supporting Wu."

"Is that all you want us to do? Uncle, I don't disagree with you very often, but that's a weak response."

"We'll respond more forcefully later. I don't want to rush into it. I want to take time to think about what could inflict maximum damage to the well-being of Wu's gang, and then plan accordingly."

"He makes most of his money from drugs," Wang said quickly. "He must have a central warehouse or a distribution centre."

"You're right about their dependence on drug money," Uncle said. "Locate their warehouse and then find out everything you can about it. It might be what we need to send a message."

"I'm on it."

"But make those phone calls first."

"Yes, boss," Wang said. "What about the rest of the day? Do you think Wu will try anything else? Maybe we should leave the betting shops closed."

"Do you have all our men on the streets?"

"Yes."

"Then we should be all right. Besides, after botching the attack on me, I can't imagine the Tai Wai gang will be keen to try anything else for a while."

"You're probably correct, but we'll keep our men on full alert."

"One last thing. Sonny was struck on the arm by a machete. He says he's fine, but I want him to see a doctor. After he drives me to the racetrack, I'll send him to you."

"Tell him to come to Dong's Kitchen. He'll be well looked after."

As Uncle ended the call, he started shivering. During the attack he'd been calm, an adrenalin rush cancelling out any fear. Now the adrenalin was ebbing, and the realization that he could have been killed had kicked in.

"Are you okay, boss?" Sonny said from the bathroom doorway.

"It's been a long time since I was a party to anything that violent. It shook me a bit."

"I couldn't tell. You looked cool enough to me."

"Never mind about that, how is your arm?" Uncle asked.

"It'll be sore for a few days at least, but it's only a flesh wound. The iodine should do the trick."

"I've spoken to Wang. Meet him at Dong's after dropping me off at the racetrack. He'll make arrangements for you to see a doctor," Uncle said. "I insist that you see one, so don't argue with me."

"Yes, sir."

"I have another phone call to make. Why don't you go downstairs and see what's going on. I'll join you when I'm finished and then we'll head to Sha Tin."

Uncle waited until Sonny was in the stairway before he phoned Fong. His old friend's reaction to what had happened was more extreme than Wang's. It took a few minutes before he finally ran out of swear words, curses, and threats — all of them delivered in raging anger. When Fong was finally ready to listen, Uncle gave him the same instructions he'd given Wang. Then he added, "I think Wu has thrown away whatever advantage he thought he'd achieved with the incident at the night market. We are now the injured party, and we have to press that fact home. If he had killed me, he might have been able to plead ignorance and convince at least some of the gangs to support him. But we know the names of the men he sent, and there will be no denying that. Their failure is going to tar his reputation. We have to capitalize on that."

"How are we going to retaliate?" Fong asked.

Uncle repeated what he and Wang had discussed.

"I would rather we killed the fucker," Fong said.

"I'm not going down that road. Nothing good would come from it," Uncle said. "I want you to make it clear that that option is off the table. Wu may choose to be dishonourable and break one of our most important unwritten rules, but we aren't going to do anything that reckless or disgraceful."

"I'll be asked what we're going to do. If we want to maintain the respect of the other gangs, they'll have to believe we're going to do something. How much can I tell them?"

"All you should say is that we're thinking about how best to respond to the attack, and that they'll find out in good time what we've decided."

CHAPTER SEVENTEEN

WHEN UNCLE ENTERED THE RACING CLUB AT SHA TIN Racecourse, he expected to see Tse and Sammy Wing. But as he walked towards their regular table, he saw another man sitting with them. His back was to Uncle, but the silver hair that reached to his shoulders made him instantly recognizable.

"Zhao, this is a surprise," Uncle said. "When was the last time you left Kowloon for the fresh air of the New Territories?"

"And I'm surprised to see you," the other Mountain Master said as he stood to greet Uncle. "Tse predicted you would come today, but I didn't entirely believe him."

"Your men have been busy spreading the word," Sammy Wing said. "Is it true? Did Wu's men try to kill you?"

"That was my morning adventure," Uncle said. "And in case anyone doubts that Wu was behind it, I questioned one of the men and he admitted it. His name is Kwan. He and his brother were two of the three men who attacked me. I think the brother died, and Kwan knew he'd be dead too if he lied to me."

"I tried to call to see how you were," Tse said.

"I wasn't answering the phone," said Uncle. "I wanted time to think."

"I told Zhao I didn't believe you'd overreact, regardless of the provocation," Tse said.

"I wonder if Wu has any idea how much damage he's done to his organization with that move," Zhao said, retaking his seat. "A lot of gangs will steer clear of him now. His businesses are going to take a hit."

Uncle sat down and looked at the track, where the horses for the first race were on post parade. "I hope that's true," he said.

"What is it between you and Wu?" Sammy Wing asked. "You've been going at each other for as many years as I can remember."

"He wants to sell drugs in Fanling and I won't let him. He tried to extort money from local Fanling businesses, and I put a stop to it. He resents that I control a large piece of the knock-off market and he has to buy the products from me. He has asked me many times to use my police contacts to help some of his men who were in trouble with the law. I refused because the trouble was drug-related, and one reason I've been able to maintain my contacts is that we avoid anything to do with drugs."

Tse looked at Wing. "Wu has no respect for anyone who doesn't want to do business his way."

Zhao had been listening carefully but now turned his attention to the racing form. "I'm told you are an expert handicapper. Which do you like in the first race?" he asked Uncle.

"The seven horse," Uncle said.

"Thanks. I think I'll place a bet on it," Zhao said.

"I'll go with you," said Wing.

"You aren't betting on this race?" Tse asked when the other two men had left.

"I placed my bet on the way in," Uncle said, then leaned towards Tse. "What's Zhao doing here?"

"He's weighing his options."

"That's not telling me much."

Tse shrugged. "It should come from him."

"I'm hoping that someone who's been my friend for as long as you have can at least give me a hint."

"He's in a difficult position," Tse said carefully. "He doesn't agree with what Man and the others want to do, but he has to share Kowloon with them. If he isn't with them, they might decide he's against them. It would be three against one, unless of course Zhao had the support of other gangs."

"What other gangs? You told me the Hong Kong Island triads want nothing to do with Kowloon."

"That's true, but Zhao has heard about the coalition you're trying to put together in the New Territories. I think he's wondering if joining it might provide him the protection he needs."

"There's no coalition yet," Uncle said.

"But assuming there was, is there a reason it couldn't include Zhao? At least part of his turf borders on the New Territories."

"It's certainly something worth thinking about," Uncle said. He saw Wing and Zhao returning. "We should talk more about it later."

"It isn't me you should be talking to," Tse said. "And some advice: let Zhao raise the subject with you."

Zhao and Wing rejoined the table and everyone's

attention turned to the start of the race. Two minutes later, the number-seven horse had won. Zhao celebrated by buying a round of drinks, and as the afternoon passed, the drinks continued to flow. The other men ate but Uncle declined. The gang members in Fanling knew about the attack by then and knew he was well, but a visit to Dong's Kitchen would be proof that nothing had changed.

It was a moderately successful betting day for Uncle, and for Zhao, who bet on all the same horses. Sammy Wing was having a bad day and grumbled incessantly about poor jockeys and bad luck. After the sixth race he expanded his complaints. "What a shit week this has been," he said. "Did the rest of you get raided?"

"From what I've heard, I think we all did," Tse said.

"I lost more than a million dollars in goods," Wing said. "I can only imagine how much worse it might get when the Communists take over."

"Are you buying Man's argument that they'll attack us after the handover?" Uncle asked.

"It makes sense after the way they treated us in China."

"Except we're back in China now and they've left us alone," Tse said.

"You're only in the sEZs and Shanghai, where you are paying government officials to leave you alone. You know that kind of bribery doesn't work in Hong Kong."

"Sammy, I've been told by a senior Chinese government official that the police system in place now will be left alone," Uncle said. "The PLA and the Ministry of Public Security won't interfere. Man's argument is bullshit."

"What's the name of this senior official?" Wing asked.

"I can't tell you his name."

"Of course you can't. He probably doesn't exist," Wing said with a dismissive wave of his hand.

"Hey, you're my guest here," Tse said sharply. "I always take Uncle at his word, and unless you can prove otherwise, I think you should as well."

"It's okay, I'm not offended," Uncle said to Tse, and then looked at Wing. "Let me ask you something, Sammy. If I could provide proof positive that the Chinese won't interfere, would you have the guts to tell Man he's wrong and that you don't support his expansionist ideas?"

"I've never said I support them."

"You also haven't said you don't, and you've been reluctant to criticize Yin's activities in Macau. People might conclude that you're onside with Man."

"The only thing I care about is my gang's best interests," Wing said. "If you forced me to choose between what Man wants to do and keeping the status quo, I'd find it hard. You could say I'm waiting to see which direction the train is going before I hop on board."

"That's fair enough, but if I provided proof positive, would you hop on our train?"

"Maybe," Wing said.

Uncle smiled. "I have to respect your consistent commitment to your own self-interest above anything else."

"None of you are any different," Wing said.

"Enough. You're giving me a headache," Tse said. "We're at the races. Let's enjoy them."

"I can't stay," Uncle said suddenly. "I have a driver now and he'll be at the pickup point in a few minutes."

"This is unusual — there are two races left. You aren't leaving because of Sammy, are you?" Tse asked.

"No, I meant it when I said I wasn't offended. I want to beat the crowds after the eighth race and I don't want to keep the driver waiting. He's also my bodyguard, and he saved my life this morning," said Uncle. "I figure the least I can do for him is be punctual."

"I'll walk you out," Zhao said.

They left the club together. Uncle noticed several women eyeing the silver-haired Kowloon Mountain Master. He was tall, graceful, and always dressed impeccably in the finest luxury brands.

Zhao waited until they were on the escalator down to the ground floor before he spoke. "I heard about your meeting with the other Mountain Masters," he said. "My friend Ng had some very positive things to say about it."

"Ng has been supportive of some of my ideas. I am tremendously grateful for that."

"Ng, like you, is a thoughtful man," Zhao said. "Do your thoughts lead you to believe you can convince the others to form a real coalition?"

"What do you mean by *real*?" asked Uncle.

"My experience with triads is that they'll agree to anything that has potential benefit, as long as it doesn't require a commitment or incur a cost," Zhao said. "The problem has often been that when they're called on to make any kind of sacrifice, they renege on the agreement. Our friend Sammy Wing is a fine example of that kind of thinking. You described him perfectly when you said his only commitment is to his own self-interest."

"Self-interest is a powerful motivator. If I have to appeal to that to get the gangs to coalesce, I will," said Uncle. "But you're correct that the possibility of gangs reneging is real.

I have some proposals to put forward that might make that less attractive."

"Such as?"

Uncle laughed. "I think I should save that for next Friday, when I meet with the group again."

They were on the main floor and working their way through the milling crowds. Hong Kong racegoers tended to arrive early, many of them as soon as the gates opened two hours before race time, and didn't leave until the last race had been run and the results posted.

When they reached the main gates, Zhao stepped to one side and came to a stop. "I have something to ask that you might find odd," he said to Uncle.

"Go ahead."

"I would like to attend your meeting next Friday, but I won't do so unless I'm invited and I'm welcome."

"Then consider yourself invited, and be assured you will be welcome," said Uncle.

"You have no interest in knowing why I want to come?"

"Yes, I do, but I figure you'll tell me when you're ready."

CHAPTER EIGHTEEN

UNCLE SPOTTED SONNY WITH THE MERCEDES IN THE area reserved for limousine pickup. The Mercedes was one of about fifty, and half of them were grey. But there was only one Sonny, and he towered above the other drivers. He was also one of the few drivers not wearing a suit.

"How is your arm?" Uncle asked when he reached him.

"Fourteen stitches, so not so bad. I've been cut worse," he said as he opened the back door for Uncle.

"I'll buy you a new shirt," Uncle said.

"I bought six yesterday. There's no need, but thank you."

Uncle settled into the back seat. "We're going to Dong's Kitchen."

It was a seven-kilometre drive from Sha Tin to Fanling. Given that traffic was light, Uncle guessed they'd get to Dong's before the eighth race began.

Uncle hadn't said much to Sonny during the ride to the racetrack, and he knew he should have. "I've been meaning to thank you for this morning," he said as the car reached Fanling's outskirts. "It was a lot to deal with on your second day in a new job, and you couldn't have done better. You saved my life."

Sonny looked at him in the rear-view mirror. "Boss, no one is ever going to get to you without killing me first. I promise you that."

"I believe you. I just hope, for both our sakes, that people don't make a practice of trying to kill me."

When they reached Dong's, all the parking spots were taken. "Drop me off in front and then join us after you find a place to park," Uncle said.

On Sundays and Wednesdays the restaurant staff put away some tables and pushed the larger ones off to one side to create as much space as possible for the bettors to mingle. Tian and his staff sat at a long table in the rear of the restaurant; the bettors stood in long lines in front of them. Twelve televisions airing the races encircled the area. Before the Hong Kong Jockey Club had opened its own off-track facilities, Dong's would be so packed that the sidewalks around the building could barely contain the overflow. Now there were only a few clusters of people outside, and most of them were there to smoke.

Uncle went inside, waved at Tian, and bypassed the betting table to go into the kitchen. He wanted to say hello to Dong, who would be supervising organizing the food that would be in demand as soon as the eighth race ended. Dong had to be in his seventies, Uncle guessed, but he never missed a day of work. He thought about Jia, and wondered if owning a restaurant was the secret to longevity.

"Hey, Uncle, I heard about this morning," Dong said when he saw him. "Some people have no sense. I hope you're going to make them pay."

"I don't want to talk about that, or today's betting handle," Uncle said with a smile. "I'm here for chicken feet, your fried salt-and-pepper squid, and maybe some short ribs."

"The ribs will be good today; I made the sauce myself. They might even be better than the chicken feet."

"Nothing is better than Dong's chicken feet," Uncle said, and then he heard a scream. He and Dong looked towards the door and both started to move in that direction at the same time. Before they got there, there was another scream, a noise that sounded like crashing glass, and then the unmistakeable staccato burst of a semi-automatic.

"Stay here," Uncle said to Dong.

There was chaos in the dining room. Some people had thrown themselves onto the floor, while others were scrambling to get under tables. People were foolishly trying to get out the front door. All that activity was accompanied by yells of fear and confusion. Tian hadn't left his seat and shook his head in grim resignation when he saw Uncle.

Uncle scanned the room, looking for signs of blood. To his relief it didn't appear that anyone had been hit, and the gunfire seemed to have ceased.

Tian stood up. "Everyone should remain calm!" he shouted. "It looks like some idiot threw a brick through the window and then took out the rest of it with a gun. Probably a sore loser. I don't think we have to worry about him coming back."

The noise in the room started to subside and people began rising to their feet and crawling out from under the tables.

"Was there a brick?" Uncle quietly asked Tian.

"Yes. And whoever was shooting aimed high. They didn't

want to hit anyone. This was an attempt to intimidate our customers and screw up our business."

"Boss!" a young man said excitedly as he approached Tian.

"Were you outside?"

"Yeah."

"What did you see?"

"A black Toyota stopped in front of the restaurant. I thought it was dropping someone off because there was nowhere to park. A guy got out of the back seat and, before I realized what he was doing, he heaved a brick at the window. When he jumped back into the car, someone lowered the front passenger window and began shooting. Then they drove off."

"What's your name?" Uncle asked the young man.

"This is Chan; he's a Blue Lantern," Tian said. "Chan, this is Uncle. He's our Mountain Master." Chan bowed his head towards Uncle.

"Can you describe the men?"

"I didn't get a clear look at the guy with the gun, but the one who threw the brick was heavily tattooed."

"Thanks," Uncle said. Then he saw Dong walking towards them.

"What's going to happen now? Will you close down for the day?" Dong asked.

"I think that would set a bad example," said Tian. "There's still one race left. If people feel safe enough to stay, I think we should let them."

"I agree, and I think Tian should make that announcement," Uncle said.

Dong nodded. "I'll have my people sweep up the glass."

"We'll pay for the window," Uncle said. Dong nodded again, as if he expected nothing less.

"I'd also like to use your phone," Uncle said to Dong as Tian informed everyone that they were still open for business.

"There's one in the kitchen and another in my office," Dong said.

Uncle turned to Tian. "Do you know where Wang is?"

"He should be on his way here. He normally arrives after the last race to help me close the books and put away the money. Then we have dinner."

Uncle saw Sonny enter the restaurant and motioned for him to join them. "Stay here with Tian while things settle. I'm going into the back to make some phone calls," he told him.

Dong's office was as small and cluttered as Jia's, and Uncle had to move paper around to get to the phone.

"Are you back from the track already?" Fong asked when he answered.

"I'm at Dong's Kitchen. The front window was just shot to pieces but no one was hurt. I suspect it was a message from our friend Wu that he isn't backing down."

"Have you spoken to Wang?"

"No, but Tian says he's on his way here. What I'd like you to do is call the rest of the executive. We need to meet, and Dong's is as good a place as any," Uncle said. He looked at the clock on the wall. "Try to get them all here by six. The bettors should have left by then."

"I'll contact them right away," Fong said.

"Before you go, how did your contacts react when you told them about this morning's attack?"

"There was a lot of professed shock, some of it real, and

there was anger, some of it real as well," Fong said. "Generally speaking, the reaction from the Territories gangs was supportive. Though I have to say, Uncle, it might have caused some of them to have second thoughts about aligning themselves with us, if it means going to war right now against Wu and Man."

"I'm not asking them to align themselves just with Fanling. There are potentially eight other gangs in this with us."

"But we're the ones pushing the idea, and most of them refer to it as 'Uncle's plan.'"

"Whatever," Uncle snapped impatiently, and then quickly added, "I didn't mean to sound like I doubt what you heard. I just find that some of our colleagues are short-sighted. But not all of them are. In fact I had a pleasant surprise this afternoon: Tse, Wing, and I were joined at the track by Zhao."

"What did he want?"

"An invitation to attend our meeting next Friday."

"That's strange."

"I suspect it might get even stranger. I think he wants to join our alliance," Uncle said.

"Shit. That would cause panic in Kowloon."

"It might also encourage any reluctant brothers we have in the Territories to jump on board."

"So did you invite him?"

"I most certainly did."

"What a coup Zhao would be," said Fong.

"The danger is, of course, that he'll come to the meeting, hear us out, and decide not to join," Uncle said.

"It's worth the risk."

"Of course it is, and I'll do everything I can to get him onside," said Uncle. "In the meantime we have to deal with

Wu. We can't let this continue. The last thing I want is a full-scale war, but unless we're committed to defending what's ours, Wu will eat us away bit by bit until there's nothing left."

CHAPTER NINETEEN

WANG WAS THE FIRST MEMBER OF THE EXECUTIVE COM-
mittee to join Uncle and Tian at Dong's Kitchen. When he
found out about the most recent attack, he stood outside
shouting at a forty-niner and a Blue Lantern before entering
the restaurant.

"Go easy on them. There was nothing they could have
done to stop it," Uncle said as Wang reached him. "It was a
hit and run."

"My blood is boiling," Wang growled.

"That's why I want you to help Tian close the accounts as
you usually do. I want things to be as normal as possible."

"What about the cops? Have they been here? Is this going
to cause a problem with them?"

"I had Dong phone the local station. He told them a dis-
gruntled customer tossed a brick through the restaurant
window and that he'll go to the station tomorrow to file an
official complaint."

"Will they buy it?"

"Thus far there's been no sign of them, and I'm assuming
that's because they believed him."

Over the next hour the other members of the committee arrived and sat down at a table Dong had set up at the back of the restaurant. Uncle had spoken to all of them in the morning, after the attack at his building, and his message had been to stay calm. Now, as he saw how agitated they were, he knew such words wouldn't be enough. He ordered water, tea, and beer and said to them, "Let's not get into this until Tian and Wang join us."

Dong helped serve the drinks and asked, "Do you want something to eat?"

"I'll let you know. For now, we're fine," said Uncle.

When Dong had left, Yu opened a beer and said, "I heard from nearly all the gangs in the Territories this afternoon. They wanted to know if you were okay. Someone has been spreading a rumour that you were injured, and one Vanguard asked if it was true you had been killed."

"Our brothers like to gossip. Maybe Uncle should take a tour of the Territories so everyone can see he's still alive," Hui said with a smile.

"There's nothing funny about this," Yu said.

"And nothing fatal on our side either, at least not yet. I'm still here, and no one who was in Dong's was hurt," Uncle said. "I'm not downplaying what happened, but I don't want to talk about it any further without Tian and Wang."

"Here they come," Hui said.

Wang and Tian sat side by side directly across from Uncle. Tian reached for a beer. "I haven't had a beer in six months. After today, I need one."

"What are we going to do, boss?" Yu asked.

"As always, direct and to the point," Uncle said, and turned to Wang. "Did you locate Wu's warehouse?"

"Yes. It's close to the railway station. I sat in my car for an hour and watched men and cars come and go. It's a busy place — a major distribution centre for rice and dry goods as well as Tai Wai's drug business. The rice and the other goods provide cover for the drug operation."

"How do you know about the drugs?" Yu asked.

"I was told by two Red Poles. And when I was at the warehouse, I saw at least six groups of guys from other gangs arriving empty-handed and leaving with boxes," Wang said. "I can guarantee they weren't buying rice."

"How many men are guarding the place?" Uncle asked.

"I'd be surprised if it's less than ten," Wang said.

Uncle nodded and then said carefully, "I asked Wang to find out where Tai Wai stores and distributes its drugs. It seems he has, and that gives us a way forward. I know all of you want us to respond to what happened today, and we will. But whatever we do has to be strategic and meaningful. I want to really hurt them, and killing a few men or shooting up a couple of massage parlours won't accomplish that. Crippling their drug business will."

"If they have ten men there, it won't be easy or quiet," Yu said. "It will cause a stir with the cops and, if we're successful, it's going to piss off some of the gangs who buy drugs from Tai Wai."

"I'm going to give the police a heads-up and trust that they'll stand by. In a sense, if we dismantle or disrupt Tai Wai's drug business, we're doing their job for them," Uncle said. "As for the other gangs, if I have to choose between pissing them off in the short term and sending them a message that Fanling hits back, there's only one choice. Besides, they'll find other sources soon enough and they'll get over it."

"Do you really believe the police will stand by?" Hui asked.

"I'll do what I can to persuade them it's the best strategy for all concerned. If we go in, take control of the warehouse, destroy what we can, and then turn the building over to the police, I think they might go along with it," Uncle said.

"They could even claim it was a police operation and take credit for it," Fong said.

"You're reading my mind," Uncle said.

"I don't mean to sound negative, but what if the police won't stand by?" Hui asked.

"We'll go ahead anyway. My contact won't give the police station in Tai Wai a heads-up. We'll just hope they don't respond too quickly."

"I trust Uncle's judgement," Tian said, then turned to Wang. "How many men will you need to take down the warehouse?"

"I've been thinking about that all afternoon. I'd like to go in at maybe two or three in the morning. There shouldn't be much regular business going on, and few civilians. I'm also figuring Tai Wai won't have as many guards in the middle of the night as they do during the day."

"I wouldn't count on that," Uncle said. "I'll be more comfortable if you make plans based on them having ten men there."

"Okay. In that case I'll take twenty men with me. We need to overwhelm them and take control as quickly as possible."

"When would you do it?" Hui asked.

Wang looked at Uncle. "I'm thinking the sooner the better."

"I agree. If we wait, they might feel emboldened to pull off another stunt like the one here at Dong's," said Uncle. "I also want to quickly eliminate any doubts the other gangs might have about our willingness and ability to defend ourselves."

"So, do we go in tonight?" Wang asked.

"Can you have twenty men ready by then?"

"I could have fifty. Everyone is on alert and itching to have a go at them."

"Then we'll do it tonight," said Uncle.

"Lau is outside. I'll give him the green light to start assembling our men," Wang said. "He was at the warehouse with me and drove around it a few times. Between the two of us we have it scoped out quite well."

As Wang left the table, Uncle motioned to Dong. "We're ready to eat now. We'll have chicken feet, squid, the beef ribs, fried noodles with seafood, and bok choy."

"Yes, Uncle," Dong said.

Uncle drained his San Miguel and opened another. "We need to fortify ourselves; this is going to be a long night. I imagine none of us will get much sleep until Wang and the men are home safely."

"I only hope tonight ends this nonsense," Hui said.

"I don't think it will, but I do believe it's a means to the end," said Uncle.

CHAPTER TWENTY

JUST BEFORE EIGHT O'CLOCK, UNCLE CLIMBED THE stairs to his apartment. With the exception of Wang, the executive committee members would be at home that evening, waiting for a call to tell them how the attack on the warehouse had gone. Wang was scheduled to call Uncle first. The group had been in good spirits during dinner. There was something about making a decision to act that had helped erase doubts and inspire confidence — especially because the entire committee agreed it was the right decision. Uncle knew that didn't guarantee a successful outcome, but the fact that the decision was unanimous would help them sustain solidarity whatever the result. And although he never took anything for granted, Uncle had confidence in Wang and his men.

Among the men heading for the warehouse in Tai Wai New Village was Sonny Kwok. As soon as he heard about the plan he had approached Wang and asked to be included. Wang went to Uncle. "Sonny wants to come with us to Tai Wai. I can't make that decision."

"Will he be an asset or a liability? What if he loses his

temper again? I want to gain control of the warehouse, but I don't want it to become a bloodbath."

"I think he'd be an asset. The other men are more confident when he's with them. They've seen him in action and know he'll cover their backs," Wang said. "Uncle, I'll talk to him. I'll stress that he has to follow my lead."

"If that's what you think, then I have no objections."

Sonny had driven Uncle home. "I know you're going to Tai Wai tonight," Uncle told him before he got out of the car. "I'm putting my trust in you not to go overboard. Do whatever Wang directs. No more, and no less."

"Yes, boss," Sonny said. "Thank you for allowing me to go."

When Uncle entered the apartment, he went directly to the fridge for a San Miguel. He carried it to his chair, lit a cigarette, and thought about how much lead time he should give Zhang Delun. *Shit. There's no point in delaying*, he decided.

Zhang's wife answered the phone, recognized his voice, and said quietly, "Just one minute, Uncle. I'll get my husband."

"I was wondering if you would call," Zhang said. "There was a rather strange event today in Fanling. Two men from Tai Wai were involved in a violent fight in front of the Blind Emperor Restaurant. If I'm not mistaken, you live in an apartment above the restaurant."

"I do. I heard about the event when I returned home after breakfast at Jia's. What did the men have to say for themselves?"

"One died, so he's not saying anything. The other won't tell us what happened or how he happened to be in that part of town."

"That's unfortunate."

"So this had nothing to do with you?"

"Absolutely not," said Uncle, pleased that Zhang was confining himself to the machete attack and not commenting on the gunfire at Dong's.

"Then why are you calling me?" Zhang asked.

"I want to give you notice that we're undertaking an action tonight that will be to our mutual benefit."

"Mutual benefit?"

"Yes. Wu's gang from Tai Wai has been trying to peddle drugs in Fanling again. We keep putting a stop to it, but they're persistent. We've come to the point where we have decided to deal with the problem at its source."

"How do you intend to do that?"

"We've identified the warehouse they use as their main storage and distribution centre," said Uncle. "In about six hours from now, a large group of my men will take control of the warehouse and destroy every drug they can get their hands on. When we're finished, our plan is to advise the police, who can take over from there. In fact, you can take the credit for closing a major drug distribution centre."

When Zhang didn't respond immediately, Uncle knew his half-truths weren't sitting well with the policeman. Would Zhang question them or let them slide? If he questioned them, how truthful should Uncle be?

"A few things occur to me, and I suspect they are connected," Zhang said slowly. "One, if your sole intention is to put the drug distribution centre out of business, a phone call to me with the relevant information would have sufficed. Why put your men at risk when we can do the job for you? Next, I have trouble believing it's a coincidence that the warehouse is in Tai Wai New Village and the two men found outside your apartment are from the same place. Do you want to tell me what's really going on?" Uncle took a deep drag on his cigarette. He knew the truth had to come out. "There weren't two men in front of my apartment this morning; there were three. They were sent by Wu to kill me. One ran off when my bodyguard foiled the attack. You know what happened to the other two," Uncle said.

"I'm glad they weren't successful, but I am concerned that they tried. I don't want the war in Kowloon and Macau to spill over into the New Territories," Zhang said, not the least bit annoyed that Uncle had initially been less than forthcoming. "Won't this venture of yours tonight aggravate the situation?"

"Zhang, I have to respond to this morning's attack somehow or risk losing my credibility with the other Mountain Masters — and, even more importantly, with my men," Uncle said. "There are those who think it should be an eye for an eye, that I should try to eliminate Wu. But I don't want to escalate the violence, so closing his distribution centre is my best option. It will cripple him financially, my men will be satisfied, and the other Mountain Masters will be reluctant to support him. I'm quite sure things in the Territories will return to being calm after this."

"How can you be so sure?"

Uncle hesitated and then thought, *What the hell.* "I'm working on a plan that has the potential to bring permanent peace. But I need time to conclude it. I'm meeting with Liu Leji in Shenzhen on Wednesday, and I have a meeting scheduled with nine other Mountain Masters this Friday."

"Why is Leji involved?" Zhang asked.

Uncle smiled, pleased with himself for having inserted

that name into the conversation. Zhang knew Leji from their university years and was well aware of the Liu family's power, connections, and influence. "I don't think he'd appreciate my saying anything until we've had our meeting," he said.

"Does that stop you from telling me something about this plan?"

"I'm still formulating it. What I can tell you is that the main objective is to bring an end to gang wars not only in the Territories but also in the rest of Hong Kong."

"That strikes me as an ambitious undertaking," said Zhang.

"It is, and I'm not sure I'll succeed. All I know is that I have to try."

"Would it help if Wu was out of circulation until the end of the week?" Zhang asked.

The question caught Uncle off guard. He hesitated before saying, "Yes, very much."

"Then tell your men to leave enough drugs in the warehouse for us to find, and not to remove Wu's men. In fact, it would be perfect if they were gagged, bound, and ready for us to question," Zhang said. "It won't take much evidence to justify locking up Wu and some of his key men for a while. I'll work with the OCTB on it."

"Thank you, Zhang."

"No thanks are necessary for a meaningful collaboration," Zhang said. "I'll tell our Tai Wai detachment to stay at the station until they hear from me. Now, when will you let me know where to dispatch them?"

"Our men intend to go into the warehouse around two a.m. It shouldn't take more than half an hour to do what needs to be done. Can I phone you that late to confirm it went as planned?"

"I'll be waiting."

Uncle put down the phone with a sense of relief. It didn't matter how many times he and Zhang worked together, Uncle never took the policeman's co-operation for granted. This request had been particularly sizeable, and then Zhang had taken it past anything Uncle had expected, by mentioning the possibility of jailing Wu. Was it because he had mentioned Liu Leji? Perhaps Zhang, like everyone else, was concerned about what the handover to the Chinese government might mean for him. He knew Uncle and Liu were in business together, because he had introduced them. Maybe he thought that cementing his relationship with Uncle would help him with Liu. Well, whatever the motivation, the outcome was welcome, Uncle thought as he called Wang.

"Is everything ready?" he asked when his Red Pole answered.

"I have twenty of our best men armed with our latest acquisitions. I've sent four of them ahead to scout the warehouse. If there's any change in activity or the number of Wu's men, they'll let me know and we'll adjust accordingly. But as it stands, we're ready to leave here about one-twenty."

"I spoke to my police contact," Uncle said. "It couldn't have gone better."

"The Tai Wai cops will stand off?"

"Better than that. We've been asked to leave some drugs on the premises and tie up Wu's men for the cops to find and question. The plan is to arrest Wu and some of his key guys. They might never get convicted of drug dealing, but if the police can hold them for a week, that will give me time to work out a deal with the other Mountain Masters without having to look over my shoulder."

"That's great," Wang said. "Please ask your contact to make sure Wu's Red Pole is one of the guys they grab. If he and Wu are both out of circulation, not much can happen."

"I'll do that," said Uncle. "Now, good luck, and here's hoping I don't hear from you again till two-thirty."

Uncle hung up and leaned back in his chair, sipped his beer, and lit a Marlboro. It had been a long and tiring day, but at the end of it he was in a stronger position than he'd been when it began. In fact, when he considered that the day had started with three men coming at him with machetes, he could never have imagined it ending any better.

The evening was going to drag. He turned on the television and found a channel rerunning the day's races from Sha Tin. As he watched, his conversation with Zhao at the track came to mind. The Kowloon Mountain Master was a serious man, and it must have taken a lot of careful thought before he decided to approach Uncle. Having him join the coalition would be a coup, but it also might alarm his Kowloon neighbours. How would they react? Uncle shook his head. The possibilities were almost endless.

"Gui-San, there are so many ideas bouncing around in my head," he said aloud. "Sometimes I feel that I've taken on too much and I'm not up to it. All I want to do is look after my own gang, but I can't do that responsibly without taking into consideration all the outside factions that impact us — and there are so many of them. There are days when I wish I could stick my head in the sand and let the world dance around me. But I'm not built that way. I just can't do it. I have this compulsion to keep moving forward, because I fear that the moment I stop, I'll get run over.

"No one is forcing me to seek this gang alliance. It's all my own doing. I don't know where the idea came from; it was just there in my mind and I couldn't get rid of it. Now I have my whole executive working with me to make it happen and I have commitments from other Mountain Masters. The thing is, I don't know if they're doing it because they think it's the right thing or because they've simply decided they have to support me."

He closed his eyes. "This is going to be an important week in my life, Gui-San. I can't tell you logically why I feel that way, but I have this overwhelming sense that there's something big out there, something to be done that will make all my other accomplishments look pale by comparison. The thing is, I sense that it will go far beyond me, far beyond the gang, and will last long after I'm dead. Am I crazy to think like that?

"Gui-San, please say another prayer for me. I think I'm getting in too deep, but I don't know how to prevent it."

CHAPTER TWENTY-ONE

UNCLE THOUGHT HE HEARD A PHONE RINGING, BUT HE knew he was asleep and figured it was in the dream. He thought if he ignored it, it would go away. But it didn't, and as he opened his eyes he realized he was in his chair. He reached for the phone and pressed it hard against his ear. "*Wei*," he said.

"I almost gave up and called Yu," Wang said, his voice full of tension. "I thought something had happened to you."

"I'm fine. I was just sleeping," Uncle said. "What happened?"

"We have control of the warehouse. There were six of Wu's men here. We caught them by surprise but they put up a bit of a fight, until they realized how badly they were outnumbered. Two of our men were wounded, but not seriously. One of theirs is dead. When he went down, the rest of them dropped their guns. We have them tied up hand and foot, and they're scattered around the room where they put the dope into small bags for the street business," Wang said. "I can't believe how much cocaine there is here. We poured a lot of it into a toilet, but we left enough for the cops to be able to brag about making a major drug bust."

"Did you tell the Tai Wai guys who you are?"

"We didn't have to. One of them recognized me."

"Are you ready to leave?"

"We are. Tell the cops that Wu's men are in the first room on the right as they come through the main entrance. We locked the door from the outside and left the key on the floor in front of it."

"Were any civilians there?"

"A night watchman, who we locked in the office. The regular work shift doesn't start until six."

"Good. It sounds like it couldn't have gone more smoothly."

"Our men were all business, although a few of them would have liked to mix it up a bit more."

"What are you going to do with the dead guy?" Uncle asked.

"We're taking him with us. I figure it will make the cops' job easier if there isn't a body lying around for them to worry about. We'll dump him somewhere between here and Fanling."

"That's good thinking," Uncle said. "What address do I give the police for the warehouse?"

"Fifty-eight Crocus Street."

"I'll give you a couple of minutes to get out of there and then I'll call my contact," Uncle said. "Tell the men I'm grateful for their efforts tonight."

Uncle sighed with relief as he put down the phone. The Fanling Triad was fortunate to have a Red Pole as experienced and capable as Wang, but things could still have gone wrong. One man dead out of twenty-six was as good an outcome as he could have hoped for. He rose from the chair and made an instant coffee, then lit a cigarette and picked up the phone.

Zhang answered before the second ring. "Uncle, you're right on time."

"The warehouse is at fifty-eight Crocus Street," Uncle said. "The first room on the right after the main entrance is where your men should go. The door is locked but the key is on the floor in front of it. That's the room where Wu's people pack drugs to sell on the street. You'll find five of Wu's men tied up there — and a lot of cocaine."

"Were there any injuries? Do we need to involve the medical people?"

"No."

"Couldn't be any better."

"When do you think you'll be able to pick up Wu?"

"The commanding officer in Tai Wai will be heading to Wu's home as soon as he confirms the presence of drugs and Wu's men at the warehouse. I spoke to him earlier this evening, so he understands the need for speed. I've already cleared it with the OCTB. I have an excellent working relationship with one of the most senior officers there. He's results-driven and doesn't ask too many questions."

"I have one more request. Could you pick up Wu's Red Pole as well? That will greatly reduce any chance of retaliation."

"I'm sure we can arrange that. You've done a good night's work, Uncle," Zhang said. "I'll take it from here."

"Will you call to let me know about Wu?"

"You will hear from me."

Uncle hung up and immediately began phoning the other five members of the executive committee. He repeated everything Wang had told him, plus Zhang's promise to keep Wu on ice for as long as possible. The news was received with an enthusiasm that ranged from Hui's calm acceptance to

Fong's excitement, but one thing in common was that no one was surprised that Wang had been successful.

"I just hope the police can indeed keep Wu out of circulation. If they can't, I don't expect Tai Wai to take this sitting down," Tian said, reflecting another common sentiment. "What do you want us to do now?"

"Nothing until we know the police have followed through. I should get confirmation in a few hours. When that happens, I want all of you to start making phone calls to your friends in other gangs," said Uncle. "I expect the newspapers will be full of stories about the drug bust this morning. I want the other triads to know that it was us who brought down the operation, and that we used the police to pick up the pieces. That should deliver two messages: first, that we're perfectly capable and more than willing to defend ourselves, and second, that our connections to the police department still run strong."

Uncle gave identical instructions to each of the committee members. Then, knowing he wouldn't be able to sleep, he went to the bathroom to get ready for the day. When he had finished, he made a second coffee and reoccupied his chair.

His plan was to start phoning other Mountain Masters as soon as he heard from Zhang. Given the speed of the triad grapevine, he expected that the third one he called would already have heard the news, but he still wanted to tell each of them personally and answer any questions. There was one person he wanted to make sure heard about it first-hand. It was maybe premature to make the call, but Uncle had faith in Zhang.

He found Zhao's number and dialled. "*Wei*," a woman's sleepy voice answered.

"I apologize for calling so late. My name is Uncle. I am an associate of Zhao's. Is he there?"

"This is unexpected," Zhao said a moment later.

"My apologies to you and your wife for calling so late."

"She's my girlfriend, not my wife, but that doesn't matter — she'll still appreciate it," Zhao said. "I'm more interested in knowing why you're calling. I suspect it's not something trivial."

"We attacked Tai Wai tonight. Specifically, we closed down their major drug storage and distribution centre. We destroyed a lot of drugs but left enough for the police to find," said Uncle. "The cops are there now. They'll arrest five of Wu's men who were working in the warehouse, and I suspect that Wu and his Red Pole will be taken into custody within the next few hours. The police will take credit for the drug bust, which should eliminate any media talk about another gang war."

Zhao paused and then said, "That's certainly not trivial. How violent was it?"

"Not very. We had them outnumbered," Uncle said. "Our objective was to destroy the business, not the men."

"Who else knows about this?"

"You're the first person outside my gang that I've contacted."

"And you're certain that Wu and the Red Pole will be taken into custody?"

"Yes, unless someone warns them," said Uncle. "The police intend to hold them for as long as possible. I'm hoping it's until the weekend."

"Is that your way of asking if I'm going to start making calls when we've finished our conversation?"

"No, it's my way of saying I trust that you won't," Uncle

said. "I won't be contacting the other Mountain Masters until everything I've told you is confirmed."

"And you fully expect it will be."

"I do."

"So the die is cast," Zhao said.

"It is. No more fake wars. We're committed. This will make Wu a mortal enemy of Fanling, though he really was one already, just not in name. It might bring Man into the fray, but I don't care if it does. We'll take on both of them alone if we have to."

"But you hope you don't have to."

"Of course I do. I don't want to go to war with anyone at any time. It's bad for business, it's bad for the brotherhood, it's bad for the people who depend on us for financial support. I think most of our colleagues understand that. How many of them that you know would embrace the idea of going to war?"

"Man, Yin, Wu, and probably Yeung."

"Which leaves fifteen gangs that wouldn't. The problem is that right now those fifteen have no way of preventing the other four from imposing their will on them."

"I am coming to your meeting on Friday. This isn't the time to pitch me on your coalition."

Uncle laughed. "Sorry. I'll wait until then."

"My hope, my dear Uncle, is that your wait will be uneventful."

"If you're referring to Wu, I'm not worried. The police will hold him and his Red Pole until Saturday. And with them out of the picture, there's not much chance of a Tai Wai response," Uncle said. "Tell me, do you really think Man will do something on his own?"

"No. And I have to say I admire the way you've managed this," Zhao said. "Although, to be blunt, you only have it managed until Wu is released."

"If he's held until the weekend, that's all the time I need."

"To do what?"

"I don't know yet, but by Friday I'll have figured it out."

CHAPTER TWENTY-TWO

UNCLE WAITED UNTIL SEVEN BEFORE LEAVING HIS apartment. Zhang had called just before six to tell him things had gone smoothly at the warehouse. The police had found a substantial quantity of drugs, had identified the bound men as members of the Tai Wai Triad, and had just arrested Wu and Lam, his Red Pole.

"You're convinced you can keep them in custody until the weekend?" Uncle asked.

"I might be able to do better than that," Zhang said. "Legally we can't hold them for longer than seventy-two hours without laying a charge. That takes us to Thursday morning. But if we lay the charge on Wednesday, we can hold them until they appear in front of a magistrate. And we can put that off for a few days, which, with the weekend intervening, would take us to the beginning of next week."

After speaking to Zhang, Uncle phoned the executive committee, then Tse and more than half of the Mountain Masters in the New Territories. The committee members were understandably pleased to hear about Wu and Lam. The Mountain Masters' initial reaction to the warehouse raid was nervousness about how Wu might respond. But when they were told he was in police custody and would be kept there for about a week, they relaxed. A week was a very long time in the life of a Mountain Master. Interestingly, no one was critical of Uncle for involving the police, and several complimented him for using them as a cover. All in all, it had been a very successful twelve hours, he thought as he exited his building.

Sonny was standing near the doorway. "You should be sleeping. It was a very late night," Uncle said.

"I couldn't sleep. I was too pumped," Sonny said.

"The men did a great job," Uncle said as he started walking towards Jia's.

Sonny fell in behind him. "Wang is a smooth operator. He was so calm and confident it made us feel like we were in complete control. If there had been thirty of their men there, we still would have taken the place. I wish I was more like him."

"Everyone has their strengths and weaknesses. The important thing is to recognize what they are, and then maximize the strengths and minimize the weaknesses."

"I'm not sure I have that many strengths," Sonny said.

"That's nonsense. In the past twenty-four hours your loyalty and courage were tested, and you showed me you have both," said Uncle. "I also don't know anyone else who could single-handedly take on three thugs with machetes."

"That isn't hard for me, because it doesn't take any thinking."

"The fact that it isn't hard doesn't make it any less impressive," Uncle said. "And as for thinking, as I told you the other day, I'll do that for both of us."

A few minutes later they reached the stand where Uncle bought his newspapers. There was no mention of the drug raid on any of the front pages. Uncle was disappointed, but he expected there would be a story in the late editions. He bought his usual papers and continued on to Jia's.

After breakfast, he and Sonny walked to the office. The four men at the entrance smiled when they saw them, and Uncle knew there would be a lot more smiles during the day. As much as he disliked admitting it, there weren't many things better than a successful skirmish to lift everyone's spirits.

"Hey, boss, there have been quite a few calls for you," Mo said as Uncle entered the office. "I wrote them down."

Uncle took Mo's notes. Two Mountain Masters wanted him to phone them back, as did Man's deputy, Chong. "I'm not calling him," Uncle muttered. He reached for the phone to call Ng in Sai Kung. But before he could, it rang, and he saw the area code for Beijing displayed.

"This is Uncle," he said.

"Good morning," Liu Leji said. "I've just finalized my arrangements for the trip to Shenzhen."

"I hope Wednesday still works."

"It does. I will arrive on Wednesday morning. My aunt has reserved a private dining room for us at the Pearl Boat Restaurant. You should be there at six."

"Will she and your wife be joining us?"

"Yes. And, as usual, you should bring Fong."

"I have no issue with that if we'll be talking about our normal, ongoing business," said Uncle. "But there is that other matter you and I have been discussing."

"You need to leave that in my hands," Leji said. "Just be at the Pearl Boat at six."

Uncle paused. He wasn't accustomed to Leji being so abrupt, and he sensed that any further questions wouldn't be welcomed. "Fine, I'll see you at the Pearl Boat," he said and hung up.

He went into the outer office and saw Fong arriving. Uncle waved him over. "We're going to Shenzhen on Wednesday to meet with Liu Leji and his ladies for dinner."

"I just met with them two weeks ago. Has something happened? Have I pissed off Ms. Gao again?"

"I am quite sure you haven't. Leji doesn't get to Shenzhen very often. I imagine he wants to take advantage of the opportunity. It will probably be social."

"I should take the up-to-date financials with me just in case they want to get into them."

"I think that's a sensible idea."

Uncle returned to his office and called Ng and the two Mountain Masters who had left messages. Ng was pleased and upbeat about the situation with Wu, while the other two seemed to be reserving judgement until they decided which way the wind was blowing. Uncle couldn't blame them. They both headed smaller gangs, and keeping out of the squabble between Tai Wai and Fanling was smart until a clear winner became apparent.

While Uncle was making those calls, Hui arrived in the office. He and Mo huddled together and then, when Uncle hung up from his last call, Hui appeared in his doorway. "Do you want to see the numbers from yesterday?" he asked.

"Will they ruin the good morning I'm having?" Uncle asked.

"No," Hui said with a smile as he sat down in front of the desk. "Despite the disturbance at Dong's, our betting shop receipts are up ten percent over the same weekend last year. Our night market sales are up over twenty-five percent. Those new knock-off purses Xu is making have really taken off, and the CDs and new clothing lines we're producing in Shenzhen are really popular."

"And we're having a record year with the warehousing and transportation business in Shenzhen," Uncle said. "If we can keep things stable until the year-end, we should be able to increase the monthly payments to the brothers and our dependants and add to the reserve fund. I would like to have enough cash in the fund to carry us for five years; that's been a dream of mine for a long time. I never want to revisit the days when we were surviving from month to month."

In theory, the White Paper Fan managed the gang's money, but given Uncle's experience in the same job, Hui was more of a co-manager. He had, for example, no involvement in the business with the Liu family. It had started before he took the position, but that wasn't the main reason. Liu Huning's wife, Ko Lan, was mistrustful by nature, and her husband's ups and downs in the Communist Party — he had been stripped of senior positions several times and was sent to a labour camp for three years during the Cultural Revolution — had proven to her that being perpetually mistrustful was prudent.

For reasons Uncle didn't totally understand, Ko Lan had made him an exception; she was completely open with him. Any major decision concerning the business was usually made by the two of them in consultation. Fong and Leji's wife, Chen Meilin, were more involved on a day-to-day basis and might sit in when those decisions were being made, but their input was rarely solicited.

Xu had been the White Paper Fan when Uncle and Liu Leji first met, but he was working in Xiamen at the time, so Uncle had taken over his duties. When Xu left for Shanghai and Hui assumed the position, Uncle tried to insert Hui into the relationship with Ms. Ko, but she wanted nothing to do with him. "I represent my family. You represent your people. That's how we'll run this business," she had said. "The more people who know about it, the more dangerous it is for all of us. I trust you and I can tolerate Fong. Let's leave it at that." So they had, and their relationship had lasted more than ten years without a major disruption or disagreement.

"By the way, Fong and I are going to Shenzhen on Wednesday to meet with Ms. Ko and Ms. Chan," Uncle said to Hui. "It might be a good time to discuss making a transfer from those company accounts into our reserve fund. I don't actually need anyone's permission, but Ms. Ko appreciates the courtesy."

"Do you want me to estimate what I think we could transfer from the accounts?" Hui asked.

"Yes, why don't you do that."

"I will. Now here are the numbers from yesterday," Hui said, sliding some sheets of paper towards Uncle. As Uncle reached for them, his phone rang.

"*Wei*," he answered.

"This is Chong. I called earlier. Didn't you get my message?"

"I did, but I've been busy. In fact, I'm still busy. Besides, if your boss wants to talk to me, he should call me directly. Tell him I don't appreciate his lack of respect," Uncle replied and then hung up.

"Who was that?" Hui asked.

"Chong, Man's deputy."

"Man must be seething," Hui said.

"He's only going to get angrier every day Wu is in custody."

"Boss, do you think it's wise to goad him?" asked Hui.

"That isn't my intention," Uncle said matter-of-factly. "Wu is a more immediate threat. Keeping him and his Red Pole in jail lessens that threat. That's my only objective. Hopefully it works and we get to the end of the week without another incident."

"By *the end of the week*, do you mean keeping things quiet until you have your meeting?"

"Yes," Uncle said, as his phone rang again. He looked at the incoming number. "It's the same as Chong's. Do you want to bet that this time it's Man on the line?"

"You're probably right. Do you want me to leave?"

"No," Uncle said, picking up the receiver. "This is Uncle."

"What the fuck do you think you're doing?" Man said in a tinny voice that sounded like he was whining.

"I'm doing a great many things, including having a meeting with my White Paper Fan. What is it I've done specifically that you object to?"

"You fucked over Wu. It's one thing for the two of you to have disagreements, but you shouldn't have gone after his business like that — and then made it worse by bringing the cops into it. Other gangs are going to suffer severe losses in the next few weeks because of what you did last night."

"Wu tried to kill me. Do you think that's the way two Mountain Masters should try to resolve a disagreement?"

"He says he didn't."

"Didn't what?"

"Try to kill you."

"That's bullshit. I spoke to the men he sent. They gave me their names."

"They did that because they knew that was probably what you wanted to hear," said Man.

"This conversation is verging on the ridiculous," Uncle said. "Is there something serious you want to discuss, or are you just calling to complain that Wu got more than he deserved? You know damn well that if I'd killed him instead of simply hurting his business, few Mountain Masters would have blamed me."

"You're always so fucking smart, aren't you. You don't care who you piss off," Man said.

"Since you seem to be pissed off already, let me give you another reason to be," Uncle said. "This story you're spinning about the Chinese government is crap. The Chinese have zero interest in harassing the triads. They have bigger problems to deal with than us. I'm telling anyone who'll listen to ignore you, and so far I'm doing pretty well. You may have Yin and Yeung onside, but I'll be shocked if you can find anyone else who believes a single word you say."

The line went dead. "He hung up on me," Uncle said to Hui.

"I'm not surprised."

CHAPTER TWENTY-THREE

THE REST OF THE DAY WAS UNEVENTFUL, AND UNCLE left the office before six. Sonny was waiting with the car. "Are you going back to the apartment?"

"Yes. Tian wanted me to join him at Dong's, but I hardly slept last night."

"It wouldn't be any trouble for me to bring you food from Dong's."

"I'll make do with my favourite, noodles with beef and XO sauce, from the Blind Emperor," Uncle said. "I enjoy a variety of foods, but when I find something I really like, I can eat it every day — like Jia's congee. I don't know what that says about me."

"You're a man who knows what he likes."

Uncle laughed. "Sonny, you're becoming rather a diplomat."

Sonny seemed uncertain if that was a compliment and said nothing.

"Don't wait for me," Uncle said when they reached the restaurant. "It takes a few minutes to prepare the noodles, and I usually have a beer while I wait. I'll see you in the morning."

"I should stay until the guy who keeps the night watch gets here."

"No, I insist you leave. Get some sleep."

Uncle didn't go inside the Blind Emperor until the car had driven away. Now that the danger of the previous day was behind him, he was again starting to feel slightly suffocated by Sonny's constant presence.

The restaurant owner greeted him effusively. "Uncle, I'm so happy to see you. When my cooks told me what happened yesterday morning, I couldn't believe it. This has always been a peaceful neighbourhood."

"It still is. None of us need to be worried," Uncle said. "Now, I want my noodles with beef, and I'll take a San Miguel while you prepare it."

"We'll add extra beef tonight."

"But not more XO sauce — I need to sleep."

Uncle was carrying his beer over to a small table when he noticed a copy of the *Oriental Daily News* lying next to the cash register. "Can I borrow this?" he asked.

"You can keep it," the owner said.

It was the afternoon edition of the newspaper, and the front page made Uncle smile. The headline read "Hong Kong Police Smash Triad Drug Ring in Tai Wai." The story said that, after weeks of surveillance, the police had raided a warehouse in Tai Wai New Village that was the major distribution centre for cocaine in the New Territories. A police spokesman was quoted as saying that a large amount of the drug had been seized and a number of triad members had been arrested, including Wu Min, the gang's leader.

Zhao was right. I did manage this well, Uncle thought. *But he's also right that it will stay managed only while Wu is in custody. All bets are off as soon as he's out.* Uncle took another sip of beer, then saw the owner coming towards him with a food container. He drained the bottle. "I'll take two beers to go with the noodles," he said.

Uncle stood in his kitchen to eat. It was his first meal since breakfast, and he quickly devoured the container's entire contents. When he was finished, he carried a beer to his chair, lit a cigarette, and checked the phone for messages. He had just missed a call from Xu in Shanghai. Uncle had meant to phone him during the day, but something kept getting in the way. Xu's message was short: "Phone me."

When Xu lived in Fanling, the two men had been each other's closest friend and confidant. Although now they spoke much less frequently, the friendship had endured. Xu owned a house in Shanghai's French Concession. Uncle had visited him there several times. He had fond memories of sitting with Xu by a fishpond in the courtyard, the two men smoking and sharing stories. He called Xu's home number.

"*Wei*," Auntie Grace answered. She was now the Xu family housekeeper, after spending years as nanny to Xu's son.

"This is Uncle. Can I speak to Xu?"

"He's outside. I'll get him," she said.

While he waited, Uncle thought about Xu's son. In his early twenties now, he would soon be entering the last year of a bachelor's degree program in economics at Shanghai Jiao Tong University. Xu wanted him to stay in school, get a master's degree, and then join either the provincial or national public service. But the younger Xu wanted to follow in his father's footsteps. Whenever he saw Uncle, he questioned him for hours about the Heaven and Earth Society. Uncle had become, for better or worse, his mentor.

"Today I felt like I was on the other side of the world," Xu said when he came on the line. "I didn't hear about the attack on you until late today, when I called Ng to talk about buying more designer bags. Are you okay?"

"I'm fine. I apologize for not calling you. It's been hectic."

"I understand. I get caught up in my own business here, and days can pass without a thought about anything else entering my head," Xu said. "Ng told me how you retaliated last night. It sounds as if it was effective, but I'm sorry you didn't kill Wu. He's a cretin. I remember how difficult he was to deal with when you were being held prisoner in China."

"Killing him wouldn't have accomplished anything. In fact, it might have worked against what I'm trying to do here," Uncle said. "Anyway, I have managed to get him behind bars for a while. I wanted him out of the way so I could focus on a meeting I'm holding this Friday with a number of the Mountain Masters. Did Ng mention the meeting or talk about what I'm trying to do?"

"He told me that Man and some of his Kowloon cohorts are making threatening noises about taking over more turf, and that you're trying to convince the other Territories gangs to form some kind of defensive coalition. He said he's not sure how it's all going to work, but he is prepared to commit to it," Xu said.

"Others have indicated they will as well. I don't know if they're doing it because they realize it makes sense or because they're simply afraid of Man," Uncle said.

"Do you care what their motive is? You're the one who always says that people usually do the right thing for the wrong reason."

"This time I'd like it to be for the right reason, but I guess I should be happy for any support I get," Uncle said. "Did Ng also tell you why Man thinks he has to take over some of the smaller gangs?"

"To fend off the Chinese after the handover?"

"Exactly, and I've been told by Liu Leji that it's completely bogus. I do believe him, but you're the triad that works most closely with the Communists. What do you think? After the handover, will they leave us alone?"

"I haven't been left alone. That's not how it works here, and not how it will work in Hong Kong," Xu said. "You know I wouldn't be here if they hadn't expressly permitted it, and I can't operate here without their co-operation. They have the power to control absolutely everything. I decided to use that to my advantage by making them partners in my businesses — not official legal partners, of course, but I look after them financially as if they were. You may not have to operate the way I do here, but you'd be wise to make some accommodations with those who are responsible for running Hong Kong."

"Are you saying there's no middle ground? If you aren't with them, you're automatically considered to be against them?"

"What I'm saying is that you can't ignore their presence. You can't pretend they don't exist. You can't act as if it's business as usual," Xu said. "Uncle, do you want my best advice?"

"Yes. That's why I'm calling."

"Listen to Leji. Whatever he tells you to do will be coming, one way or another, from his uncle. The old man knows the system inside and out and still has formidable influence."

"I'm meeting with Leji on Wednesday. I believe he wants

to talk about the handover, although he was vague when I spoke to him this morning."

"You and the Lius have been successful partners for a long time. I'm sure that's a relationship they'll want to maintain, and one important way of doing that is to help keep your organization intact. So whatever advice he has to give will also be self-serving, and I think that's a very good thing."

"You make sense, of course. You always do. My thought process gets too convoluted at times."

"That's not true. Your mind just works differently," Xu said. "Most of us see the world in black and white, but you are able to see all the shades."

"I will try to convince myself that has some value," said Uncle.

"Stay in touch, and let me know how things go this week."

"I will. This was a good conversation, Xu. I appreciate the advice."

As Uncle put down the phone he chided himself for not having called Xu sooner. He had always been a good man to bounce ideas off. Uncle rose from the chair and went to the kitchen to get another beer. On the way back he was overtaken by an enormous yawn. It was still early in the evening, but he knew he needed to get to bed. *One more phone call,* he thought.

Zhang answered. "I thought I might hear from you tonight. Did you read the late newspapers?"

"It seems the Hong Kong police are doing a bang-up job fighting drug trafficking."

"Well, it was a major bust, and it made some people happy at headquarters and in the OCTB."

"Are they happy enough to make sure Wu is kept out of circulation until the beginning of next week?"

"I think you can count on that," Zhang said. "And there's an additional wrinkle that you might find to your liking. Lam, the man you say is Wu's Red Pole, had a gun on him. He didn't have a permit for it and he happens to be on probation. That probation will be revoked tomorrow, and Mr. Lam will be spending the next six months in Tong Fuk prison on Lantau Island."

CHAPTER TWENTY-FOUR

ON TUESDAY, UNCLE RESUMED HIS NORMAL WORK schedule. After the drama of Sunday and Monday, the day seemed to drag, and by four Uncle was thinking about leaving the office early. Then Wang barged through the door.

"I just got a call from Song, the Red Pole in Tsuen Wan," Wang blurted. "There's big trouble."

"What kind of trouble?"

"The town has been overrun by members of Man's gang. He says there has to be sixty of them."

"What are they doing?"

"Harassing some business owners and loitering in front of restaurants and stores, driving customers away. And according to Song, they've been taunting his men, trying to draw them into a confrontation."

"Why did he call you?"

Wang drew a deep breath as he sat down in front of the desk. "He's looking for help."

"How many men do they have?"

"Song says he might be able to put together a force of thirty," Wang said.

"Wasn't it his boss, Chow, who said at our meeting that he doesn't need anyone else's help, that his gang is capable of handling its own affairs?"

"Yeah, but Song is more realistic. He knows they need help and he's not too proud to ask for it."

"Did he tell Chow he was going to ask for it?"

"No."

Uncle knew Wang wanted to provide assistance to Tsuen Wan, but he couldn't agree to it based on Song's request alone. "Unless I hear from Chow, there's nothing we can do."

"And if Chow does call you and ask for help?"

Uncle's look became more intense. "Is Song a capable Red Pole?"

"Yes."

"Would you trust him to lead our men?"

"I would, but why do you ask that question?"

"I think Chow and Song would resent it if someone from another gang took the lead. They have to save face. If we send men, I want you to stay in the background. Let Song call the shots," Uncle said.

"Will you talk to other Mountain Masters about contributing men?"

"Absolutely. I don't want this to become Tsuen Wan and Fanling versus Kowloon. This is an opportunity to present a united front, and the more gangs we involve, the better."

"How many of our men would you send?"

"If I can get Ng and Tan to participate and we each send twenty-five men, that will give Chow more than a hundred to fend off Kowloon with. Do you think that will be sufficient?"

"It should be. But it would send more of a message if we each sent thirty."

"Okay. But nothing happens until I hear from Chow."

"I'll call Song right now and tell him," Wang said.

Uncle picked up his phone as soon as Wang left. He reached Ng, explained what was going on in Tsuen Wan, and asked him if he would contribute men if Chow made a direct request. Without the slightest hesitation, Ng agreed. "I'll let you know if this is going to happen or not," Uncle said. "If it is, then we should let the Red Poles sort out the logistics."

He next called Tan. There was no answer, and he left a terse message. "Man is making a move on Tsuen Wan. If Chow asks for help, Ng and I are each going to send thirty men. Would you be willing to do the same?"

Uncle walked into the main office. Wang's door was open and he was sitting behind his desk, looking grim. "I'm going to chat with Wang," Uncle said to Mo. "Answer my phone. If there's a call from Tan or from Chow in Tsuen Wan, transfer it to Wang's."

"How did Song react to our offer?" Uncle asked Wang as he entered his office.

"He was grateful and was going to talk to Chow right away, but he wasn't sure what Chow would decide to do."

"We can't help people who refuse to help themselves," said Uncle. "Do you think he'll say no? Is that why you're looking so tense?"

"I've been sitting here wondering what kind of message it will send to the other gangs if we don't react to what's going on in Tsuen Wan. They might think all this talk about a defensive alliance is just that — talk."

"Ng has agreed to contribute thirty men. I'm waiting to hear from Tan and I'm optimistic that he'll join with us. That wouldn't have been possible a week ago, so already we've gone beyond talking," Uncle said. "And Wang, we can't walk into Tsuen Wan without an invitation from Chow. If we did, we wouldn't be acting any differently than Man."

"I didn't mean to sound dismissive about the progress you've made pulling the gangs together, Uncle," Wang said. "I'm simply worried that Man is testing us and I'm itching to show him we're up for it."

Wang's phone rang. The two men made eye contact before Wang picked it up. He said, "*Wei*," listened briefly, then passed the phone to Uncle.

"This is Uncle."

"This is Chow. Song is with me. I have him on speakerphone."

"I have Wang, my Red Pole, with me. I'll put us on speaker as well. I understand you're having a bit of trouble," Uncle said.

"Man's men are swarming the town centre. I was hoping they'd come to pester us and then leave, but they're getting more aggressive by the hour. Our men are on the verge of losing control," Chow said.

"I spoke to Ng a few minutes ago. Between us we have sixty men that we're prepared to send to help you. I also reached out to Tan, but we haven't connected yet. When we do, I'm hopeful he'll send thirty more."

"If those men come here, who will be giving them instructions?" Chow asked.

"Whoever you designate. I assumed it would be Song," Uncle said. "I'm sending my Red Pole with the men, but he'll play whatever role Song wants him to. Ng's Red Pole will do the same. It's your turf and your call."

"I didn't want Song to reach out for help," Chow muttered,

almost as if he was talking to himself. "We're very proud of our independence."

"Chow, Ng and I aren't forcing you to take our men. It's your decision entirely, but I predict that not accepting them will be a greater threat to your independence than taking them."

"He's right, boss," Uncle heard Song murmur.

"I appreciate your offer, but I have to ask — what strings are attached?"

"None. Although I'd like to think that if either Ng's gang or mine faced a similar threat, you'd send men to support us."

There was a long pause. Then Song said, "Excuse us for a minute."

Uncle looked at Wang and whispered, "He may know he needs our help, but he's afraid to lose face."

"Uncle, we're back. Send the men," Chow said abruptly. "However this ends, you have my thanks. I'll call Ng to thank him as well."

"I realize that was a difficult decision, but I genuinely believe it's the right move for the future of your gang," said Uncle. "Now I'm going to turn things over to Wang. He and Song should contact Ng's Red Pole and coordinate their approach."

Uncle left Wang to sort things out. Yu was the only other executive committee member in the building, and Uncle made his way to his office.

"I thought you should know that Man is causing a disruption in Tsuen Wan. At Wang's suggestion I have offered assistance to Chow and he's accepted it. Wang will be heading there with thirty of our men and will be joined by thirty of Ng's. Do I need to call a committee meeting to get approval?"

"No, but we should let everyone know what's going on."

"Uncle, Tan is on the phone," Mo called from behind him.

"I need to talk to him. I'll let you make the calls to the other committee members," Uncle said, then hurried to his office. He picked up the phone. "Tan, I assume you got my message."

"I did. Those pricks from Kowloon are going to try to do in Tsuen Wan what they did in Macau. The actors may be different, but the script is the same."

"I just spoke to Chow. He asked us to send help."

"That surprises me. After his comments at the meeting, I thought his pride would get in the way."

"Truthfully it took some persuasion, and I think his Red Pole pushed him into the decision, but I care more that he got there than how," Uncle said. "Ng and I have committed to send thirty men each, and we're placing them under Chow's command. Our Red Poles are coordinating their efforts now."

"Ask Wang to involve my Red Pole in that discussion," Tan said.

"So you're sending men?"

"Yes, although I have to say it makes me nervous. It's been a while since most of them were in a scrap. They're hardly battle-hardened."

"I expect there will be a lot of posturing, but when the Kowloon triads see ninety brothers showing up to support Tsuen Wan, I think they'll back off."

"I hope you're right," Tan said. "The past few days have been crazy enough."

"I've certainly kept my Red Pole busy," said Uncle. "Speaking of Wang, I should let him know that you're on board. Tell your guy to expect a call in the next few minutes."

"I'll do it right now. Let's touch base later," Tan said.

Uncle hung up, feeling pleased with the reactions from Tan and Ng. He hadn't taken it for granted that they'd agree to go into Tsuen Wan. He did believe, though, that they had bought into his ideas for the New Territories, so he hadn't been surprised. Still, getting that confirmation increased Uncle's confidence that the meeting on Friday would go his way — assuming, of course, that the foray into Tsuen Wan was successful. *It had better be, or I'm going to look foolish,* he thought as he walked back to Wang's office.

"You need to call Tan's Red Pole. Mai Po is contributing thirty men, so you have the ninety you wanted," said Uncle from the doorway.

"There's a large shopping mall on the outskirts of Tsuen Wan. We'll meet up there with Song and his men. I'll let Mai Po know where to go," Wang said. "I'm rounding up our men now. We should be ready to leave in less than an hour."

"Great," Uncle said, then stepped inside the office and closed the door. He leaned towards Wang. "You know there's a lot riding on what happens in Tsuen Wan. I've convinced Tan and Ng that working together is the best way to survive. This is the first test, and I need it to be successful. Or, frankly, there won't be much point in having that meeting on Friday."

"We will drive the Kowloon men out of Tsuen Wan," Wang said.

"Getting them to leave is the goal. It would be ideal if you could send them packing without a shot being fired or a knife being drawn," Uncle said. "But, if they won't leave peacefully, you have my full support to do whatever is needed."

"I'll share that message with the other Red Poles. Although I know you told Chow that Song would be in charge, he quietly asked me to take control," Wang said. "I won't let you down."

"I know you won't," Uncle said, then hesitated.

"Is there something else?" Wang asked.

"Yes. I'm thinking I might go to Tsuen Wan with you and the men," Uncle said. "I wouldn't interfere with how the Red Poles manage the situation, but I'd like to demonstrate to Chow how committed I am to this alliance."

"Your physical presence would certainly do that. And, I can tell you, our men would be thrilled to have you alongside them," Wang said.

"So no objections on your part?"

"None whatsoever, although I do think you should contact Chow to let him know. If he has objections, it could be awkward."

"I'll call him right now, and if he's okay with it, I'll let Tan and Ng know as well. Who knows, they might want to be in on this too."

CHAPTER TWENTY-FIVE

WHEN THE TRIADS FROM FANLING REACHED THE REN-dezvous point at the shopping mall, the men from Mai Po, Sai Kung, and Tsuen Wan were already there. Uncle was in the lead vehicle with Wang and Sonny. As the Mercedes rolled to a stop he saw Chow, Ng, and Tan walking towards them. *Stay calm,* he thought, but the combination of adrenalin and excitement was difficult to restrain. Chow had been elated when Uncle suggested he come to Tsuen Wan, and when Ng and Tan found out he was going, they quickly decided to go as well.

"I'm so pleased to see you all," Uncle said as he got out of the car.

"I wouldn't have missed this for anything," Ng said, and turned to Chow. "It was good of you to welcome us."

"Looking at all these men, I'm almost embarrassed to admit that my Red Pole had to persuade me to accept help," Chow said. "But once I got past my pride, I realized how important this could be — not just for my gang, but also for this notion that Uncle has been promoting."

Wang had been standing off to one side with Sonny while

Uncle and the Mountain Masters greeted each other. Now he moved closer to Uncle. "Boss, I should be meeting with the other Red Poles."

"Of course. Go," said Uncle.

"Wang, could you wait just one minute?" Chow said, and then he addressed the other Mountain Masters. "Song, my Red Pole, believes this small army we've assembled should have a clear leader. Uncle suggested putting the men under Song's command, but he would rather defer to Wang. Song says the other Red Poles feel the same."

"If the Red Poles want Wang to be in charge, I have no objection," Ng said.

"Me neither," added Tan.

"It would be an honour," Wang said.

"Then go and brief your men," Chow said.

Uncle watched as Wang went to join the other Red Poles. "We have more than a hundred men gathered. Has Man added to his corps or do they still number around sixty?" he asked Chow.

"When we pulled our men out of the town centre about an hour ago to come here, there were still about sixty. Given that they probably think we've run off, I can't imagine they've called for reinforcements."

"How were they behaving?"

"They were very aggressive and insulting. They acted like they owned the place."

"Is Man with them?"

"No, his Red Pole, Fok, is in charge. His men have occupied the town square and may be fanning out by now to let the local businesses know there's a new gang in charge," said Chow.

"Where are the police?"

"Nowhere to be found. They either don't know what's going on or are prepared to let things play out," Chow said. "We certainly wouldn't go to them for help."

"Of course you wouldn't," Uncle said. "How far is the square from here?"

"About a ten-minute walk."

Uncle looked over to where Wang was huddled with the other Red Poles. Around them, some men stood patiently, while others seemed jumpy or anxious to get started. After a few minutes more of discussion he saw Wang nod, and then the four Red Poles joined hands. They were obviously in agreement about how to proceed.

Wang turned to face the men, flanked on either side by the other Red Poles. "We are going to walk as a single group to the town square," he said loudly to the men. "Our main objective is to get Man's gang to leave as quickly and quietly as possible. Our hope is that they will be unwilling to fight and will leave voluntarily. We're going to start by talking to them. If that doesn't work, then we'll use force."

"Remember, using force is Plan B," Song added.

"Exactly. No one is to take it upon themselves to initiate an action of any kind. We need to function like a cohesive unit. You have to follow orders, and only the Red Poles are allowed to issue them," Wang said. "Does anyone have questions?"

"If we have to use force, how much are you talking about?" a forty-niner asked.

"We don't want gunfire in the town square; there's too great a risk that a civilian could get hit. We don't want a repeat of Macau," Wang said. "Let's try to limit it to fists and, if it really comes down to it, knives."

"What if they fire at us?" another man asked.

"Don't return fire unless your Red Pole gives you permission," Wang said.

Uncle could see that some of the men were unhappy with that answer. He only hoped they would be disciplined enough to follow orders.

Wang held up his hand. "That's it. We leave in a few minutes. The Red Poles will form a line at the front. The men from each gang should fall in behind their own Red Pole," he said, then turned and walked over to the Mountain Masters.

"How will you gentlemen be playing this?" he asked.

"I don't know about the others, but I'm going with you," said Uncle.

"Will you fall in behind with the men?"

"No, I want to be at the front, next to you. I know Fok, and I want him to see that I'm here. I want him to understand that we're committed."

"I'll do the same," Chow said.

"Me too," chimed in Ng and Tan.

"But if it turns violent, it would be irresponsible to let any of you get caught up in it," Wang said.

"If it turns violent I'll find a way to fade into the background, and I'm sure my older colleagues will do the same," said Uncle. "I have no interest in taking on one of Fok's young forty-niners."

Wang looked at Sonny. "I'll be right next to Uncle," Sonny said.

Wang nodded. "Okay, then let's head to town."

"I'll lead the way," Chow said.

Chow and Song started walking in the direction of the setting sun. Uncle, the other Mountain Masters, and the

Red Poles fell in alongside, while behind them the four gangs of triads followed, the air around them buzzing with excitement.

Uncle knew there would be a confrontation. His hope was that it wouldn't be violent, but he also sensed that wasn't the wish of many of the men behind him. Being a member of a small triad sometimes meant giving way when you didn't want to and accepting things you knew were wrong because you had no choice. The mood of this group was different. They were finally feeling the power of superior numbers, and he worried that they were too eager to use it.

"We're almost there," Song said as they passed a train station.

Two hundred metres later they entered a square. Directly in front of them were knots of men drinking beer and surrounded by goods that had obviously been looted.

"They didn't waste any time," Chow said.

The men didn't seem to notice them at first, but as the four gangs approached they leapt to their feet and formed a line. Uncle could hear them talking among themselves, and then a man he recognized as Fok stepped forward.

"What the hell is this?" Fok asked.

"We are from the brotherhoods in Fanling, Tsuen Wan, Sai Kung, and Mai Po. We have come to ask you to leave this place," Wang said.

"We are here peaceably. What's your problem?" Fok said as his men bunched closer together.

Uncle saw that most of them were armed, although knives and machetes seemed to be more prevalent than guns.

"Our problem is that you're trying to exert control over Tsuen Wan. We're not going to let that happen."

Uncle kept his attention focused on Fok, who in turn was eyeing the men facing him. *He's trying to count how many we are,* Uncle thought. *If he has any sense he'll realize he's badly outnumbered.*

"We are here peaceably," Fok repeated. "There's no reason to threaten us."

"We are here to defend Tsuen Wan's right to operate in their own territory without outside interference," Wang said. "You are most definitely trying to interfere. There's nothing peaceable about that."

Fok turned to speak to a couple of men standing next to him, and then faced Wang again. "I need to speak to my Mountain Master about this. I'm not going anywhere unless he directs me to."

"Then go and speak to him. We'll wait. We're not going anywhere," said Wang.

Fok nodded and walked away from his men towards a bank of payphones. His men stayed where they were.

"Man will tell them to leave," Song said.

"We'll see," said Wang.

Uncle watched Fok make the call. His back was turned to them, so he couldn't see if Man's Red Pole was doing most of the talking or if he was listening. Regardless, the conversation didn't last long, and Fok quickly made his way back to his men. He said something to them before turning to face the four gangs.

"My boss told me he doesn't want our presence to be the cause of any problems between gangs, so we're going to leave, but he says you should enjoy this meaningless exercise while you can," Fok said. He pointed a finger directly at Uncle. "He also wants me to tell you that no one is interfering in other people's business more than you. He says if you keep it up, there will be a price to pay."

Sonny twitched. "Stay calm," Uncle said to him. "Wang, don't acknowledge that last remark."

Wang nodded. "Leave the square in an orderly manner," he said. "Leave the things you've stolen, and don't loot or damage property on your way out of here."

Fok muttered something to the men standing next to him, and the group began to turn away. They started to walk from the square, but they hadn't gone more than fifty metres when a group of ten men peeled off to one side. Uncle saw they had knives and machetes clenched against their legs.

"What are they doing?" Song asked Wang.

Before he could answer, the group screamed and charged forward, brandishing their weapons.

"Hold your ground!" Wang shouted. "Don't go to meet them."

They can't be that crazy, Uncle thought. He felt a sense of relief, even if it was somewhat puzzled, when the men stopped ten metres short and began shouting and laughing as if it was all a game.

"Get the fuck out of here," Wang said.

"We're going," one said with a smile.

He and his colleagues turned away, and then suddenly they pivoted and ran directly at Uncle.

Uncle's view was instantly blocked as Sonny stepped in front of him. The Fanling men closed ranks on either side and moved forward. Man's men were on them in seconds, but whatever element of surprise they'd thought they had was immediately gone. Uncle saw Sonny's right elbow crash into the head of one of the attackers, and almost before he'd reached the ground, Sonny's foot bore into his groin and then rocketed into the side of his head. Out of the corner of his eye, Uncle saw Wang stick a knife into the side of another man.

"Move back!" one of Fok's men shouted. They did, but only five were still standing. On the ground in front of Uncle, the rest lay in pools of blood or writhing in pain from less visible damage.

Wang reached down, grabbed the man he had stabbed, and rolled him towards his gangmates. Sonny did the same with the man he'd taken out. "If you drop your weapons, you can retrieve your friends," Wang said to Fok's men. "If you don't, we'll leave them here to rot."

Machetes and knives fell to the bricks. The men tentatively moved forward to help their wounded away from the front line.

"Are any of our men hurt?" Uncle asked.

"Chan took a knife to the groin. We'll get him to a hospital," Wang said.

Uncle looked across the square to where Fok had been watching the action from a safe distance. He shook his head at the Red Pole. Some of Fok's men ran across the square to help remove the injured. Two of them could walk, two others had to be supported, and the fifth, who was being carried by his feet and arms, wasn't showing any signs of life. Fok waited for them to reach the main force. When they did, he turned and led his men from the square.

CHAPTER TWENTY-SIX

BY TEN O'CLOCK, DINNER AT DONG'S WAS OVER. UNCLE, Fong, and Wang were working on their third beers and Tian was drinking his second pot of tea.

What had started as a celebration of their success in Tsuen Wan soon found the four comrades sharing stories about their years as triads. Old friends, enemies, and business acquaintances were remembered. Fong was a particularly good storyteller and, given his many interactions with people, he had a lot of stories to tell. At one point, after Tian asked him why he was so drawn to Macau, Fong spoke uninterrupted for twenty minutes. Stories about mama-sans, the grimy casinos, wildanimal restaurants, and his various gambling systems — all of which had ended in failure — tumbled out of him.

Uncle listened as best he could, but he couldn't stop thinking about Tsuen Wan. He left the table several times to call the hospital, enquiring about Chan, the wounded forty-niner, and didn't relax until he was told the man would be released that night.

"You seem distracted," Tian said to Uncle as he returned from making his last call. Fong was still talking about Macau.

He was predicting that Las Vegas casino operators would be allowed to set up in Macau when Stanley Ho's decades-long gaming licence — which gave him a monopoly — came up for renewal.

"I'm thinking about Tsuen Wan," said Uncle, then looked at Wang. "Do you believe the men we left there will be enough if Man's people return?"

"I don't think there's much chance they will, but if they do, Song should be able to handle things."

"Okay . . . I just can't stop worrying. I would hate to see a reversal of the success we had today."

"Speaking of which," Tian said as he pushed himself to his feet, "I have something to say to you."

"I hope you're not going to spoil my night by telling us you're going to retire," said Uncle.

"There's no chance of that," Tian said. "Today four gangs came together as one and drove off a bully, and three of those gangs had nothing to gain and a lot to lose. I can't remember that ever happening before. It's a remarkable thing, and it happened because of you. So congratulations, Uncle. You make me proud to be a member of this triad."

"I feel the same," Fong said.

"You two must really want a ride home," Uncle said, with a smile that he hoped hid how touched he was. "We should leave now. I have calls to make."

"I'm going to stay a bit longer," Wang said. "You can reach me here if you need me."

Sonny was waiting by the car when the three men left the restaurant. Uncle had invited him to join them for dinner, but he had declined, saying it provided better security if he was outside.

"Drop Fong off first, then Tian," Uncle said.

Uncle and Tian sat in the back seat. Fong slid into the front next to Sonny and said, "Uncle told us you did well in Tsuen Wan today."

Sonny shrugged. "I did my job. Nothing more."

Fong's apartment was near Dong's Kitchen, and even driving slowly it took less than five minutes to get there. Before getting out, Fong turned to Uncle. "What time do you want to leave for our meeting in Shenzhen tomorrow?"

"I thought about three."

"Could it be a little earlier? Ming would like to pick us up at the train station and take us to his office for a short meeting."

Ming Gen was their partner in the garment trade and had been their first connection in Shenzhen. He manufactured an ever-expanding variety of quality knock-off clothing in his two factories. "Would this meeting have anything to do with him wanting to build Ming Garment Factory Number Three?"

"Yes. He tells me that both of the plants are running at full capacity now and can hardly keep up with demand. To be fair to him, we do keep asking him to add more brand lines. Something has to give. We either have to cut some brands or help him increase production."

"Have you seen a plan?" Uncle asked.

Fong managed day-to-day business with Ming. "Every time I see Ming, he pulls out the plan."

"Okay, we'll leave at one, and you can tell Ming he can present his proposal," Uncle said. "Now, can you do something for me tonight?"

"Sure."

"Call the rest of the executive committee and let them know we were successful in Tsuen Wan."

"I'll do it right away," Fong said. "See you in the morning."

"Those garment factories have been a fantastic investment," Tian said as the car pulled away.

"They saved us financially," said Uncle. "We were dipping into the reserve fund to maintain our cash flow, and that was only a short-term fix leading nowhere."

"We were fortunate you had the foresight to realize what would be happening in Shenzhen."

"We were even luckier to connect with the Liu family," Uncle said, and then lowered his voice slightly. "By the way, I told our mutual friend that I'm meeting with Leji tomorrow, and that I hoped he would have information that could help calm things down among the gangs. I think it might have bought us a little time with the police."

"I'm sure he's heard about what happened in Tsuen Wan today. I hope that doesn't cause him to become impatient."

"I'll find out soon enough. He's the first person I'm going to call when I get home."

They reached Tian's apartment and Uncle got out of the car to help his old friend. "Thank you for your kind words at the restaurant," he said.

"You know I meant them. I'm so very proud of you. I have no sons, and there is a very special place in my heart for you and Delun," Tian said, his voice catching.

"And we both feel the same way about you," Uncle said, slightly uncomfortable with the display of emotion.

The nighttime bodyguard was standing outside Uncle's apartment building when he and Sonny arrived. Uncle nodded at him, headed upstairs, and went directly to the phone to check his messages. A number of Mountain Masters had called to congratulate him on Tsuen Wan. There was no rush to call them back, he decided. The priority was Zhang.

Uncle took a San Miguel from the fridge, settled into his chair, and phoned the police superintendent.

"*Wei*," Zhang said.

"It's Uncle. Did you hear about what happened in Tsuen Wan today?"

"I did, and I'm not pleased with how the detachment office handled things."

"I saw no police," said Uncle.

"Precisely, and that's the problem. It's a small detachment, but that doesn't excuse the fact that they ignored multiple calls from shop owners asking them to intervene when the town was invaded by triads."

"I was wondering why they didn't show up," Uncle said. "But before you say anything else, let me explain why today could be a very good thing."

"I have no idea how that's possible, but I will listen. Do yourself a favour, though, and don't stretch the truth. I'm not in a mood to play games."

"Thank you, I won't," Uncle said, taking a few seconds to gather his thoughts. "You know how aggressive Man and some of the Kowloon gangs have been. What happened today was the latest manifestation of that aggression. Sixty of Man's crew descended on Tsuen Wan. The triad gang there is one of our smallest, and I guess Man thought they'd be easy to pick off. Instead, the Kowloon men found themselves confronting more than a hundred from Tsuen Wan, Fanling, Mai Po, and Sai Kung. In other words, the four gangs united to fend off Man. I can't begin to tell you how significant that is."

"I think you should begin to tell me. In fact, I insist that you tell me."

"I mentioned to you before that I've been working on a plan to bring peace to the Territories."

"You did, but you neglected to give me any details, and I'm hard pressed to understand how a pitched battle in Tsuen Wan can be described as peaceful."

"It was a skirmish, not a battle."

"Not according to some civilian witnesses — but I'll let that go."

"The point is, I've been trying to convince all the gangs in the New Territories to form a defensive alliance. None of us are large enough on our own to fend off the big Kowloon or Hong Kong gangs, but together we're far more than they could handle. Simply put, I'm trying to get the other gangs to buy into the idea that if you attack one of us, you'll have to take on all of us. Today was the first physical manifestation of that idea."

"You said four gangs put up men to ward off Man. There are ten gangs in the Territories, and that includes Wu's. I can't imagine he'll be joining what you're proposing, but where were the other five?" Zhang asked.

"We didn't ask them to help today. But everyone I asked came."

"Do you think you can get the others to buy into your idea?"

"Yes," Uncle said with a certainty that surprised him. "By Friday it will be done. And once it is, there will be peace. All the nonsense that's been going on between the gangs will be over."

"Maybe the gangs here won't be sniping at each other, but you still have the triads in Kowloon and Hong Kong Island to contend with."

How far can I go? How sure am I that I'm right? Uncle thought. Then he said, "What the hell."

"What the hell?"

"Sorry. I was debating whether I should tell you what I'm certain will happen or what I believe might happen. Under the circumstances, I'm going to go out on a limb," said Uncle. "I know that not all the Kowloon gangs share Man's expansionist views. In fact, I think one of them is considering joining our alliance. Similarly, I think there may be two gangs on the Island that can be persuaded to join. If I can pull that off, there isn't a gang or any combination of gangs not in the alliance that could be a threat to us. They'd be left to squabble among themselves."

"And you believe you can achieve this by Friday?"

"There are specifics that need to be worked out, but I'm confident I'll have an agreement in principle that encompasses as many as twelve gangs."

"And between now and then, what am I supposed to do? That was a disgrace today in Tsuen Wan. It made us look like we have no control over triad activity in the Territories. I've been called to Hong Kong tomorrow, and I know it isn't to exchange pleasantries."

"I need three days. Give me until Friday night."

Zhang sighed. "If I do, you need to be completely honest with me after your meeting. I can't accept the possibility of another Tsuen Wan."

"You will know precisely how things stand. You'll know who's in and who's not."

"I don't doubt you'll tell me what you think is true, but this time, Uncle, I also need you to tell me about all the potential problems, even if they seem far-fetched. I can't afford surprises."

"I'll share with you every thought I have," said Uncle.

"Okay, I'll let things stand as they are until Friday night. But I'm going to have to tell my superiors there's a plan in the works to bring a complete end to the current hostilities."

"What if they ask for details?"

"I have to be credible, but I'll tell them as little as possible," Zhang said.

"You know I trust your judgement," Uncle said. "You'll hear from me Friday night."

Uncle felt his body sag as he put down the phone. He hadn't realized how tense he'd been. The business with Man and Wu had tested his relationship with Zhang as it hadn't been tested in years. He went to the fridge for another San Miguel and drained half the bottle in several large swigs. *I shouldn't have told him I'd get twelve gangs to join. That was rash,* he thought suddenly. *I'm always telling my men to underpromise and overdeliver, but Zhang had to hear that I'm confident. I hope it doesn't backfire on me.*

He went back to the phone and called Chow.

"Uncle, it's good to hear from you."

"Are things still quiet in Tsuen Wan?"

"They are, thanks to you."

"Thanks should be extended in equal measure to Ng and Tan. They contributed as much as Fanling."

"I've spoken to both of them already to express my gratitude."

"I know we agreed to leave ten men each with you, but if you need more, don't hesitate to ask," said Uncle.

"I know. Your Red Pole told Song. Thanks for that also."

"The four Red Poles seemed to work very well together."

"They did. And Uncle, I know I've been skeptical about this alliance of yours, but after seeing it in action today, I'm impressed," Chow said. "You can consider Tsuen Wan part of it now."

"I told you there were no strings attached to our help."

"I know, but we're still in. We'll stand with you and the others."

"I'm pleased to hear it," Uncle said. "Will you make that announcement at the meeting on Friday?"

"I'll do more than that. I'm going to call the Mountain Masters I'm closest to and encourage those who haven't already committed to do so."

"That would be very helpful. Thanks, Chow. Hopefully things will stay peaceful in Tsuen Wan and we won't have to talk again until Friday."

Uncle's optimism ticked upwards after speaking to Chow. Twenty minutes later, after he'd spoken to Ching in Yeun Long and He in Sha Tin, it had risen even further. They told him they had been leaning towards joining the alliance, but now they too were ready to commit.

Maybe I wasn't too rash with Zhang after all, Uncle thought as he headed for bed.

CHAPTER TWENTY-SEVEN

SHENZHEN HAD PLAYED A SPECIAL ROLE IN UNCLE'S life. As he boarded the train with Fong on Wednesday afternoon for the ten-kilometre trip, memories came flooding back.

It was from Shenzhen that he and his friends had swum to Hong Kong in 1959. It was then a small, nondescript town with a population of thirty thousand who worked mainly in agriculture and fishing. Uncle hadn't taken much notice of the place except for the town square, which when darkness fell had become crowded with throngs of people carrying homemade flotation devices. They were making their way to Mirs or Shenzhen Bay to attempt the four-kilometre swim to freedom. On many nights thousands of people slid into the treacherous waters, but only about half of them made it to Hong Kong.

Uncle hadn't returned to Shenzhen until 1981, by which time it had been designated a special economic zone. The SEZs were Deng Xiaoping's vehicle to modernize and grow Chinese industry, opening a door to the West that Uncle had stepped through. He recognized the opportunity presented by the sezs and had invested Fanling money to upgrade Ming's existing garment factory. Over the next few years his gang financed the construction of a second factory and fell into the warehouse business with the Liu family. By then Shenzhen had a population that exceeded a hundred thousand, and its old agricultural base had been replaced by sprawling industry. Now the city was the source of most of the Fanling gang's income.

"What's the population of Shenzhen these days?" Uncle asked Fong.

"About three million, I think, but it could be more than that. It grows so damn fast it's hard to keep track."

"I was thinking about the first time we came here to meet Ming. He had that beat-up old Toyota, he was wearing a stained Mao jacket, and some of his teeth were missing."

"And now he owns a high-end bmw — with driver — and dresses like he's the president of a bank," Fong said. "But he's still quick to acknowledge that he wouldn't be enjoying the life he has now without us."

"He's been a good partner."

"Yeah, he has. I don't think he's ever lied to me, and I've never found anything to suggest he might be trying to cheat us. He has completely honoured our agreement, which isn't always the case with deals between foreign investors and their Chinese partners. I hear stories all the time about foreigners getting fucked over as soon the locals figure they can go it alone."

"What do you think of his plan for a third factory?" Uncle asked.

"It is ambitious. It would double our current production capacity. I don't think we'll be able to use all that capacity right away, but if we push the sales hard enough, we'll get there eventually."

"I went over our money situation this morning with Hui. We're in great shape. I don't think we'll have any problem approving a third factory," said Uncle.

"I'm surprised you found time to look at the numbers. You seemed to be on the phone all morning."

"It was a memorable morning," Uncle said. "I spoke to every Mountain Master in the Territories — except for Wu, of course. Yesterday's events in Tsuen Wan had more of an impact than I expected. First there was the fact that Man made a move on Tsuen Wan. I think some of our colleagues thought I was exaggerating his ambition, but he put that to rest. Next, four gangs came together and routed his men. That proved we have the will and the manpower. The question I posed to the Mountain Masters was 'If all of us are prepared to stand together, who is there for us to fear?'"

"No one," Fong said.

"That may be true in the world of the triads, but not in the outside world. We mustn't get cocky or careless; we can't give the Hong Kong police or the Chinese government a reason to come after us. Even collectively, we'd be like a bug under their boot."

"Did anyone disagree with you?"

"No. They listened, but not many of them care about the outside world. Their focus is on the Heaven and Earth Society and their position within it," Uncle said. Then he smiled. "Fong, I'm happy to tell you that all nine gangs have declared their intention to join the alliance. You're the first person I've told."

Fong looked astonished, then bowed his head. "Uncle, I'm

honoured you are sharing this with me. That's terrific news."

"There are still some things to sort out, but we've made a strong start to bringing everyone together."

A sign beside the track indicated they were nearing their destination, Lo Wu Station, in the southern part of the city. "Before we reach the station, can I ask you to do me a favour when we meet Ming?" Fong asked.

"Of course."

"When he meets us at the station, don't tell Ming you're going to approve the plan. He's been working on it for ages and has been desperate to present it to you. I'm the one who's been holding him off, so let him present it and then make him wait before you give him an answer. It will seem like more of an accomplishment for him that way."

"That's thoughtful of you," Uncle said.

"I know Ming well, that's all."

The train came to a stop at the station. To neither Fong's nor Uncle's surprise, a stampede of disembarking passengers raced towards the customs and immigration booths. The two of them waited until the worst of the rush was over before leaving the car and walking to the end of the line. The station was almost ninety years old but had undergone several major renovations to accommodate the increased traffic. Fong looked at the queues and said, "Ten minutes."

Twelve minutes later they exited Lo Wu to find Ming, wearing a double-breasted pinstriped blue suit, standing near his gold-coloured BMW.

"It was good of you to meet us, Ming. We could have taken a taxi to the factory," Uncle said.

"Have you ever come to Shenzhen when I haven't been here to greet you?" Ming asked.

"Now that you mention it, I can't remember when you weren't," Uncle said.

"I think of it as a tradition — and, more importantly, as a portent of good luck."

"You assume I'm going to approve your plan."

Ming glanced at Fong. "No, I'm just pleased that you're prepared to listen. Fong explained that you're in Shenzhen for other reasons. I appreciate that you're making time for me."

"Let's go to the factory, and let's not talk about the plan until we get there, so you can present it properly," Fong said.

Ming sat in front with his driver but kept looking back at Uncle as the BMW left the city centre.

"Fong and I were talking on the train about our first trip here," Uncle said to him. "You had that old Toyota."

"How things have changed," Ming said. "If you remember, to get to my old factory we had to drive into the countryside, along narrow roads that were full of potholes. Now we have six-lane highways and there isn't a patch of land left to build on between the train station and our factories."

"When will all this development come to an end?" Uncle asked.

"I was at an SEZ meeting last week with about fifty other company heads. The meeting was called to encourage us to keep investing. The SEZ is projecting that the city will have a population of ten million in ten years. That should be great for our business."

"Ming, I asked you to wait to talk about your plan until we're at the factory. I sense that you're starting already," Fong said.

It had been some time since Uncle had visited the

Shenzhen factories, and on his previous trip there were still a few acres of farmland nearby. Now there were none, and as the BMW turned into the road leading to the factories, Uncle saw another change. Instead of bicycles, the courtyard in front of the buildings was filled with cars and scooters. There were also four buses used to transport workers back and forth to various parts of the city. Ming had managed to keep his workforce intact and had made a point of hiring local people, so, unlike many of the neighbouring factories, he didn't need dormitories.

As they came to a stop outside the main office, the front door opened and the senior staff filed out to form a line. Ming introduced each of them to Uncle, a ritual that was repeated at every visit he made. So was the invitation issued when he reached the man at the end of the line.

"Sir, can we take you on a tour of our facilities? We are producing a new line of polo shirts, and we have been experimenting with sports caps for the North American market," the man said.

Uncle knew the man was the head of production. "I would love a tour," he said.

The tour took half an hour. When it ended, Uncle and Fong accompanied Ming to his office and took seats around a small conference table. "As always, I'm impressed with the efficiency of your operation," Uncle said to Ming.

The three men were the only people at the table. Uncle expected that, during the course of the meeting, others would be invited to expand on any financial or marketing questions that might arise. Ming had built a competent management team and wasn't afraid to delegate — a trait that Uncle shared.

"So tell me, why should we build Ming Garment Factory Number Three?" Uncle asked to start the conversation.

Ming picked up three thick binders from the credenza next to the table. "It's all in here," he said.

Two hours and several briefings later, Uncle closed his binder and nodded at Ming. "That was an excellent presentation."

"I particularly like the idea of dedicating a large part of the new factory to the production of sports jerseys and caps. The profit margins on those are enormous," Fong said.

"What do you think, Uncle? Do we have your approval to proceed?" Ming asked.

"I think you've made a strong case, but it's going to require a lot of money, so I need to run the idea past my executive committee. I'd also like my White Paper Fan to go over your projections," Uncle said carefully.

When Uncle saw Ming's face fall, he turned to Fong. "Give your binder to Hui and tell him to read it over the weekend. We'll schedule a committee meeting for Monday," he said.

"So I can expect an answer on Monday?" Ming asked.

"Yes."

Ming smiled. "I appreciate that you're going to decide quickly, but it will make for an anxious weekend."

"My weekend is going to be anxious as well, but for a different reason," Uncle said, and then looked at his watch. "Fong and I have to be at the Pearl Boat Restaurant for six o'clock. What time should we leave here?"

"We should leave now," Ming said. "Traffic can be bad at this hour."

"You needn't come with us, but I would appreciate the use of your car and driver," said Uncle. "Can he wait for us at the restaurant and then take us to the train station after dinner?"

"Of course. Let's go and find him."

They left Ming's office and went into the courtyard, where the driver was sitting in the car. Ming gave him instructions and then turned to Uncle and Fong. "He should get you there by six."

"Thanks for this. I enjoyed the afternoon," Uncle said.

As soon as the partition was up and the car was leaving the factory lot, Fong said, "I thought you handled it perfectly, but that's hardly a surprise. Do you really want me to give the binder to Hui? Are you going to be calling a meeting?"

"I wouldn't mind Hui's opinion, but there's no need for a meeting. Ming's plan is solid."

"He will expect me to call him tonight, when I get back to Fanling. I'll tell him that you were favourably impressed. That should tide him over until Monday."

"Shit," Uncle said suddenly.

"What? Is something wrong?"

"No, but I meant to call Tsuen Wan before we left Ming's. I'm still worried that Man might try something stupid."

"I told everyone where we were going and to call us if anything happened. There were no calls, so I'm sure things are still calm," said Fong.

"I should have thought of that."

"You have enough on your mind."

The driver turned left onto a boulevard and then, a kilometre later, the BMW climbed a ramp onto an expressway going north. Traffic was heavy but moving steadily.

"You haven't told me why Leji is in Shenzhen," Fong said. "He hasn't been here in a while, and when he does come, it's normally because his aunt wants him to get the customs department to send more business our way."

"That could be part of the reason, but there's more to it. I just don't have anything specific I can tell you. I've been talking to Leji about Man's claims that the Chinese are going to run roughshod over the Hong Kong triads after the handover. He told me that's completely untrue, and I'm hoping he brought some tangible proof with him."

"Why do you need it if the Mountain Masters are already onside?"

"The gangs in the Territories are onside, but I still want to convince those in Kowloon and Hong Kong Island. I would like to destroy whatever credibility Man has left," Uncle said.

Driving on the expressway was like riding in a canyon, except instead of being flanked by rocky cliffs, the cars were dwarfed by row upon row of towering apartment buildings and office skyscrapers. *If Ming was right about the population tripling to ten million in ten years, what will the skyline look like then?* Uncle thought.

Uncle almost felt a sense of relief when they left the expressway for another boulevard. They were still flanked by tall buildings, but at least spaces were visible between them that made the experience seem less oppressive. The Pearl Boat was on the ground floor of a thirty-storey office building. The driver parked behind a black Mercedes out front.

"That's Ms. Ko's car," Fong said. "She's always early. I'm sure Leji and his wife are with her."

The Pearl Boat was Ms. Ko's favourite restaurant in Shenzhen. They had been meeting her there since it opened many years before. Uncle thought the food was only passable and not worth the trip across the city. Fong claimed — without proof — that Ms. Ko was a part-owner, and that's why she always chose it.

Uncle mentioned Ms. Ko when they were greeted by the host at the door. Her name generated a slight bow of respect and an escort to a private room off to one side of the main dining room. The host knocked on the door, opened it slightly, and said, "Your guests are here, Ms. Ko."

"Send them in," she replied.

Leji stood up and came towards them with his hand extended. He was wearing a grey suit, a white shirt, and a colourful Hermès tie, and looked every bit the successful senior official. He was still lean and fit; the only change Uncle saw in him was his greying hair, and that just made him look more distinguished.

The men shook hands and then Ms. Ko appeared at Leji's side. "My dear Uncle, it's so wonderful to see you."

Ms. Ko was a tiny woman; when she offered her cheek for him to kiss, even Uncle had to bend down. Both she and Chan Meilin, Leji's wife, were fashionably dressed and elegantly coiffed and made-up. There was nothing casual about either of them, and their attitude was equally formal with everyone except Leji and Uncle. Fong, who dealt with them most often, couldn't understand why the two women didn't seem to like him. Uncle had never detected any animus directed at Fong by Ms. Chan, but he couldn't help but notice that Ms. Ko treated him with something bordering on disdain. On this occasion, after the kiss on the cheek from Uncle, she said, "Ah, I see you brought Fong with you."

"Lan, my understanding was that building some additional cold-storage warehouses could be on our agenda, and Fong does handle our day-to-day business affairs with

Meilin," Uncle said. He used Ms. Ko's given name, something she had requested he do as a sign of the respect she had for him.

"Of course I'm not unhappy to see him. I'm just happy to see you," she said.

"Let's sit down," Leji said. "We have a variety of drinks on the table and my aunt has already ordered dinner. The food will start appearing shortly."

"I hope you don't mind," Ms. Ko said to Uncle, "I ordered some of your favourite dishes."

"I don't mind at all," Uncle said, reaching for a Tsingtao beer. "How is your husband? Is he giving any thought to retirement?"

"None whatsoever," she said, and laughed. "It was so hard and it took so long for him and Deng to get to the top that now they're there, they can't let go."

"I thought Chairman Deng had retired," Uncle said.

She furrowed her brow and looked at Uncle as if he'd told a joke. "Death will be his only retirement, and we hope that isn't for many years. China still needs Deng to show us the way. He may no longer carry the title, but make no mistake, he's still the paramount leader."

"I admire their dedication."

"We all do. And Uncle, you should know that my husband has the greatest admiration for you. There is no one he respects more than a person whose word can be trusted, even when sticking to that word comes at a horrific cost. This family will never forget how bravely you refused to denounce us when our enemies made it easy for you to do so."

Uncle took a sip of his beer, hoping to disguise his discomfort. In the years since he had been held and tortured by elements within the Chinese government opposed to the Liu family, the subject had never been raised by him or by them. "Those were difficult times. I only did what I thought was right," he said, wondering what had caused her to mention it.

Ms. Ko began to say something else but was interrupted by a loud knock at the door.

"Who's there?" Leji asked.

The door opened and an officer in a People's Liberation Army uniform appeared. "The Minister has just arrived and is ready to meet with you," the officer said to him.

"We'll be right there," Leji said as he stood up. "Ladies and Fong, Uncle and I have to attend another meeting. Start dinner without us, and by all means discuss the cold-storage additions. I'm all for them."

Uncle looked at Leji. "What is this?"

"Come with me and you'll find out."

The PLA officer waited for them by the door, then led the way across the main dining area to another private room. Two PLA soldiers with guns held across their chests stood on either side of the door. The officer knocked, waited a few seconds, and then opened it.

Uncle followed Leji into the room. Three people sat at a round table with a pitcher of water and glasses on it. Two of them leapt to their feet when they saw Leji; the third remained seated, his eyes fixed inquisitively on Uncle.

"This is Uncle Chow Tung," Leji said, and then gestured with an open palm towards the seated man. "And Uncle, let me introduce you to Tao Siju, Minister of Public Security of the People's Republic of China."

CHAPTER TWENTY-EIGHT

UNCLE STOOD ROOTED TO THE FLOOR. HE COULDN'T remember being more surprised, and he found himself struggling to find something appropriate to say.

"Come and sit," Tao said to Uncle and Leji. Then he turned to the young man and woman who had been sitting at the table with him. "You can leave now. I'll send for you if I need you."

Uncle and Leji took seats directly across from Tao. He smiled at them. "I am told you are a prominent triad leader in Hong Kong," he said to Uncle.

Uncle glanced at Leji.

"The Minister has met with my uncle. They were candid with each other. There is nothing to fear here," Leji said.

"Yes, I am a triad, a member of the Heaven and Earth Society. I am also the leader of my gang, but it is only one of about twenty triad gangs in Hong Kong."

"You are not what I expected a senior triad leader to look like," Tao said.

"We come in all shapes and sizes."

"As do senior members of the Chinese Communist Party."

Who could have imagined what an impact a man of Deng Xiaoping's physical stature would have on the world?" Tao said.

"I was fortunate enough to meet the Chairman some years ago," Uncle said. "He is a truly remarkable man."

"My colleague Liu Huning describes you in the same way. On our flight here, his wife expanded on that. I think I can say from experience that she is the harder of the two to impress," Tao said.

"The Minister and my uncle have a shared past, not dissimilar to the one my uncle has with the Chairman," Leji said. "The Minister knew success early in his career, was purged, then resurrected, and is now a key member of the Party's Central Committee, as well as being in charge of public security."

As Leji spoke, Uncle looked at Tao. He was in his sixties, he guessed, thick across the shoulders and chest, with a broad face, large eyes, and a thick head of jet-black hair parted on the right. He wore a navy-blue suit, white shirt, and plain light-blue tie. Unlike Deng and Liu Huning, he wasn't a man who would stand out in a crowd.

Tao smiled again. "I'm sure Uncle is interested more in hearing why I want to meet with him than listening to a recital of history," he said.

"Of course. I'm sure he is, but I wanted him to understand that you are here representing more than just yourself, that there are connections and friendships that go back many years," Leji said.

Tao looked at Uncle. "That is true, so let me tell you why I'm here, on their behalf as well as my own."

"You have my complete attention," Uncle said.

Tao nodded. "As you know, in two years Britain will return Hong Kong to its rightful owner. It will be an exchange fraught with complications, some of them immediate but others that are anticipated to appear some years from now," he said. "Although we will reclaim Hong Kong, there are conditions that will impede our ability to integrate it as fully as we'd like. One of those conditions is that my ministry and the PLA will have no presence in the new administrative region. We are to leave policing in the hands of the Hong Kong Police Force, and we have committed not to interfere with the way they carry out those duties."

"I know this may not sound pleasing to you, but I can tell you the prevailing opinion among triads is that retaining the status quo with the Hong Kong police is a good thing," Uncle said.

"Leji has explained that to me, and I can understand why you think that way. But does that mean you wouldn't consider establishing a relationship with us? Given that we will never cede control of Hong Kong again, and that the terms of the handover agreement will end in 2047, wouldn't it be forward-thinking to find a way to work with us? Your society hasn't lasted for nearly three centuries by being short-sighted."

Uncle felt a jolt as he struggled to contain his surprise. He reached for the pitcher of water and poured himself a glass.

"I know this might have caught you off guard, and I apologize for not briefing you earlier, but I thought it should come directly from the Minister," Leji said. "After you and I talked about the triads' uneasiness over how the Chinese government might treat them after the handover, I went to see my uncle. He spoke to the Minister, and they both spoke to Chairman Deng."

"In fact, we spoke several times over several days," Tao said. "Although Liu Huning's initial idea came spontaneously, it required a lot of additional questioning and reasoning before we reached a conclusion."

"And the conclusion was that you want to work with the triads?" Uncle said. "I hope you understand why I have a problem believing that."

Tao leaned forward. "After we sign the handover agreement, Hong Kong will be China's, but, as I said, it won't be completely ours for another fifty years. For some parts of our government, that's a tolerable situation. For my ministry, it isn't. We will have no presence. We can't openly impose one without breaking the agreement, and trying to create one covertly would pose tremendous risks. If it were to be discovered, we would receive international condemnation for breaching the agreement. And besides, my experience is that no covert operation stays covert very long, especially if it's trying to function in a hostile environment full of smart, mistrustful people. Does that type of environment sound like the Hong Kong of today as far as attitudes towards the mainland Chinese are concerned?"

"I think it does. Not everyone feels that way, but a majority do."

"So tell me, how successful do you think we'd be if we tried to insinuate mainland officers loyal to my ministry into the Hong Kong Police Force?"

"I don't think it would work."

"Neither do we, which is why we're having this meeting."

"What are you trying to say?" Uncle asked.

"We would like your organization to be our presence in Hong Kong."

"Which organization? As I said, there are twenty or so gangs in Hong Kong, and they all operate independently."

"We'll come back to that later. For now I'd like to know if you think it's possible for us to work together," said Tao.

"Work how? Do you want us to be spies or act like police?" Uncle asked. "I can tell you now, those are roles we aren't fit to play, even if we wanted to."

"We envision a relationship that is less structured, more fluid, although its exact nature is difficult to predict. After all, no one knows what challenges will present themselves over the next fifty years. But for now, let me give you an example," Tao said. "To our certain knowledge, a large number of hardened criminals are using Hong Kong as a sanctuary. Some are hiding beneath the cloak of Hong Kong's British legal system to avoid Chinese laws. Others were convicted in China but contrived to flee. Among them are murderers, kidnappers, drug dealers, swindlers, and so on. None of them has — as far as we know — any triad connections, and if a few do, we can leave them aside for now. As for the rest, we want them returned to China to serve their sentences or face trial."

"You can't get them extradited?" Uncle asked.

"Extradition is a complicated business. Matters of nationality are involved. The impartiality of the Chinese legal system is considered questionable by Hong Kong authorities. Even the evidence we present when we make a request is regularly dismissed as being fabricated."

"I have had dealings with your legal system and the way evidence can be gathered," Uncle said.

"Yes, I know. Liu Huning told me you were arrested and abused by a rogue military element. Please don't draw a comparison between them and us," Tao said softly. "My understanding is that your ordeal was ended by people who represent the system I am part of, and that, moreover, there was compensation for the suffering you endured."

"Uncle, in the ten years since then," Leji said, "you have been back and forth between Hong Kong and China countless times. You have deep-seated business relationships here that have lasted just as long. Your friend Xu has been living and working in Shanghai for years. Do either of you feel unsafe? Do you feel oppressed by the weight of the Chinese legal system?"

"No, in truth I do not, and neither does Xu," Uncle replied, and then looked at Tao. "But that aside, Minister, what did you mean by *issues of nationality*?"

"Let me answer that by asking you a question," Tao said. "I know you were born in Hubei province and that you are also a citizen of Hong Kong. When you are asked what you are, how do you respond? Do you say you're a citizen of Hong Kong or do you say you're Chinese? Or do you say that you are Chinese *and* a citizen of Hong Kong?"

"I've never been asked that particular question. But if I was, I'd say I'm Chinese and a citizen of Hong Kong."

"I'd like you to note that you placed your Chinese birth before your Hong Kong citizenship," Tao said. "That's how we view anyone born in China. They will always be Chinese, and we claim them as such. Just as many ships fly flags of convenience as a way to avoid paying taxes in their real home country, we think of the foreign passports carried by Chinese criminals living in Hong Kong as their way of avoiding justice at home."

"You believe we can help you bring them to face that justice."

"Yes, but carefully and selectively. It isn't something we'd want you to rush into. We'd start with individuals whose departure from Hong Kong would go unnoticed," said Tao.

"Uncle, these are people who have committed horrendous crimes," Leji said.

"I have no doubt that could be true. What I'm struggling to understand is what's in it for us."

"You have my promise that neither the Ministry of Public Security nor the PLA will interfere, now or in the future, with any of your business dealings in Hong Kong," Tao said. "And we'll pay you for any specific services you provide."

"That's not enough," Uncle said quickly. "My colleagues are naturally mistrustful. In fact, when I told one of them of Leji's assurance that triads would not be persecuted, he asked me for the source of that information. When I told him I couldn't breach a confidence, he accused me of lying. And that colleague, gentlemen, is someone I consider to be more friend than foe."

"What more do you want?" asked Tao.

"I need to think about that," Uncle said. "This has caught me off guard."

"I am here only for this evening. Can you think quickly?"

"Can I have a few hours?" Uncle asked.

"How about two? That will give me time to have dinner and finish some work with my assistants."

"Yes, two will be fine."

"Then off you go."

"Before I leave, there's another matter I want to return to," said Uncle. "I told you earlier that I lead just one gang. I have no right to speak for any of the others."

"I thought we could talk about that, and the opportunities

and challenges it presents, after we reach some form of agreement," Tao said.

"What value is an agreement if I can't bind my brothers to it. If it's simply between you and me?"

"Leji mentioned that the gang structure in Hong Kong could be an issue, and we did discuss it," Tao said. "We won't make a commitment to just one gang. You need to persuade all of them, or at the very least a majority of them, to accept the agreement."

"A majority might be a possibility if the offer is tempting enough," Uncle said. "Are there any other conditions I need to know about?"

"There is one," Tao said. "Even if all the gangs agree to work with us, we can't deal with each of them separately. They will have to appoint a representative with whom we can deal directly, who can speak on their behalf and manage the relationship with us. You are here for a reason, Uncle. We want you to be that representative."

"While my colleagues may accept that you want to deal with a single voice, they won't take kindly to your imposing me — or anyone else — on them," said Uncle.

"Well, frankly, we're not interested in dealing with anyone else. So factor that into what you think you'll need from us to persuade your brothers to support you."

CHAPTER TWENTY-NINE

"I WISH I HAD KNOWN WHAT TO EXPECT," UNCLE SAID to Leji as they made their way back to Ko Lan and the others. "I apologize, but the Minister wanted to do it this way. I hope you aren't disappointed with his basic proposal. It could be good for all the parties involved."

"Does your uncle support this?"

"Yes, and so does Chairman Deng. My uncle was particularly insistent that you be the triad representative moving forward," Leji said. "I realize that may put you in an awkward position with your colleagues, but I also think it could strengthen your negotiating position with the Minister."

"Do you have any idea what he's prepared to offer?"

"No, but I know there's more than a handful of people in Hong Kong he is desperate to get back into China."

Leji opened the door to the private dining room. Ms. Ko looked at them and smiled as they entered. *She knew what that meeting was going to be about,* Uncle thought.

The table was covered with platters of food and a large ice bucket filled with bottles of Tsingtao. Uncle reached for a beer. "Ladies, you'll have to excuse me, but I need to speak to Fong in private. We'll go outside to our car. Save us some food for when we get back," he said.

Fong looked questioningly at him but didn't say a word as he got to his feet, picking up the beer he'd been drinking.

"We won't take two hours," Uncle said to Leji.

As Uncle and Fong left the room, Fong noticed the armed guards standing outside the other door. "Is that where you were?" he asked.

"Yes, but let's not talk about it until we're in the car."

The BMW was parked at the curb about fifty metres from the restaurant. The driver saw them approaching and leapt out to open the back door.

"We aren't going anywhere right now. We just need to speak in private. Go grab something to eat," Uncle said to him.

Uncle slid into the back seat. Fong joined him and said, "What the hell is going on?" before the door closed behind him.

"I just met with Tao Siju, China's Minister of Public Security."

"What did he want?" Fong asked, his voice immediately full of concern.

"Don't panic. He's not here to cause us grief. It's actually rather the opposite. He's offered us what I think could be a fantastic opportunity. The thing is, I can't decide whether it's legitimate or a ploy to get us to do some messy work for them, at the end of which they'll dump us, or worse," Uncle said. "What makes me want to believe it's legit is Leji's involvement, and the fact that Tao is a friend of Liu Huning. Tao told me — and Leji concurred — that Huning and Deng both approve of the offer."

"What offer?" Fong asked, his concern still evident.

It took Uncle twenty minutes to relate in detail everything he and Tao had discussed. Fong listened intently. When Uncle had finished, Fong placed his hand on his colleague's forearm and squeezed. "This is incredible, almost unbelievable. No wonder you have questions about whether it's real or not," he said.

"Assuming it is, what do you think we should ask for in exchange for helping?"

Fong finished his beer and wiped his mouth with his sleeve. "They want us to do their dirty work in Hong Kong, right?"

"Yes. And taking so-called criminals back to China might just be the start of it. Who knows what else they'll ask us to do next, so we can't completely give up the right to say no to them."

"For what Tao is talking about, we could attach a big price to every head. Make them pay."

"He mentioned that they'd pay us, but I don't like that idea. It would make us look like hired goons instead of partners," Uncle said. "I want something more substantial, something with a longer-term payback, something that ties us closer to them and gives us extra protection in the process."

"Like what?"

"Xu is doing well in Shanghai, and we're established in some of the special economic zones, but the rest of China is still off-limits to triads," said Uncle. "What if we asked them to open up more of the country to us? Allow us to set up shop in specific cities and operate freely without having to worry about police or the PLA."

"That's a huge request. Do you think they'd consider it?"

"I don't know. And I won't know unless I ask," said Uncle.

"If you could pull that off, it would give us all kinds of leverage with the other gangs, especially if you were the one deciding who got to set up where."

"I'm not sure making those decisions by myself would be smart. Which brings us to the issue of the Communists wanting to deal directly with me. How do we make that work without alienating every other gang?"

"You could be overthinking that one," Fong said. "Let's face it, you're already the de facto leader in the Territories."

"I'm not going to pretend that I don't think of myself as a leader, but there are a lot of egos out there that need to be massaged, and I've always been careful to consult and ask for advice. Making the other Mountain Masters feel that they're part of the decision-making process is one of the reasons I think we're close to a real coalition. And truthfully, they have to be part of the process, because at the end of the day we are equals."

"Some are more equal than others. They all know that, even if they won't say it, and they also know you're the most equal."

"Still, I have to be careful not to get too far ahead of myself. I need to keep everyone moving with me at the same pace."

"Then you need a structure that will satisfy both the Mountain Masters and the Communists, because you can't keep having meetings with sixty people," Fong said. "I also think you have to accept that, no matter what you do, some of those pricks in Kowloon and on the Island will never be satisfied."

"You could be right about Man, but if I can cut a deal — providing proof positive that the Chinese government's attitude towards triads is the exact opposite of everything he's been saying — I have to believe he'll lose his allies. We'll isolate him."

"If you do, and if you can get some Kowloon and Island gangs to buy into the proposal, you'll have to make them part of the decision-making process. You won't be dealing solely with our friends in the Territories."

Uncle shook his head. "This is getting more complicated by the minute. All I wanted was to surround Fanling with allies and secure the Territories from outside aggression."

"However this turns out, you're going to achieve that. This is gravy. This could be win-win-win," Fong said.

Uncle laughed. "Listen to us, making plans when I haven't even reached a deal with Tao."

"Knowing you, Uncle, you will."

"If I do, then is the time to talk about how we convince the other gangs to join us. For now, I'm going to focus on how to get the best possible deal."

"Do you want me to leave you alone?" Fong asked.

"No. We should get back to our partners," Uncle said. "How was your meeting with them?"

Fong smiled. "I knew we hadn't been invited here to discuss cold-storage warehouses. Ms. Ko barely spent ten minutes on them, and then she told me she'll agree with whatever you decide."

"Does she want to build two of them?"

"Yeah."

"What do you think?"

"They make sense. I think we should spend the money, but she wants to hear that from you."

"Then let's go tell her and get something to eat."

CHAPTER THIRTY

THE TABLE HAD BEEN CLEARED WHEN UNCLE AND FONG rejoined the Liu family. Uncle's disappointment must have been obvious, because Ms. Ko was quick to say, "Uncle, I can't have you eating cold food. I told the manager to bring you something fresh and hot when he saw you return. It should be here in a few minutes."

"Thank you, Lan," said Uncle. "Fong told me you had an excellent discussion about the cold-storage warehouses."

"He agrees with Meilin and I that we should build them, but what do you think?"

"Let's do it."

She smiled. "I won't ask about your other meeting, but I want to say that my husband is very hopeful some agreement will be reached."

A knock at the door deflected everyone's attention. "Come in," Leji said.

The table was reset for Uncle with plates, bowls, spoons, and chopsticks. A moment later the food arrived, and conversation dwindled as he ate. When he had finished, Uncle looked at his watch. "I'm going outside for a smoke and a

walk. I think better when I'm walking. I'll be back in time
to resume our meeting," he said to Leji.

One cigarette turned into four as Uncle paced back and
forth along the sidewalk. His challenge had been clearly
identified by Fong. Somehow he had to find a way to give the
Chinese government what they wanted while protecting the
long-term interests of the triad gangs. What he didn't know,
and what was causing him concern, was how the Chinese
would react if they couldn't reach an agreement. He wished
he'd discussed that with Fong or, better yet, with Leji.

He kept thinking about something Xu had said during
their last call — that remaining neutral wasn't an option. Was
that really true? Would inability to reach an agreement be
interpreted by the Chinese government as a rejection rather
than a failed negotiation? And if it was considered to be a
rejection, what would be the consequences? Could it put the
existing triad footholds in China at risk? What else had Xu
said? One thing came immediately to mind: Xu had told
him he should take Leji's advice.

Leji was waiting outside their private room when Uncle
returned. "One of the Minister's assistants came to tell me
he's ready for us," he said.

"Before we head over there, I have something I want to
ask you. I'd like you to be brutally honest with your answer,"
Uncle said.

"That sounds ominous."

"It's an important question," Uncle said. "Tell me, am I in
a position to say no to the Minister's offer?"

"Have you decided to say no?" Leji asked, looking
uncomfortable.

"No, I haven't. My mind is still open. What I'm asking is,

if I chose to say no, what would be the consequences?"

"You would be throwing away the chance to establish a very beneficial relationship."

"I understand that, but would there be repercussions?"

Leji hesitated, then looked directly into Uncle's eyes. "I think it would be sensible to expect some. I don't know what form they might take but, despite his pleasant demeanour, the Minister can be vengeful. He was sent here to arrange a deal. If he goes back to Beijing without one, it won't sit well with some people we know, and he'll be blamed."

"So I'm going to walk out of here either his friend or his enemy."

"I think that's an accurate assessment."

"What's your advice?"

"Make a deal," Leji said quickly. "My uncle wouldn't have arranged this meeting if we didn't think it's the right thing to do. But don't feel that your hands are tied when it comes to negotiations. Make your demands clear. No offence will be taken; the Minister respects you."

"Thanks for your honesty, Leji," Uncle said. "I'm ready to speak with the Minister."

The officer who had escorted them earlier in the evening opened the door as they approached. Tao Siju was alone in the room.

"Uncle, I hope your time was productive," Tao said.

"There was a lot to think about," Uncle said as he sat down.

"Indeed. And what conclusion did you reach?"

"We are prepared to work with you and we are pleased that you think enough of us to have made the initial offer," said Uncle.

"But not pleased enough to accept it as presented?"

"Obviously your promise that we will be allowed to conduct our business without fear of reprisals is important, and readily accepted," Uncle said. "But your offer to pay us for our services is something we would rather decline."

"No money? That's a surprise. I expected you to be a hard bargainer when we got into the details of payment."

"If we take your money, we'll be nothing more than contract employees working from project to project. If you want a long-term relationship — you're talking about more than fifty years — we would like to view ourselves as your partners, albeit very junior partners. Money is not that important to us if that's the situation. We'd rather build trust based on performance and earn the right to ask for favours."

"I see the logic behind that decision. But if you don't want money, what is it that you do want?"

Uncle leaned towards Tao. "My associate Xu has been permitted to conduct business in Shanghai for the past ten years. Several other associates operate enterprises in the special economic zones. In every case we are making investments, contributing to the local economy, and working in concert with government officials at all levels," he said. "We want assurance that those businesses will be as equally protected as those in Hong Kong."

"That's a given."

"Thank you. And we would like to expand into other parts of China. To start with, I would like from you a list of five cities with a population of more than one million where we would be allowed to do business. The operations would be conducted in the same manner as in Shanghai and the sezs, and that includes working with anyone you choose to designate."

"*Five* cities?"

"To start with. If after five years you're satisfied with our working relationship in Hong Kong, we will ask that you designate another five cities."

"That is an intriguing proposal, but it's not something I can offer without consulting my colleagues."

"If this will help with the consultation, you can tell them I've requested a list of the ten criminals on your list you most want to have returned to China. If we reach an agreement, we'll start rounding them up immediately. You'll find that we're a very efficient organization."

"I've been told that is true," Tao said. "But, going back to your request, being allowed to expand in China is your priority?"

"It is."

"Is that all you want in addition to protection for your current businesses?"

"No, there's one more thing. And I'll preface my request by saying that I think it's necessary if I'm to persuade the majority of my colleagues to accept your proposal."

"I can't imagine what that might be," Tao said.

"I need your direct involvement in convincing them that this is a genuine offer."

"They won't take your word for it?"

"Some will, some might, and some most certainly won't. I believe that if you can persuade those who might, it will give us a majority," Uncle said. "Another reason for this request is, if they accept a deal based solely on what I tell them and it doesn't work out, I'll be the target of more criticism than you can imagine. And truthfully, it might not be limited to verbal criticism. I can't risk the possibility of being hung out to dry like that."

"Assuming I am prepared to help, what do you have in mind?" Tao asked.

"A meeting of Mountain Masters is scheduled for this Friday in Fanling. Only about half of them were going to attend, but I'm sure I can convince more to be there. Assuming that you and I have finalized a draft agreement by then, it would be the ideal opportunity to present it."

"Are you suggesting that I attend the meeting?"

"I am."

"That would be totally inappropriate. It isn't possible," said Tao.

"Then send a representative. My colleagues need to see for themselves that this is real."

"And what would you expect this representative to do? Sell the proposal to your colleagues?"

"No, I would do that. I think it's enough for whoever you appoint to confirm that you and I met and that the Chinese government has agreed in principle to an agreement that I will explain. The representative can leave after that's done."

Tao looked doubtful and turned to Leji. "What do you think of this idea?"

"If the representative didn't work for the ministry, it wouldn't compromise you. And if Uncle thinks it will give him the support he needs, then I think we should do it," Leji said.

"We'll have to talk to Beijing," Tao said after a long pause. "I have to discuss the five-city proposal anyway, so let's find a secure phone and make the call."

"You should join my aunt and the others," Leji said to Uncle. "I'll come and get you when we're done."

Uncle nodded and left the room without speaking. He started across the main dining area but then pivoted and headed for the front door. Once outside, he lit a cigarette and leaned against a wall. He thought he had presented his case as well as he could; now it was up to Beijing. But who in Beijing would be making the decision? Uncle hoped it would be Liu Huning, who he was certain would be involved in the process. But what if they turned down his request or tried to alter it? How much wiggle room did he have? How much could he compromise and still have something worth presenting to the other Mountain Masters? *This could turn out to be a complete disaster*, he thought, and suddenly felt tense. What gave him some level of comfort was that, regardless of how it turned out, he was confident he'd still have the support of the Liu family.

Uncle went back into the restaurant and made his way to Ms. Ko's room. She was sitting in a corner chatting with Meilin while Fong sat by himself on the opposite side of the room.

"Where's Leji?" Ms. Ko asked.

"He's making a call to Beijing."

She frowned but didn't say anything.

Uncle went to sit with Fong. "How did it go?" Fong asked softly.

"I presented our proposals and Tao decided he had to talk to Beijing."

"I can't stop thinking about it. And the more I do, the more I realize this is a really big deal," Fong said. "If you can make it happen, you'll secure our future for years."

"*If* I can make it happen, and that's a huge if."

"I've also been thinking about how you could structure things in Hong Kong. Are you interested in listening or is this the wrong time?"

Uncle's initial inclination was to tell Fong to wait, but when he saw how intensely focused his friend seemed, he said, "Sure, go ahead."

"When I thought about it, I realized you had already started the process by pulling together the gangs in the New Territories, and that if you could persuade some gangs from Kowloon and Hong Kong Island to join with us, we'd have a fairly representative group. It has always frustrated me — and some other Straw Sandals — that there's never been a mechanism to address problems we all share or to resolve disputes between gangs. Your coalition idea got me thinking that we could use it for other things, in addition to mutual defence."

"What are you suggesting? That we create some kind of formal body?"

"Why not?"

"I don't want to sound negative, but can you imagine twenty Mountain Masters sitting in one room trying to resolve disputes? It would be chaotic."

"I know, but we could set it up the way the Communists do. The twenty Mountain Masters would be like their Central Committee. It has about two hundred members and meets only once a year, to set policies. Implementation of those policies is controlled by the Politburo Standing Committee, which usually has between seven and nine members."

"We don't have the equivalent of a Politburo Standing Committee. And if we did, I can't believe the Mountain Masters would cede any control to it," said Uncle.

"We could create one, and I've even come up with some possible names," Fong said, becoming quite animated. "The twenty Mountain Masters would comprise something we could call the Triad Council of Hong Kong, and the smaller group could be the Executive Council."

"And how small do you suggest this Executive Council should be?"

"Three Mountain Masters, one each from Kowloon, Hong Kong Island, and the New Territories. The gangs in each of those districts could elect their own representative," Fong said. "And if it were decided, as the Communists want, that one of them be designated leader, we could let all twenty Mountain Masters vote to see which of the three they choose."

Uncle smiled. "That's very clever of you, Fong. But given that there are more gangs in the New Territories than Kowloon and the Island combined, the leader would more than likely come from there. That wouldn't go over well in Kowloon or Hong Kong."

"I'm not saying my plan can't be improved, but it is a start. And if the gangs agreed that disputes should be brought to the executive group to resolve, it would be a terrific start. Just think how many feuds have been dragging on for years."

"You do make some good points. I'm not being dismissive, but I need time to think about this, and right now I have enough to worry about," said Uncle.

The two men fell into silence. Fong had surprised Uncle with his idea, and though at first it had seemed overly ambitious, there was a thread of common sense running through it. Uncle's attempt at forming a coalition had proven that the gangs were capable of working together, and if they could agree on one common objective, why not two or three?

He pondered the possibilities, and as he did, one random thought came to him. He was about to express it when the door opened.

"Uncle, the Minister is waiting for you," Leji said.

CHAPTER THIRTY-ONE

THERE HAD BEEN TIMES IN UNCLE'S LIFE WHEN, IN THE midst of confusion, he suddenly knew how things were going to end. It wasn't a logical process. Clarity simply entered his mind and took hold, and that's what he felt when he re-entered the meeting room with Leji and saw Tao's blank expression.

Uncle poured a glass of water and sat back, waiting for Tao to speak.

"Your request caught our people in Beijing off guard," Tao said.

"How so?"

"Your refusal to accept payment for your services surprised them."

"I haven't refused payment; what I'm declining is cash payments. There are other ways to provide compensation. Granting us access to more cities in China is one."

Tao placed his fingertips together and touched his lips. "Beijing is reluctant to grant you that access."

"Why? If we contribute to the economic well-being of

those communities the way we've done in the SEZs, it's to China's benefit as much as ours."

"Even so, there is a reluctance," Tao said. "How firm are you about this request?"

Uncle said, "There's no agreement we'd accept that didn't include it."

Tao looked at Leji with resignation. For a second Uncle's confidence wavered, and he braced himself for a possible rejection.

"In that case, we are prepared to give you three cities," Tao said.

"I asked for five."

"Bend a little," Tao said.

"I'll accept four, but give me a list of ten from which I can choose."

"No, we'll do the choosing," said Tao. "This is a practical consideration, not one intended to inhibit your ability to conduct business. We know the abilities of the officials in the cities, and we need to ensure that your activities are properly supported. Neither party wants to risk failure."

"In other words, you want to choose which officials are rewarded by our presence."

Tao smiled. "Uncle, you won't succeed unless you have strong local support. Let us guarantee it."

"Then you choose the cities — four of them," said Uncle.

"Four it is."

"How soon can I have the names?"

"It will take a little time. People need to be consulted. We can't rush into anything."

"I would appreciate a time frame," Uncle said.

"Within a month," said Tao.

"We think that's fair," Leji added.

Uncle glanced at his friend, and he knew the interjection was meant to signal that Liu Huning had agreed to it. "I can live with that," he said. "Now, what about adding cities further down the road? I suggested five more in five years."

"We aren't opposed to the idea. We will agree to consider it when the time comes, but we can't commit. We hope you're prepared to accept that in good faith."

"Uncle, if you are successful in the four cities you're being given now, Beijing would be foolish not to permit you to expand your presence," Leji said. "But I think you would agree it's prudent on our part to let the results dictate what comes next."

"That is a reasonable position. As long as you can guarantee reconsideration in five years, I can live with that as well."

"There will be no problem with a guarantee," Tao said.

"Can I also assume that our current businesses in Shanghai and the SEZs will be allowed to continue operating without interference?"

"Those businesses and your activities in Hong Kong are one and the same in Beijing's eyes. You are free to operate as you have been doing," Tao said.

"Excellent."

"Now, if I may, I'd like to change the subject. You asked me to give you a list of ten people we want repatriated. I'll have it for you by Friday," Tao said.

"And do we have a timetable?" Uncle asked.

"Why don't we say a month as well. All I expect is for you to do the best you can, but I will be disappointed if you don't get them all. We know they're all in Hong Kong. The list will contain addresses and any other personal information we have," said Tao.

"We'll get on it right away. Where should we deliver them?"

"We don't care, as long as they return to China, but Shenzhen, Guangzhou, and Zhuhai are close and might be easiest. Contact information for our office in Beijing will be included with the list. You should give us advance notice so our people can make arrangements to receive whoever you pick up."

"That is agreeable," said Uncle.

"Then all that's left is to discuss your meeting on Friday," said Tao. "After talking it over with Beijing, the decision has been made to send Liu Leji."

"I'm pleased to hear that," Uncle said, hiding his surprise. "What will he say?"

"That has yet to be finalized. By Friday you will know," said Tao. "For now, be satisfied that he will be there to support you."

"An additional point of clarification," Leji said. "I won't be there representing the General Administration of Customs or the Ministry of Public Security. I will be there as chief of staff to the third-ranked member of the Politburo Standing Committee. My uncle has wanted me to assume that position for several years, and we've agreed that the timing is finally right."

"Are congratulations in order?" Uncle asked.

"Not until I've proven I can handle the position. Friday will be a test," Leji said.

"The meeting is scheduled for noon at the White Jade Restaurant in Fanling. When can we expect to see you?"

"I'll stay in Shenzhen until Friday morning. Can you meet me at the train station in Fanling?"

"Let me know your schedule. I'll be there with my car and driver."

"We'll talk before then," Leji said. "In the meantime, I think you and Fong should head back to Hong Kong. The Minister and I still have things to discuss with Beijing."

"That's fine, but I have one last question. Assuming we can pull everything together, who will be my contact moving forward?"

"Our requests will come directly from me to you," Tao said.

"My group hasn't agreed that I'll be their representative," Uncle said.

"They'll need to. Beijing won't work with anyone they don't know and trust."

"Making that point will be part of my mandate on Friday," Leji said.

Uncle nodded and stood up. "Minister, it was a pleasure meeting you," he said. "It appears that our paths may cross again, and when they do, I hope it's after our plans have been successfully launched and we're both happy men."

"I am committed to making it work from our side, and I can't stress enough how important it is, for your sake and ours, that you make it work in Hong Kong."

"I'll do everything I can. And with Leji's help, I don't see why it won't be possible."

"I'll walk you out," Leji said.

Uncle followed him into the main dining room. As they crossed the floor, Leji said, "There's still a lot to be decided about what I can say on Friday. There's an understandable reluctance to openly endorse triads, but I'm working on it, and my uncle is quietly supporting me. I've been making the point that if they want a deal they need to give you the tools you're asking for, because you're the only person who can make it happen."

"Does this new position increase your influence?"

"In terms of prestige it's a lateral move from the customs department, but it puts me right in the middle of the political mix. How much influence I have will depend on how well I can manoeuvre. My uncle thinks I've inherited some of his political genes. I hope he's right."

They reached Ms. Ko's private room and stopped outside the door. "Will this affect our businesses in Shenzhen?"

"If anything it will make things easier, but what would make them easier still is getting a deal on Friday."

CHAPTER THIRTY-TWO

FONG STARTED ASKING QUESTIONS AS SOON AS HE and Uncle left the restaurant, but Uncle quieted him. "Let's wait until we're on the train."

They rode in silence to the station and rushed to catch a train that was already at the platform. When they were seated, Fong looked expectantly at Uncle. "Now can you tell me what happened?"

Uncle nodded. "The Chinese have made an offer that seems acceptable on the surface, but I won't be completely sure until I hear what Leji tells the Mountain Masters on Friday."

"Why is Leji going to speak to the Mountain Masters?" Fong asked, his confusion evident.

"I asked that a representative from the Chinese government come to the meeting to confirm that they had met with me and made us an offer. I thought it would add credibility to the proposal. I was hoping it would be Tao. They gave us Leji, which isn't a bad thing, because we don't have to worry about him doing anything that would undermine me. In fact, I'm sure he'll be as supportive as his government permits him to be."

"I agree. We can count on Leji."

"I know, but he will be operating under orders. We have to expect him to say only what has been authorized."

"And if you like what he has to say, where does that leave us?"

"It doesn't matter if I like it. It only matters that the other Mountain Masters believe him and are willing to listen to me with open minds," Uncle said. "To make this work, we need the support of a clear majority, and that support has to be broad-based. I want at least two Mountain Masters from Kowloon on board, and two or ideally three from Hong Kong Island."

"You said Zhao is interested in the coalition, and I'm sure Tse will support you. That gives you a foothold in both places."

"And I have some leverage that might bring a few others over to us."

"Did Tao agree that we can expand our presence in China?" Fong asked.

"The agreement came from a higher source than Tao."

"That's even better. How many cities did they give us?"

"Four, but we don't know which ones yet. They'll tell us within a month, after they figure out who they want to reward on their end."

Fong smiled and jabbed Uncle lightly in the arm. "So you've come around to the idea that you'll decide which gang gets which city?"

"It does appear that the Chinese government thinks I

should be the one making those decisions, and there's no point fighting them on it," Uncle said. "But Fong, it can't be a blatant process. That would only alienate the other Mountain Masters. We'll have to manage things subtly."

"I understand."

"Truthfully, the fact that the Chinese government has committed to let us operate in Hong Kong, Shanghai, and the SEZs without interference is almost enough in itself to justify doing a deal with them. I don't think the Mountain Masters would believe that if it was simply coming from me, but Leji's presence should convince most of them. Being allowed to expand further into China is a huge bonus."

"What are they expecting in return? What you told me earlier, or do they want more?"

"The same, but that doesn't mean they won't want us to do other things for them down the road. In fact, the more I think about it, it's possible that Tao wants us to be a para-military extension of his ministry. If that's how he views us, then god knows what we'll be asked to do," Uncle said. "But for now they're going to give us a list of ten criminals they want rounded up and shipped back to China."

The train began to slow as it approached Fanling. "Is Sonny meeting you?" Fong asked.

"No. I didn't have a chance to tell him when we'd be arriving."

"Then we'll share a taxi," said Fong.

"I'd rather walk, and if you don't mind, I'd rather be alone," Uncle said. "I have some phone calls to make when I get to the apartment, and I need to organize my thoughts."

"Is there anything I can do?"

"Yes. I want you to call the executive and tell them to meet

FORTUNE 245

with us at ten tomorrow morning," Uncle said. "Then I want
you to phone some of the Straw Sandals you trust and talk
about your idea for a council. I'd like to know their reactions. But Fong, make sure they know that you're doing this
on your own, that the idea didn't come from me. You also
mustn't mention anything about China."

"I can do that. I'll tell them that the coalition in the
Territories got me thinking."

"Perfect."

"Do you want to hear from me tonight?"

"No, it won't be necessary. We'll talk in the morning,"
Uncle said.

It was a twenty-minute walk from the station to Uncle's
apartment. Most of the businesses were closed and the sidewalks virtually empty. Still, he walked slowly, his mind preoccupied with the day's events as he continued to process
them. Part of him had trouble believing that Tao's offer was
genuine. Perhaps it was just a carrot being dangled to entice
the triads to deliver the ten men to China, and when that
was done, the carrot would be pulled back. Except the Liu
family was party to the offer, and Uncle could not imagine
them participating in anything that would adversely affect
their business arrangements.

No, Uncle thought, the offer was real. The thought almost
took his breath away as he conjured up what it could mean
for the future of the triad gangs of Hong Kong. *Slow down,*
he thought. *I'm getting too far in front of myself.* Even if the
offer was real, it wouldn't be realized if he couldn't convince
his brothers to come together in a way that satisfied Tao and
Beijing. How hard would that be? Uncle didn't know, but he
was going to find out.

When he neared his apartment, Uncle saw a silver Mercedes parked outside the Blind Emperor. As he approached, the driver's door opened and Sonny stepped out.

"Your shift is supposed to be over," Uncle said.

"I wanted to make sure you made it home safely," Sonny said.

"How was the afternoon? Were there any problems in Tsuen Wan or elsewhere in the Territories?"

"Wang called me an hour ago to ask when you were coming back. I told him I didn't know and asked about Tsuen Wan. He said it was quiet."

"I'll call him when I get upstairs," Uncle said. "First I want to get some beer. You can wait here until I come out, but then I want you to go home."

"The night-shift guy is coming at midnight. I'll stay until he arrives. Wang wouldn't want it any other way."

Knowing there wasn't any point in arguing, Uncle shrugged and went into the Blind Emperor. A few minutes later he came out with two San Miguels and made his way upstairs. He took off his jacket, opened a beer, and settled into his chair to phone Wang.

"You're home," Wang said.

"I just arrived. Sonny was waiting outside."

"He'll leave at midnight."

"So he told me," said Uncle. "He's a good man. I'm pleased we found a way to keep him."

"Me too. How was your day in Shenzhen?"

"Eventful, but I don't want to talk about it tonight. Fong is organizing an executive committee meeting for tomorrow morning."

"I spoke to him five minutes ago."

"I'm calling to ask about Tsuen Wan. Evidently it's quiet."

"I spoke to Song five times today, the last time two hours ago. There's been no sign of trouble but he's still nervous, so we're leaving our men there for another day," Wang said. "He's really appreciative of what we did yesterday. He says Chow is as well and has been calling other Mountain Masters to tell them he's joining your coalition."

"That's excellent. I'm beginning to think we have a chance to get every gang in the Territories — except Wu — to join."

"Who would have thought that was possible? We should thank Man for his help. Nothing demonstrated the need for an alliance more than his move on Tsuen Wan."

"I would thank him if I could," Uncle said. "But I imagine I'm the last person he wants to speak to."

"With Chow on board, this should make for a different meeting on Friday."

"A very different meeting, but I'll talk more about that tomorrow," Uncle said. "I'll see you then."

Uncle felt a fleeting sense of satisfaction as he put down the phone. He had been convinced of the need for an alliance, but to see his judgement confirmed was gratifying. Now it was time to see if Tao Siju's offer would be welcomed by the people whose support was crucial. He phoned his old friend Tse first.

They spoke for close to an hour. Uncle began by getting Tse to agree to hold in confidence what he was about to hear. But then it took him five minutes to convince Tse that he wasn't drunk or playing a joke on him. When he finally got his friend to listen seriously, Tse constantly interrupted him with questions. Finally there was nothing more for Uncle to say, and Tse became quiet.

"What do you think?" Uncle asked.

"It's hard to believe."

"I know, but it's true. My hope is that Liu Leji's presence at the meeting on Friday will provide the credibility I need to persuade the others."

"If it is true, this could be a turning point for us."

"Do you think some of the gangs will be opposed to working with the Communists?"

"No one cares about politics. It's all about money and the well-being of the gang. Most of them would work with the devil if they thought it would be good for them," Tse said. "Besides, they've all seen how well you and I have done in China."

"What about Beijing's insistence that they deal with only one person with the authority to speak for everyone?"

"It could be a stumbling block, but if that authority is well-defined and limited, and if the rewards are sufficient, you'll get some of them to come along."

"Will you?"

"Yes," Tse said without hesitation.

"Thank you."

"Listening to you has made my gang a lot of money. I'd be a fool not to."

"The thing is, Tse, I want you to do more than listen," Uncle said. "I want you to work with me to make this happen."

"How?"

"I'd like you to attend the meeting at the White Jade Restaurant in Fanling, and I'd like you to convince your Island neighbours to attend as well."

"What reason should I give them? Do you want me to mention the Chinese offer?"

"That's the last thing I want," Uncle said sharply. "I want them to learn about the offer at the same time as everyone else, and I want them to hear out Liu Leji and understand that this is a serious and crucial moment for our organization."

"Okay, I'll come up with something. Sammy will be easy to persuade, and Feng in Causeway Bay usually does what I ask if I frame it as a favour. Yeung and Ling in Central will be more difficult, but I'll do what I can."

"Thank you again."

"Will it just be Mountain Masters attending?"

"No, we've invited their senior people as well. We had close to sixty at our first meeting."

"Will you be inviting anyone from Kowloon?" Tse asked.

"Zhao and I spoke after the races on Sunday," Uncle said. "He actually asked to be invited, so I expect him to be there. I'm going to call him after you and I finish."

"Will you tell him about China?"

"Yes, and I'll ask him to speak to Weng, Yin, and Man about attending. I'm not expecting any of them to accept, but I don't want to exclude them. That would only give them a reason to complain later."

"And Wu?"

"He's in jail. I'm told he won't be released before the weekend, but if he is, he's welcome too."

"I hope he's not, and I hope Zhao talks the Kowloon gangs into attending," Tse said. "That would make for a very interesting meeting."

"It's going to be interesting enough without them," Uncle said.

"I was trying to be funny," Tse said.

"I know, but I don't find any humour where they're concerned."

"I'll bring my serious side to the meeting. And I'll do everything I can to drag Sammy and the others along with me."

"That will be much appreciated. I'll see you on Friday," Uncle said, and ended the call.

CHAPTER THIRTY-THREE

THURSDAY WAS A BLUR FOR UNCLE AS THE MEETINGS and phone calls piled up, one on top of another. By the time he sat down for dinner with Tian and Fong at Dong's Kitchen, the last thing he wanted to do was talk, but he hadn't seen Fong since that morning's executive committee meeting. There was a lot to discuss.

"You look tired," Tian said as Uncle sat down.

"I was barely out of the shower this morning when my phone started ringing," Uncle said. "I had a quiet hour at Jia's for breakfast, but the rest of the day has been frantic."

"There's a lot of excitement out there, and for once it isn't because brothers are shooting each other or trying to strong-arm their way into someone else's territory," said Fong.

All three men were drinking beer. Tian sipped at his tentatively, but the fact that he was drinking at all surprised Uncle. "Are you sure you should be doing that?" he asked.

"I sense that you're going to have a successful day tomorrow. Since we may not be able to celebrate together when it's over, I want to take advantage of this time with you."

"What have you heard?" Fong asked Tian.

"I was told an hour ago that all the Mountain Masters from Hong Kong Island are coming to the meeting," Tian said. He looked at Uncle. "Is that true?"

"It appears to be a strong possibility. Our friend Tse has been encouraging their attendance," Uncle said. "But I won't know for sure until I see them in person."

"What about Kowloon?" Fong asked.

"Zhao will attend, and at my request he has invited the other Kowloon Mountain Masters. I haven't heard that any of them have accepted."

"With all the buzz in the air, it might be difficult for them to stay away," said Fong.

"Have the details of what we're going to discuss been leaked?" asked Uncle.

"I don't think so. I haven't heard anything relating to the offer. People are just guessing that there has to be a major reason why Tse and Zhao are pushing for the Mountain Masters to attend the meeting."

"If there is a leak, it didn't come from Fanling. You made it clear enough this morning that we aren't to talk about it with anyone. No one would think of violating that," said Tian. "Who else did you tell?"

"Only Tse and Zhao, and they both promised to keep it to themselves until tomorrow."

"People are just speculating," Fong reiterated.

A server arrived at their table with platters of chicken feet, salt-and-pepper fried squid, and Hokkien fried rice laden with seafood. Conversation dwindled as they dug into the food.

Uncle had briefed the executive committee that morning on his meetings with Tao and Liu Leji. The response had been enthusiastic, with everyone wanting to know what they could do to help make the offer a reality. Uncle had asked them to keep it confidential but said there was something else they could assist with. Then he asked Fong to explain his idea for a council.

When Fong had finished, Uncle said, "I think this is an idea whose time has come. What I'd like you to do is reach out to your most trusted colleagues and friends in other gangs. Share Fong's reasoning with them and make especially sure they understand that the council wouldn't have authority over any of the gangs and wouldn't be making decisions for them. Instead, stress that it would exist to resolve disputes that the gangs are unable to sort out on their own."

For the remainder of the afternoon Uncle had various committee members popping into his office to report on the conversations they'd had about the council. He was pleasantly surprised that most of the reactions, while not necessarily supportive, weren't negative.

"We haven't had a chance to talk since this morning," Uncle said to Fong as Tian plucked the last chicken foot from the platter. "What are the Straw Sandals saying about your council idea?"

"There was some initial resistance and skepticism, but most agree that the idea has some merit," Fong said. "But I think they'll need a concrete reason or reward to support it."

"We could link it to the expansion into China," Uncle said. "Any gang that declines to join the council could be shut out of those cities."

"That would get their attention," Tian said. "But, speaking

of China, if we're given only four cities, how will you decide who gets what? You run the risk of pleasing four and alienating the other gangs."

"I went to sleep thinking about that last night," said Uncle. "Why do we have to restrict ourselves to one gang per city? Tao said all the cities will have a population of more than a million. We could assign multiple gangs to each city and help them sort out who does what. I would have to coordinate that with Beijing, but their main focus seems to be ensuring that the right officials get paid. More gangs would mean more payments."

Fong raised an arm in the air, indicating to the server to bring more beer. "It's almost unbelievable that we're sitting here talking about these things," he said. "Early yesterday we were still recovering from Man's attack on Tsuen Wan. I never expected this, and when I think about tomorrow, I get goosebumps."

"It does have the potential to be a memorable day," Tian said. "What's the agenda?"

"I spoke to Leji this afternoon and we're scheduled to talk again tonight. Our tentative plan is for him to speak first," Uncle said. "I'm not entirely sure what he's going to say, because he isn't either. There's still discussion going on in Beijing about what will be permissible. But his sole reason for being here is to support us, so we have to trust that his message will be tailored accordingly."

"What happens after he speaks?" asked Tian.

"He'll leave the restaurant and then it will be my turn. I'll explain what happened in Shenzhen with Tao and present Beijing's offer. Then, hopefully, we'll have a fruitful discussion."

"There will be a lot of questions," said Fong.

"I've been trying to anticipate them. I think I'm prepared for just about anything."

"Our friends in the Territories will support whatever you recommend," Fong said. "I spoke to every gang today, and they all mentioned what went down in Tsuen Wan. You've made believers of them."

"That's reassuring, but to make this work we need Kowloon and the Island gangs on board as well," Uncle said.

"Aren't Tse and Zhao enough?" Fong asked.

"No, and although they told me I have their support, I sensed that they aren't totally committed. I expect they're waiting to see how their neighbours react."

"Will they speak at the meeting?"

"They told me they might, but I didn't press them on that. My priority was to get them to bring the other Mountain Masters to the meeting. And that brings me back to the agenda," Uncle said. "After everyone has had a chance to express his opinion, I'm going to press for answers from them — simply, are they in or are they out?"

"You want them to declare tomorrow?" Tian said. "Isn't that rushing things?"

"It is, but Leji was talking about a deadline this afternoon. He didn't set one but he made it clear that this can't be a long, drawn-out process. Beijing wants an answer as soon as possible. I figure, why not push for one while we have everyone in the same room? We've invited all the members of the executive committees, so if the gangs want to huddle in individual groups, they can do it at the restaurant. My fear is that, once they're out of there and back on home turf, we'll have a lot of second thoughts and requests for more time to think it through."

"Do you think the gangs from the Territories might do that?"

"No, I think we've got them onside. It's the others I worry about. If my instincts are right, the active support of the Territories gangs should create a feeling of momentum, maybe even excitement, at the meeting. That's why I want to push for commitment from the others."

"Do you want us to make more phone calls? We could urge our supporters to come to the meeting ready to be enthusiastic," Fong asked.

"How many gangs do you need to commit?" asked Tian.

"Beijing didn't set a number, but they'll expect a majority. My goal is fourteen, with Kowloon and Hong Kong Island well represented."

"Assuming you get the majority you want, what happens next?" asked Tian.

"We'll need to create a structure that can deal with the Chinese government. I don't know if Leji will touch on that during his remarks, but it would be helpful if he did. I'll recommend it to him tonight."

"And the structure is based on Fong's notion of a council," Tian said.

"Exactly. That won't come as a surprise to the people he spoke to today, but it will be to the gangs from Kowloon and the Island. So when you explain it, Fong, you should focus on them. They need to understand it takes nothing away from them, and in fact opens up opportunities."

Tian was still working on his first beer. "That's a lot for those guys to absorb in one meeting, especially those who aren't from the Territories. Don't you think it might be too much?"

"We don't need them to approve every detail of Fong's proposal. I'll be satisfied if they simply agree that we need a structure of some kind and commit to working to create one," said Uncle.

"Will that satisfy Beijing?"

"As long as I'm the contact person, and we start shipping people from their list across the border, I don't expect any opposition from them."

Tian shook his head. "What a strange world this is becoming. Who would ever have thought that the British handing Hong Kong back to the Chinese would lead to the strengthening of the Heaven and Earth Society."

"Not Man, that's for sure," Fong said.

Uncle looked around the restaurant for Dong. "I should get going. Leji will be calling me soon."

"Go ahead. I'm going to stay and have one more beer. My wife won't let me bring it into the house," Tian said.

"I'll keep you company," said Fong.

"Don't drink too much. I need you both fresh and alert tomorrow," said Uncle, and then he headed for the exit, where Sonny was waiting.

Once again Uncle had invited Sonny to join them for dinner, and once again he'd declined. Uncle was starting to realize that, in addition to being fearlessly loyal, Sonny had his own idea of what his job should be and was sticking to it.

"I'm going home," Uncle said as he slid into the back seat of the Mercedes.

"Yes, boss," said Sonny.

Sonny waited until they were halfway to the apartment before he spoke. "I hope you don't mind me saying, boss, but there's a lot of excitement among the men."

"Are they still talking about Tsuen Wan?"

"A bit, but more about the meeting tomorrow. A couple of forty-niners told me that all the leaders of the gangs from Hong Kong Island are going to be there. They think you're going to unite those gangs with ours in the Territories and take down Kowloon."

"That's the last thing I would think of doing. There's zero truth to any of it." Uncle said. "How do rumours like that get started?"

"So the Hong Kong gangs aren't coming to the meeting?"

"They'll be there, but for a different reason," he said. "Listen Sonny, after you drop me off, call those forty-niners you were talking to and tell them I want them to stop spreading rumours. The last thing we need is for something like that to reach Kowloon ears."

"I'll do that."

The night bodyguard was already in place when the car arrived at the apartment. He waved at Sonny and then stood at attention to one side as Uncle approached the door leading to the stairs. Uncle turned back before he opened it. "I have a visitor from China arriving tomorrow morning," he said to Sonny. "I think it might be a good idea to have an extra bodyguard in the car while he's here."

"I'll tell Wang. He'll assign someone."

"Fine. I'll see you in the morning."

As he climbed the stairs, Uncle checked his watch and saw he had fifteen minutes to spare before his call with Liu Leji. He hung up his jacket, lit a cigarette, and went to his chair. The message light on the phone was blinking. He pressed the button and seconds later heard Man's voice.

"I don't know what game you think you're playing by getting Zhao to invite me to your meeting tomorrow," Man said. "He probably expected me to tell him to fuck off, and I bet you thought that as well. But I may surprise you and show up. And if I do, I'll speak my mind — unless you try to silence me. I wouldn't if I were you, because that would look like you're afraid of what I have to say. I know you think you're a smart little fucker, but I warn you, we aren't stupid in Kowloon. So I'll see you tomorrow — or maybe I won't. And maybe I'll come alone — or maybe I won't."

What did he mean by that last remark? Uncle thought as he reached for the phone.

"*Wei*," Zhao answered.

"This is Uncle. Man left a message on my phone. I take it you spoke to him."

"I spoke to him, Yin, and Weng."

"How did it go?"

"Weng actually listened to me, and I think there's a chance he'll come tomorrow," Zhao said. "The other two heard me out but were equal parts dismissive, insulting, and threatening."

Uncle butted out his cigarette and lit another. "Frankly, I'm a bit concerned about something Man said in his message. He mentioned that he might come tomorrow, and that if he did, he might not come alone. Do you think it's possible he'll try to disrupt the meeting?"

Zhao hesitated. "I don't know . . ."

Uncle was starting to ask another question when he saw that Leji was on the other line. "Zhao, I have another call I have to take. I'll phone you back when I'm finished."

"I'll be here."

"Leji, you're right on time as usual," Uncle said after he'd switched lines.

"It's a trait you and I share, though I'm not quite so fanatical as my aunt and uncle. They're completely unforgiving if someone is more than a minute late for anything."

"Which is why Fong worries about trains and traffic every time he has to meet with her," Uncle said, laughing.

"You sound like you're in an excellent mood. Was the remainder of your day successful?"

"It wasn't bad, but hardly perfect," Uncle said, his concerns about Man resurfacing. "How was yours? Has a decision been made about tomorrow?"

"For the most part we're set, although there has been a change since we talked earlier."

"What kind of change?" Uncle asked warily.

"I had assumed I would be coming alone to your meeting, but that's not the case. One of Tao Siju's assistants and a senior officer attached to the Ministry of Public Security will join me. My uncle told me I should have expected it. They'll be observers only, so they won't disrupt your agenda."

"Observers of what?" Uncle asked.

"I'm sure Beijing wants to hear from another source what I had to say and how well I said it," Leji said. "And undoubtedly they will also be interested in the reactions of your colleagues to my message."

"They sound like spies."

"I prefer to think of them as professional companions. Truthfully, it won't change my approach or my message."

"Are your travel plans the same?" Uncle asked.

"No. We will be crossing the border together in a government car. We'll meet you at the restaurant."

"That's too bad. We'll miss the opportunity for a last-minute talk."

"I don't think anything will change between now and then."

"But if it does . . ."

"You will hear from me."

"Then safe travels, and we'll see you at the White Jade around noon," said Uncle, and put down the phone.

He sat completely still, staring blankly out at the street below, until he felt the heat of the burned-down cigarette on his fingers. He dropped the butt into the ashtray and fought back the feeling of foreboding that had crept into his mind. This wasn't a time to overreact, he told himself, but neither should he take anything for granted. He called Zhao again.

"Sorry I had to cut short our call earlier," Uncle said when Zhao answered. "I had to speak to Liu Leji about tomorrow."

"Is everything set?"

"Yes, but I keep thinking about Man," said Uncle. "Leji won't be alone; there will be two government functionaries with him. They'll be there to observe and report on the meeting. We can't let things get chaotic or out of control. Have you thought more about the possibility that Man will try to disrupt things?"

"I have, and I think it would be careless to discount that possibility," Zhao said. "He could do it in the meeting or stay outside and try to prevent people from attending. I wouldn't put anything past him."

"I won't allow that."

"How will you stop him?"

"I don't know yet, but I have to come up with something," said Uncle. "I'll speak to Wang."

"Are you sure that involving your Red Pole is the right approach? The last thing you want is a physical confrontation. As successful as you were in Tsuen Wan, a repeat of what went on there wouldn't reflect well on us in front of our guests."

"Wang is one of my most reliable sounding boards. Besides, he has always preferred avoiding confrontation over seeking it."

"I'm not being critical of Wang, but if Man shows up with a horde of men tomorrow looking for trouble, how will Wang or anyone else avoid it?"

"I understand the challenges we might face. Let me think about it," said Uncle.

"If you need to talk further, I'm here," Zhao said, and hung up.

Uncle slumped in his chair. He had resolved not to drink after leaving Dong's, but this situation called for a San Miguel. He took a deep swig as soon as he opened the beer. Then he stood rooted in the kitchen as he calculated what had to be done next.

It all began with the assumption that Man would try to disrupt the meeting. To believe anything else would be irresponsible. So the first question was, how could Man be prevented? And if he did make an attempt, how could he be stopped with the least amount of fracas?

Uncle needed to speak to Wang. When it came to Man, he knew that half-measures wouldn't work. That meant he and Wang had to come up with a plan and mobilize a team that could block any disruption. Was there enough time?

Uncle left the kitchen and went back to his phone. He had an idea. The first call he was going to make was to Zhang Delun.

CHAPTER THIRTY-FOUR

UNCLE FINALLY FELL ASLEEP AROUND THREE AND WAS up again at six-thirty. He drank three cups of instant coffee as he made some final phone calls, then left his apartment at eight-thirty.

"The congee place?" Sonny asked.

"Not today. I'm going straight to the office."

Uncle closed his eyes as soon as he got into the car, and rested his head against the back of the seat. He knew he wouldn't nap, but he thought ten minutes of quiet might recharge his mental batteries. Somehow, though, he did nod off. He woke with a shock when he felt Sonny gently pushing his knee. "Boss, we're here."

Sonny held the car door open for him and Uncle slid out. "When will we be picking up your Chinese guest?" Sonny asked.

"There's been a change of plan. We won't be meeting him at the station after all," Uncle said. "I want to leave here at eleven to go directly to the White Jade."

Sonny nodded; no explanation was necessary.

Uncle walked towards the office entrance, where four men

were standing guard. "Has Wang arrived?" he asked one of them.

"He got here ten minutes ago, boss."

Uncle climbed the stairs to the office. When he entered, he saw Fong and Wang standing together in front of Wang's office and went over to them. "Good morning. Did anyone get any sleep?" he asked.

"A bit," Fong said.

"Maybe two hours," said Wang.

"How many Red Poles have you heard from?" Uncle asked Wang.

"Everyone from the Territories except Wu's. And Tse's called half an hour ago."

"Tse told me they would be joining us," Uncle said.

"They are."

"That was a good night's work," Uncle said.

"What time are you heading to the White Jade?" Fong asked.

"Around eleven. Leji is driving across the border with two Chinese officials, and I want to make sure I'm there to greet them when they arrive at the restaurant."

"Yes. Seeing that crowd could be a shock to them."

"You can ride with me."

"Thanks, I'll do that," said Fong.

"Have you worked on your presentation yet?"

"I'm about to do that now," Fong said. "I have to admit it's making me nervous."

"Keep it simple. Just repeat what you said to me in Shenzhen."

"How about what you're going to say? Have you prepared anything?"

"No. I'm going to my office to do that now," Uncle said, then checked his watch. "But first I have to make a phone call."

Wang had been hovering in the background as Fong and Uncle spoke. When it appeared they were finished, he said, "I want to leave about nine to go to the restaurant. There's still some organizing to do. I want everything mapped out by the time people start to arrive."

"Wait until I make that one phone call," Uncle said. "It could have a bearing on how things proceed today."

Wang looked questioningly at Uncle.

"Just wait," Uncle repeated, and headed for his office. He sat down behind his desk, stared at the phone, and wondered if he'd gone too far this time. Then he dialled Zhang Delun's home number.

His wife answered and said, "Just a minute. He's been waiting for your call." Uncle felt a touch of apprehension.

Seconds later, Zhang was on the line. "Uncle, did you accomplish what you set out to do last night?"

"Yes, but I'm more interested in whether you had any success."

"Before I get into that, I would like to confirm how you did."

"There will be more than a hundred — actually, several hundreds — of triads at the White Jade Restaurant. I don't have an exact number, but I can guarantee it will be the largest gathering ever seen in the New Territories."

"Did your colleagues agree that the men would be unarmed?"

"They did."

"In that case, I'm pleased to tell you I've been authorized

to deploy a substantial force, including armoured vehicles. I'm still working on the final numbers, but we will have at least sixty officers at the restaurant."

"The armoured vehicles shouldn't be obvious. Can you keep them on a side street unless they're absolutely needed?" Uncle asked.

"Yes, we can do that. They'll be there for backup only. We don't want to provoke an unnecessary response."

"And your men will not be in riot gear?"

"That's correct, but they will be well armed."

"Of course. I wouldn't expect anything else," said Uncle.

"Then we are, as usual, in accord. Hopefully it will all go as you anticipate and my officers will be nothing more than spectators at a large, peaceful gathering of triads."

"Did you have any difficulty selling this to your side?"

"I have kept the OCTB aware that an attempt is being made within the triad communities in the Territories to broker a lasting peace, and that meetings are being held," Zhang said. "When I told them about your meeting today, they didn't understand why we needed to get involved, until I mentioned the possibility of trouble. I stressed that for once we are in a position to prevent an armed conflict from occurring in a public place, rather than cleaning up afterwards and having to explain why we weren't on top of it."

"Did you tell them that I requested your presence?"

"Not precisely, but I did say I'd been advised of the meeting by a senior triad leader, and that he'd expressed concerns about the meeting being crashed by people opposed to it."

"All of which is perfectly true."

"But Uncle, given that we're going to be present, do you still need to have so many triads there?"

"We worked for hours last night to get commitments from the other gangs, because we couldn't risk the chance that your superiors would say no. We can't go back to them now and tell them they're not needed. Besides, if the meeting goes as I hope, they'll have a chance to be part of history."

"What do you mean?"

Uncle hadn't mentioned that Liu Leji would be at the meeting and saw no need to now. "For the first time — at least, the first time in memory — the Hong Kong triads will be more than a collection of individual gangs."

"I'm not sure if that's a good or a bad thing," Zhang said.

"It will most definitely be a good thing if it reduces friction between the gangs. Everyone, including the Hong Kong police, will benefit."

"I hope you're right," Zhang said. "Now, let's talk about what should happen at the restaurant. I've assigned Commander Choi, one of my deputies, to head up our detail. Who should he coordinate with at the White Jade?"

"Wang, my Red Pole. He'll communicate with the other Red Poles. He'll be going to the restaurant as soon as I have a chance to talk to him. He doesn't know about your involvement yet."

"Then talk to Wang. Choi will look for him there."

Uncle put down the phone and smiled. The police presence would add a second layer of protection around the restaurant, and they would be the first to confront Man if he showed up. Uncle got up, went to the office door, and shouted to Wang.

The Red Pole hurried over to him. "You look pleased with yourself," he said.

"Is it that obvious?"

"It is to me."

"I'll try to be more subdued when I address the Mountain Masters this afternoon," Uncle said. "But we've just had some very good news. The Hong Kong police are sending a contingent of men to the White Jade."

"What?" Wang exclaimed. "You're confusing me. I thought you said you had good news."

"I spoke to my police contact last night and requested that they send the men. Even though we have enough of our own men to repel Man, that isn't an ideal situation. The best thing that can happen is nothing at all. Having the police at the restaurant will make that more likely. Man isn't crazy enough to take them on, and if he does, we'll be there to back them up."

"So your contact knows about the meeting."

"He does, although I didn't give him all the details. He thinks we're meeting to finalize our coalition. I've kept him updated on that, and he's kept his bosses informed. They're in favour of anything that decreases the chances of gang violence, and coming to the restaurant is their way of helping us achieve that."

"I guess that makes sense," Wang said, sounding not quite convinced.

"It does make sense," Uncle said. "A Commander Choi will be in charge of the police squad. He knows who you are and has been told to coordinate with you. Introduce him to the other Red Poles and make sure they understand that we're all on the same side today."

"We were going to surround the restaurant," Wang said.

"You still can. Our men can form the inner circle, and Choi's the outer."

Wang said, "I'd better get over there. This is going to take some explaining."

"If any of the Red Poles don't like the arrangement, they should leave, with their men," Uncle said. "I don't want some hothead to mess up a perfectly amicable arrangement."

"They'll be okay. In fact, a few of them said their men would be happy to go even if there wasn't a threat. That brawl in Tsuen Wan fostered a sense of camaraderie among the men that has spread from gang to gang. You must have felt it when you were on the phone last night, when you talked to the Mountain Masters who didn't send men to Tsuen Wan."

"You're right. There was a sense of collaboration that was new."

Wang looked at his watch. "I'd better get going. I don't want the police to arrive before me."

"And I need to call some Mountain Masters and then work on my speech," said Uncle. He went into his office and in rapid succession called Zhao, Tse, Tan, and Ng. He told them what he'd arranged with the police, and all of them seemed to feel it had been the smart thing to do. Uncle asked them to contact the other Mountain Masters to explain.

With that finished, he turned to his speech. Uncle didn't want to read from a piece of paper. Instead he was trying to organize his thoughts so that the message was structured but his delivery would come across as spontaneous and unrehearsed. He wrote down headings and listed points under them. Then he tried to memorize them, turned over the page, and repeated them. He did that seven times before he was satisfied that the talking points were locked in his head.

"I'm as ready as I'll ever be," he muttered, and closed his eyes. "Gui-San, please watch over me today. I am afraid my ambition may be greater than my ability, but I take comfort in knowing I'm not alone in chasing this dream. I'm so fortunate to have friends I can depend on for support. I've always had Wang, Fong, Tian, and others in the gang, but now that circle has expanded. Today will be a test for those who have joined with me. I pray, I hope — no, I *expect* that we will succeed. It may be foolish to be so optimistic, but I'm committed to the path I've taken. I can't permit any negative thoughts or actions to get in the way. So please, watch over me."

CHAPTER THIRTY-FIVE

UNCLE WAITED UNTIL HE AND FONG WERE IN THE CAR before telling him about the police presence. As it had been with the Mountain Masters, there was immediate understanding. "That almost guarantees the meeting won't be disrupted," Fong said. "Man won't pit his men against the police."

"I agree it's unlikely, but we have to make sure that, if he does come, we allow only Man and his executive committee inside the restaurant. I think you should stay at the entrance to verify that everyone going in is legitimate."

"I'll ask Zhao's Straw Sandal to stand with me. He knows all of Man's executive committee members."

"Good thinking," said Uncle.

They fell into silence, Uncle's attention on the road ahead of them. They were still some distance from the restaurant when he noticed that many more cars than normal were parked along the street. "You might not be able to find a parking spot near the restaurant," he said to Sonny.

"I'll drop you off, then double back," said Sonny.

"That's fine," Uncle replied.

A few moments later, Sonny said, "A parking spot ahead just opened up. Should I take it? It's still half a kilometre to the restaurant."

"Grab it. We'll walk. The fresh air will do us good," said Uncle.

After Sonny had parked, the three men piled out of the car and began walking. They hadn't gone more than a hundred metres before Uncle began to hear a dull buzz. With each step the noise grew louder, until it seemed to fill the air around them. They were on a street that ran parallel to the restaurant's, and as they turned the corner the source of the buzzing came into sight.

"My god, look at that!" Fong said.

The restaurant sat at the intersection of two streets. Directly ahead of them was a wall of men, stretching along the sidewalk and down the side street. The wall was five men deep. On the pavement in front of them clusters of police were walking back and forth, guns strapped across their backs.

"There must be five hundred triads here," Fong said.

"Maybe even more," said Uncle.

As they approached the restaurant, Fong nudged Uncle. "Look, down there to the left. The armoured vehicles."

The vehicles were parked at least a hundred metres from the restaurant, Uncle guessed. Close enough to be a presence but not a provocation. He looked across the street and saw Wang standing at the curb with an officer. They were talking, and it looked amiable. *So far, so good,* he thought.

Uncle stepped off the curb in the direction of the restaurant. He was halfway across the street when he heard someone yell, "There's Uncle!"

"Uncle!" another voice shouted. Then another, and then more joined in, repeating his name until it became a chant of "Uncle! Uncle! Uncle!" voiced by a hundred men or more. He felt his face flush. Should he act embarrassed or gratified?

"Those are our men to the left of the entrance," Fong said.

Uncle looked in that direction and was able to pick out familiar faces among the throng. He waved at them, and that initiated another chant of "Uncle! Uncle! Uncle!"

"The men are in good spirits," he said to Wang as he approached.

"So far, no worries," said Wang. "It's like a big social gathering. Our men don't get together in numbers like this very often, and some of them are seeing old friends from other gangs for the first time in ages."

"Have any other Mountain Masters arrived?" Uncle asked.

"You're the first."

"Good. I wanted to be here to greet the others," he said, and then looked at the police officer. "You must be Commander Choi."

Choi bowed his head ever so slightly, a deferential acknowledgement that caught Uncle by surprise. What had Zhang said to him?

"It's a privilege to meet you, Uncle. We're pleased to be here to help make this day as peaceful as possible," Choi said.

"I must say, I like the way your men are comporting themselves. Hopefully they'll have nothing to do but observe."

"Wang and his colleagues have your men well under control. I'm confident they'll be able to maintain order without any assistance from us," said Choi.

"All the same, we're pleased you're here," said Uncle.

Wang looked past Uncle's shoulder. "Here comes Ng with his executives," he said.

Uncle smiled in Ng's direction and moved towards him. As he did, a voice shouted, "Ng!" and almost at once a chant like the one that had welcomed Uncle greeted the Mountain Master from Sai Kung.

"What's this shouting about?" Ng asked Uncle as they shook hands.

"The men seem excited to be here," Uncle said.

"How many are there?"

"Fong guessed about five hundred."

"Closer to seven hundred," Wang said. "The other Red Poles and I did a rough count. We had about five hundred committed from the Territories, and we think they've all showed up. Then Tse and Zhao each sent more than eighty men."

"What a turnout," Ng said. "Who would have thought this was possible."

Uncle heard Poon's name being yelled and saw the Mountain Master from Mong Kok getting out of a car on the other side of the street. He looked slightly perplexed but then smiled and waved. Another chant began, and for the next half an hour, chant followed chant as the Mountain Masters and their executive teams arrived and were greeted by Uncle, then led into the restaurant by Fong.

By ten to twelve there were fifteen Mountain Masters inside the White Jade. That number comprised all the gang leaders from the New Territories except Wu and Uncle, along with Zhao and Weng from Kowloon and five from Hong Kong Island. The Kowloon and Island groups had arrived together, causing a ripple of unease among the men encircling the restaurant until they saw Uncle welcoming them warmly.

Uncle stayed outside the restaurant with Wang, Fong, and Commander Choi. Fong tried to keep a conversation going, but Uncle was too distracted. His eyes darted up and down the street, looking for Liu Leji and, in the back of his mind, fearing he'd see Man approaching with a group of his triads.

Man came first. He marched down the same street Uncle had used, surrounded by at least fifty men. Uncle stiffened, but before he could speak he saw Wang and Choi move towards the perimeter where the police were gathered. He thought briefly about joining them, but realized they had a plan and that he'd just be in their way.

Uncle watched Choi speak to his men. In quick succession the police formed two straight lines that stretched across the street, unstrapped their guns, and stood at attention. Man hesitated, then came to a stop. Fok, his Red Pole, moved to stand beside him. They stared at the police, then at the wall of triads behind them. There was silence on both fronts, and a tension in the air that Uncle feared could easily ignite.

Man spoke to a couple of men behind him. Their conversation seemed animated, and Uncle wondered if the outcome was going to result in more foolishness. Finally Man seemed to make a decision. He took ten steps forward, until he was just five metres from the police line. Fok went with him.

Man stopped, planted his feet, and folded his arms across his chest. He was a tall man, a bit over six feet, but looked shorter because he was so broad. He wore jeans and a black T-shirt that displayed the tattoos on both his arms. His hair was shaved close to the scalp and his face was deeply creased. He projected menace as he shouted at Wang, "What do you think you're doing? We're here to attend the meeting."

Wang moved past the police line to face Man. Uncle and Sonny joined him. "You and the rest of your executive committee are welcome to join us, but your other men will have to stay where they are," Wang said. "Commander Choi and his men are here to ensure that nothing foolish happens."

"Why the fuck are the police involved in this?"

"We are here to maintain public order," Choi said. "If you doubt we have enough manpower to do that, I suggest you look to your right. I won't hesitate to call for support."

Man glanced to his right and saw the armoured vehicles stationed down the alley. He smiled at Wang and Choi and said, "I have a large executive committee."

Wang shouted in the direction of the restaurant. "Ko, could you come over here for a moment, please."

"What the fuck are you doing here? You're Zhao's Red Pole," Man said to Ko as he approached.

Ko ignored him. "Yes?" he asked Wang.

"Can you identify the men who are members of Man's executive?"

"Sure," Ko said, moving a few steps closer. A moment later he said, "There's only the Red Pole, Fok, present here."

"Then you and Fok can go inside. No one else," Wang said to Man.

"What does your boss have to say about that?" Man said, turning his attention to Uncle. "I should be allowed to have seven or eight men inside, like the rest."

"No," said Uncle.

"You little fuck," Man said, spitting on the ground.

Uncle heard the men behind him starting to stir. He turned and saw a lot of angry faces among the group from

Fanling. "Don't react to his provocations," he told them. "I don't want anyone to give Man an excuse to cause trouble."

Man tried to stare them down, his focus switching from Uncle to Wang to Choi. "I'll take five men in with me," he said to Uncle.

"No, only two," Uncle said.

Man shook his head and threw his hands in the air. "I came here as a gesture of goodwill, but it's obvious I'm wasting my time. I've had enough of you. Have your fucking meeting. It won't change anything."

"You're entitled to your opinion," said Uncle.

Man spat again, this time aiming in Uncle's direction but not coming close. Uncle saw Sonny stiffen. "Stay calm. That's his way of saying goodbye. He'll be leaving now," Uncle said. "It was good of you to come, Man, and it was good to see you and Fok again. I hope the rest of your day goes better."

Fok stepped forward. "You little fuck," he said, and spat directly at Uncle, hitting his shoes.

Before anyone could realize what had happened, Sonny leapt forward. He grabbed Fok by the neck and lifted him off the ground.

"Don't, Sonny!" Uncle shouted.

But Sonny wasn't listening. He carried the Red Pole towards Man's men, stopping just short of them, raised Fok high in the air, and shook him. Fok was gasping for air and his feet swung madly in all directions. "Any of you who wants to disrespect my Mountain Master has to get through me to do it. Never forget that!" he yelled.

"Sonny, drop him," said Uncle.

Sonny looked back at Uncle, nodded, and then threw Fok at Man's feet.

"I think you should take your Red Pole and leave," Uncle said to Man.

Man looked down at Fok, then turned and walked back to his men. He didn't stop when he reached them, and soon they were following him back up the street along which they'd come. Fok was left lying on the ground.

"Stand down," Choi shouted to his force. Then he and Wang approached Uncle.

"Please excuse my driver, Commander. He doesn't take kindly to my being abused," Uncle said.

"When will your meeting begin?" Choi asked. "The sooner it can get started, the better."

"We're still waiting for some guests. They should be here any moment," Uncle said, and then smiled as he saw a black limousine driving up the street. "I think that's them now."

CHAPTER THIRTY-SIX

THE LIMOUSINE STOPPED DIRECTLY IN FRONT OF THE restaurant and the driver leapt out to open the doors. The first person to exit was one of the assistants who had been with Tao in Shenzhen. Behind him was a balding middle-aged man with a thin black moustache. Liu Leji was the last to emerge. The three men stood transfixed on the sidewalk, their attention torn between the police squad on the street and the throng of triads around the restaurant.

"Welcome to Fanling, Leji. We thought we would greet you in style. Don't concern yourself about the police. They're here to make sure the streets don't get too congested," Uncle said, and turned to Choi. "Isn't that correct, Commander."

"Absolutely."

"This is Commander Choi of the Hong Kong Police Force," Uncle said to Leji. "Standing next to him is Wang, a member of our executive team."

"Pleased to meet you. The gentlemen with me are Lin Wenyan and Wu Shen. I'll introduce them properly inside."

"Speaking of which, we should go in," Uncle said. "Sonny, please help Wang clear the way for us."

Between the limousine and the restaurant door was a solid wall of men. There had been a clear path earlier, until Man made his appearance and the men had closed ranks to seal it off. "Excuse us, we need to get past," Sonny said, motioning for them to move back.

"Follow him in," Uncle said to Leji.

The restaurant owner greeted them at the door. "I hope you'll find the setup to your liking, Uncle," he said. "As before, Fong wanted each gang to have their own table, but this time we put the tables in two rows with the chairs facing the back of the restaurant, so everyone can see you when you speak. There's a portable microphone on your table if you need it."

"I'm fine with whatever arrangements you and Fong have made," Uncle said.

"Good. We'll start serving food as soon as you take your seats."

As Uncle and his group walked towards their table, there wasn't an eye in the restaurant not trained on them. Uncle knew there would be sharp curiosity about the three men with him, and the Mountain Masters would also want to know what had happened with Man. When he reached the table, he picked up the microphone. There was no reason, he had decided, to withhold that information.

"Gentlemen, welcome again to those of you who were here last week, and a warm welcome to those joining us for the first time," Uncle said. "As we did last week, we'll eat first and then talk. But before they start serving the food, I want you to know that we just had a visit from one of our Kowloon colleagues. Man arrived about fifteen minutes ago with sixty men. He was received by Commander Choi of the

Hong Kong police and persuaded to leave. It was all quite uneventful."

He heard murmurs of approval and waited for them to diminish. "I would also like to point out that we have three guests joining us for lunch. After we've eaten, one of them has a few things he'd like to say to us. Then they'll leave and we can start our meeting with only brothers in attendance."

"Who are they?" someone shouted.

"I was coming to that," Uncle said with a smile. "The man in the grey suit is Liu Leji. He was the director of Customs in Shenzhen for many years before returning to Beijing. He has just been appointed chief of staff to Liu Huning, the third-ranked member of China's Politburo Standing Committee. And if he wouldn't mind, I'll ask Leji to introduce his companions."

"Thank you, Uncle," Leji said as he took the microphone. "In the blue suit is Wu Shen. He is an assistant to Tao Siju, Minister of Public Security for the People's Republic of China. Seated next to him is Lin Wenyan, a senior director in the ministry. I want to thank Uncle for inviting us to join you for lunch, and I look forward to speaking to you after we've eaten."

As Leji sat down, the murmurs returned, in greater number and volume.

"That was a terrific move," Fong said to Uncle. "You've completely captured their attention. Lunch won't go fast enough for most of them."

Lunch also couldn't go fast enough for Uncle. He poked at his food, sipped tea, rehearsed his speech in his head, and wondered what Leji might say. Fong, as gregarious as ever, kept trying to engage Lin and Wu in conversation, without much success; all his questions were answered with the briefest of replies. Leji, like Uncle, seemed lost in his own thoughts and ate almost absent-mindedly.

When the dishes had been cleared, Fong stood up. "My name is Fong. For those of you who don't know me, I'm the Straw Sandal in Fanling. We'll start the proceedings in ten minutes. So if any of you need to go to the bathroom or want to go outside for a smoke, I suggest you do it now."

"Assuming anyone can get outside," Leji said to Uncle as Wu, Lin, and Fong left the table. "That was quite a scene out there."

"This is an important meeting. People are anxious to see what happens. There are great hopes that we'll achieve a unity we've never had. The fact that so many triads are here shows in real terms that they understand the need for it."

"Is that the only reason for the crowd?"

"Of course."

"How much do they know about what was discussed in Shenzhen?"

"Those outside? Nothing. In this room, my executive team and a few Mountain Masters know, but they don't know everything."

Leji looked at Uncle. "I have to tell you, I'm nervous about today."

"So am I."

"Really? I've never seen you appear anything less than confident."

"Some days I have to will myself to be like that. Today is one of those days," said Uncle. "Tell me, how were your conversations with Beijing?"

"Productive. I think you'll like what I have to say. But

beyond that, you'll have to wait — like everyone else," Leji said, smiling.

Fong, Wu, and Lin returned to the table, and Uncle saw that the rest of the room was filling up again. Fong waited for several more minutes, until everyone was seated, before he stood up. "I would like to call this meeting to order. Sixteen gangs are represented here, which is a remarkable thing. Now I'd like to turn things over to my Mountain Master, Uncle," he said.

Uncle took the microphone from Fong. "Welcome, all of you. This has already been a special day in the history of the Hong Kong triads, and by the time we're finished, my hope is that it will be one you remember as vividly as the day you took the Thirty-Six Oaths," he said. "I introduced Liu Leji earlier, and now I'm going to invite him to speak to us again. Before he does, there's something I want to say. I've known Leji and his family for more than ten years. During that time he has always been honest and direct with me. I don't know what he's going to say today, but whatever it is, I'll take him at his word."

Leji reached into his jacket pocket and extracted a piece of paper. Then he took the microphone and walked around to the front of the table, so he was clearly visible to everyone in the room.

"As Uncle said, I am the chief of staff for Liu Huning, the third-ranked member of the Politburo Standing Committee. What he didn't say is that Liu Huning is my uncle, but in reality he is more like a father to me," he began. "I am here today to speak on his behalf. I have also been authorized to speak on behalf of Tao Siju, the Minister of Public Security, and he has sent his two associates, Mr. Lin and Mr. Wu, to lend support. Lastly, I am here with the knowledge of Deng Xiaoping. Chairman Deng is officially retired, but he has a voice that is still listened to in Beijing, and he approves of what I'm about to say."

The room became so quiet that Uncle was almost afraid to draw a breath. Every eye was locked onto Leji, and he wanted to do nothing that would break that spell.

"In two years Britain will return Hong Kong to its rightful home, the People's Republic of China," Leji continued, his tone neutral. "The terms and conditions for the handover have been clearly delineated, but of course not every subject has been covered. Among those is the question that I imagine matters most to you — what impact will the handover have on Hong Kong's triads?

"I understand there has been considerable speculation about this among your community. I've also been told that one theory being put forward is that the Chinese government will prosecute triads even more strenuously than the current Hong Kong authorities." Leji looked slowly around the room, then pointed a finger at his audience. "I am here to tell you that is an absolute lie," he said, his voice rising. "In fact, the complete opposite is true."

He fell silent for several seconds, letting the message sink in, then continued. "That's why I and my two colleagues from the Ministry of Public Security are here today. We have a message for you, and that message is, we believe the People's Republic of China and the triad brotherhoods in Hong Kong will be able to co-exist."

Uncle saw heads swivel as the triad leaders looked to each

other for confirmation of what they had just heard. Zhao, though, stared directly at Uncle, a smile breaking across his face.

"How, you must be asking yourselves, is this possible?" Leji went on. "I'm going to leave it to Uncle to explain the details. On Wednesday he met with me and Tao Siju, the Minister of Public Security, in Shenzhen. We proposed ways in which the PRC and your triad organizations could co-operate. Uncle heard us out and responded, and then we clarified some fine points. When we were finished, Uncle made it clear that the decision to accept or reject our proposal wasn't his to make. He said he would have to consult with his brethren — and here you are today.

"You might ask why we chose to meet with Uncle. The answer is simple and complicated at the same time. The simple part is that my family has known Uncle for more than ten years, and there's no one in Hong Kong we respect and trust more than him. We knew he'd be thoughtful and honest with us, and that if he believed our proposal had merit, he'd communicate it in the same way to you.

"The complicated part is that we were told — and Uncle confirmed — that your organization is a loose amalgamation of individual enterprises. That poses a problem for us, because it's impossible for the government to strike an agreement and then work with ten, twenty, or thirty gangs individually. You need a structure we can work with and a single voice to represent you. We make no demands in terms of the structure or how you organize yourselves to deal with us, but we do insist that the lines of communication be clear and that we can be assured that the person who speaks for you represents your decisions and commitments.

"Our preference for that single voice is Uncle, a man we know, respect, and trust. But if he isn't your choice, we will consider the person you put forward. You will determine that. All we insist is that when he speaks to us, he speaks for you all.

"Lastly," Leji said, looking down at the paper in his hand, "and notwithstanding everything I've told you, we understand there might be doubts about our sincerity. To emphasize just how serious we are, and how committed the most senior levels of our government are, I have been instructed by Tao Siju to read you the following. This is a statement prepared by the Minister, in his own words. He has authorized me to tell you that if you can agree to work with us along the lines we discussed with Uncle, he will make this statement public. It will be sent to every newspaper and media outlet in Hong Kong."

Leji stopped, looked around the room, and raised the paper he was holding. He began to read from it slowly, emphasizing every word, imbuing them with meaning. "The Minister's statement reads as follows: *Triads are not always gangsters. As long as they are patriotic, as long as they are concerned about Hong Kong's prosperity and stability, we should treat them with respect, and we should unite with them.*"

Leji turned to Uncle. "What more could you ask from the People's Republic of China than the Minister of Public Security openly endorsing your continued existence, recognizing your contribution to the economic well-being of this fantastic city, and making a commitment to work with you." With that, he offered him the microphone.

The room was silent. Uncle had been caught off guard by Tao's statement, and evidently so had his colleagues. But it was a welcome change to be surprised like that. He thought for a few seconds about commenting on the statement, and then decided it spoke for itself. Instead he said, "I want to thank Liu Leji, Lin Wenyan, and Wu Shen for joining us today. They'll be leaving now and heading back to the mainland. We wish them safe travels."

He moved closer to Leji and said quietly, "You did very well. I couldn't have asked for more. You'll hear from me tonight, one way or another. Judging from the reactions of my colleagues, I think it will be positive. Now let me walk you to your car."

The two men, joined by Wu and Lin, started walking towards the restaurant entrance, only to be stopped immediately by Zhao, who stepped in front of Leji with his hand extended. "Thank you for this," he said. "Today has exceeded my expectations."

"I hope we can work together," Leji said.

"I'll do what I can to make that happen," Zhao said.

"Me too," Tse added as he moved next to Zhao and held out his hand to Leji. "I can say with confidence that if your proposal has any substance, Uncle will have the support of the gangs on Hong Kong Island."

Sammy Wing and the other Island Mountain Masters had formed a line between Tse and the door leading outside. Beyond them, other Mountain Masters were beginning to queue up.

"Getting to your limo could take some time," Uncle said. "It looks like everyone wants to show their appreciation."

"I don't mind," said Leji.

It took another ten minutes for them to get to the door. Every Mountain Master in attendance wanted to shake Leji's hand and offer a comment. Leji took it in stride, not rushing and carefully thanking all of them. When they finally reached the exit, they were met by Wang and Ko, Zhao's Red Pole.

"Is everything okay?" Uncle asked.

"Yes. We're just trying to keep the path clear. The men keep crowding in and making it tighter," Wang said.

"Is Liu Leji's limousine nearby?"

"It's at the curb to the right."

Despite Wang's efforts, the sidewalk was so crammed they couldn't use it to get to the car. They had to step into the street, which placed them in clear view of the men. "How did it go in there, Uncle?" someone yelled.

Uncle looked in the general direction of the voice, smiled, and gave a thumbs-up.

"Uncle! Uncle! Uncle!" someone shouted. As before, other voices picked up the chant until it was almost a roar.

"This is so silly," Uncle said to Leji.

"And also very nice," Leji said. "There are leaders in Beijing who would pay to hear a crowd salute them like that."

Uncle shook his head. "Believe me, it isn't normal. I don't know what's got into the men. I only hope that those inside the restaurant are as receptive."

"Go and find out," Leji said. "We'll talk tonight."

Uncle made his way back to the White Jade, trying to ignore the hundreds of eyes fixed on him. It wasn't in his nature to be self-conscious, but this crowd of hard men had managed to make him feel that way.

Wang opened the door for him and he stepped inside. As he did so, he thought about the notes he'd made that morning and started formulating his opening remarks. It was one thing for the Mountain Masters to react so warmly to Liu Leji, he thought, but with him he knew they'd be all business. There would be difficult questions, and there could be no evading them. *Be honest. Be direct. Be blunt,* he told himself.

Most of the men had stood up as Leji left. Many of them were still on their feet, gathered in small clusters and talking animatedly to their executive committees. His presence wasn't remarked upon until he was about halfway to his table.

"Hey, Uncle, well done!" Ng said loudly.

"Yes, that's a job well done," Tan added. He began to clap and was immediately joined by the others in his group, and then by the people in the group next to them. Soon everyone in the room was clapping with the kind of enthusiasm usually generated by a ten-to-one winner at Happy Valley.

Maybe this isn't going to be as hard as I thought.

CHAPTER THIRTY-SEVEN
Friday, March 17, 1995

UNCLE LEFT HIS APARTMENT AT SIX-THIRTY, JUST AS the sun appeared on the horizon. He had told Sonny he didn't need him for the day, preferring to take a taxi for the twenty-kilometre ride from Fanling to the town of Yuen Long. His destination was something he kept a secret. It was the most private thing in his life, because it was where the remains of his fiancée, Lin Gui-San, were interred — or at least his memories of her. Gui-San's body had never been recovered from Shenzhen Bay, so Uncle had filled an urn with sand from the beach, pressed into it the jade bracelet he had intended to give her on their wedding day, and placed it in a niche with a picture of her.

He directed the taxi to the Ancestor Worship Hall on Fo Look Hill in Yuen Long. He hadn't been there since January 31, the start of the lunar new year, and he knew the niche would need to be cleaned and freshened up.

Uncle had thought of visiting Gui-San a few weeks earlier, but the details and commitments arising from the meeting at the White Jade Restaurant were still being ironed out.

Until things were finalized, Uncle hadn't wanted to risk inviting bad luck into his life. But regardless of what was going on, he always went to the hall on the anniversary of her death, the first day of the lunar new year, and during the Qingming Festival. Other visits were reserved for the times when he had special news to share with her. This was such a time.

It was just past seven when the taxi stopped at Fo Look Hill. Uncle got out and began the hundred-metre climb to the top, carrying a folding stool and a paper bag. There were no other cars parked at the base of the hill, and Uncle didn't expect to see anyone else in the worship hall. He always came early so he and Gui-San could have time alone together, and with the exception of the Qingming Festival, that was usually the case.

The path was uneven and Uncle took his time, taking care not to step on anything that might cause a sudden ankle twist. It was flanked by a hillside covered in shrubs and wild-flowers. On the anniversary of her death he always picked some flowers to take to the niche. On this day he headed directly to the hall.

As he neared the summit of the hill, Uncle was relieved to see that the hall was indeed empty of people. The building faced northeast, so it overlooked the sea and caught the morning sunlight. It was a quiet and beautiful place at that time of day. About thirty metres across and fifteen metres deep, the worship hall had a red tile roof and sweeping curved overhangs. The front was completely open to its surroundings, and this openness and the wonderful sight-lines contributed to its feng shui. A small stream ran along one side and a fountain gurgled near the entrance. It was a place that welcomed *qi,* promising peace and tranquility to the people being memorialized there.

Uncle reached the hall and climbed the five steps that led inside. He walked past a statue of the seated Buddha and another of a Taoist god. He approached the hall's back wall, which was a mass of small alcoves and niches, each devoted to a loved one. The niches were small and could accommodate only an urn and some small mementos. Most of them also contained a photo of the deceased.

Gui-San's niche was in the left end of the wall at about chest height. Uncle stopped in front of it, unfolded his stool, and put the paper bag on it. From the bag he produced a small whisk broom and approached the niche. He removed the urn and placed it gently on the ground. The two oranges he'd left on his previous visit were now dry and shrivelled. He took them out, and the bowl of dry tea leaves that had been left with them. The niche was now empty except for a photo of Gui-San, taken in Wuhan on her twenty-first birthday. Uncle had had it enlarged and laminated and had affixed it to the back wall. Under the photo, gold lettering read:

LIN GUI-SAN
BORN IN CHANGZHAI, HUBEI PROVINCE, 28 OCTOBER 1934
DIED NEAR HONG KONG, 28 JUNE 1959
FOREVER LOVED
FOREVER MISSED

He stared at the photograph. She had been dead for thirty-six years, and she would have been sixty-one on her next birthday. But for him Gui-San was perpetually twenty-four and became increasingly more beautiful as the years passed.

Uncle swept out the niche with the whisk and returned it to the bag. He took out a cloth, wet it in the fountain, and returned to the niche. There he wiped away the dust and grime that had collected on the photo and the floor of the niche, and then bent down and carefully cleaned the urn. When that was done, he put the urn back into the niche, off to one side so that Gui-San's face was visible. Then he placed two fresh oranges and tea in the bowl next to it.

He turned and went back to the stool, put the cloth back in the bag, and extracted six sticks of incense. Facing the niche, he lit them with his faded black crackle Zippo lighter, which had belonged to Gui-San's father and had been her most prized possession. He inserted three sticks into slots in the front of the niche and held the others between his palms. Then he raised his hands to his chest, lowered his head, and began to pray. He prayed until the sticks began to burn his flesh. Then he stopped, dropped what was left of the incense into a receptacle, and sat down on the stool facing the niche.

He lit a Marlboro with the Zippo, took a drag, and blew the smoke sideways, away from the niche. Uncle stared up at Gui-San's photo and marvelled again at her beauty. They had found each other in hard times and had hardly ever been apart until she was ripped from him by Shenzhen Bay. He had no doubts they would have had a long, happy life together, perhaps filled with children. Now, instead of children, he had brothers. Now, instead of a wife, he had the Heaven and Earth Society. It wasn't the same, but at least he wasn't alone in the world.

Uncle stubbed out his cigarette on the ground and

deposited the butt in a trash bin. When he returned, he sat down again and tried to gather his thoughts.

"Gui-San, my love, there are going to be changes in my life. More changes, in fact, than at any time in the past, including when I became a Mountain Master and when I went into business with the Liu family and the Communists," he said. "It won't affect us, of course. I'll still visit you. In fact, when I think about it, I might be able to visit more often.

"About six weeks ago things started to go badly between the gangs. You know there's always been tension, jealousy, and rivalries, but this was different. A group of gangs in Kowloon decided, without provocation, to take over other gangs through sheer violence. They succeeded in Macau, and there were rumours that their next targets were in the New Territories. I decided that even if the rumours weren't true, I couldn't just sit back and wait.

"Over the years I have made many friends among the other Mountain Masters, so I reached out to some of them, first for information and then to gauge their interest in forming a defensive alliance. Their responses were heartening, and they confirmed that I had made friends and that my judgement was trusted. When I talked to them, I learned that Man, the leader of the largest Kowloon gang, was using the British handover of Hong Kong as an excuse for his aggression. He claimed that the Communists would come down hard on the triads, and that the best defence would be for gangs to amalgamate — voluntarily or otherwise. I thought that was nonsense but I had no proof, so I called my friend Liu Leji in Beijing, told him about Man's claim, and asked if there was any truth to it. That one phone call, Gui-San, started a chain of events that I still can scarcely believe." Uncle shook his head. "Sorry for what must seem like confusion on my part, but I'm trying to relate things in their proper order, and there was a lot going on at the same time.

"Anyway, Leji promised to find out what he could in Beijing that might be used to discredit Man. While he was doing that, I tried to persuade other gangs to join with us and together fight off any aggression. At that point my old enemy Wu, from Tai Wai New Village, re-entered my life, determined once again to impose his presence in Fanling. And, Gui-San, he decided the best way to do that was to send three men to kill me." Uncle could hear his voice tremble. He reached for his cigarettes, lit one, and walked over to the worship hall entrance to smoke it. When his emotions had steadied, he returned to the stool.

"I hope that didn't alarm you," he continued. "Perhaps I shouldn't have mentioned it, but I keep no secrets from you. This is the first time I've thought about it since it happened, and I didn't expect to get so emotional. In all the years I've been a triad, I've never violated the Thirty-Six Oaths, and the idea that a brother would violate the most sacred of those oaths shakes me to the core. Obviously Wu didn't succeed. A few days before, Wang had insisted that I accept a body-guard. I resisted the idea but eventually gave in to help save a young man's membership in our gang. Then that young man saved my life. What hand lay behind that twist of fate?

"Ironically, Wu's attack had the opposite result of what he'd intended. We retaliated and did tremendous damage to his gang's drug business, with only one loss of life. And his attack convinced more Mountain Masters that we needed to form a coalition committed to protecting each other. I said 'Attack one of us and you attack us all' so many times as I tried to persuade gangs to join us that I would wake up in the middle of the night with those words on my lips. Anyway, enough gangs expressed interest in my idea that we held a meeting to talk it through. We didn't ask them to commit there and then, but to come back in a week with an answer. What a week that became!

"It started when Man made a move to take over Tsuen Wan. Even though my idea of a coalition was still up for discussion, I decided to try putting it into action. I reached out to two Mountain Masters who I knew supported the concept and enlisted their aid. Our three gangs put together a small army that, with Tsuen Wan's approval, joined with their men to beat back Man. Chow, the Tsuen Wan Mountain Master, had been opposed to the idea of an alliance. After our victory he changed his mind and became an ardent supporter. And others who had been uncertain came on board as well. By mid-week we had virtually every gang in the Territories with us and — just as satisfying — there were indications that Zhao from Kowloon and maybe some gangs from Hong Kong Island would join.

"I have to say, Gui-San, that I was feeling very pleased with myself. If the week had ended there, I would already have considered it a success. But then I went to meet with Liu Leji in Shenzhen, and it took a turn I hadn't anticipated. Good friend that he is, Leji had been trying to find something definite that I could use to discredit Man's claim about the Communists' plans after the handover. I thought the meeting would be about that, but there was so much more."

Uncle smiled at Gui-San's photo, and for a second he thought she smiled back. "The Chinese government wants us to partner with them," he said, his smile broadening. "They have promised not to interfere with any of our activities in Hong Kong and are going to let us expand our operations in China into four new cities. In exchange, we'll be their men on the ground in Hong Kong. If that's confusing, let me explain. The handover agreement explicitly prohibits them from having a military or police presence in Hong Kong until 2047. But there are things they want to do, and returning convicted criminals to China to carry out their sentences is one.

"Over the past three weeks we've sent ten men over the border to face Chinese justice. I have to confess I'm not completely comfortable with the idea. There was one man, for example, who hadn't been convicted of anything and was carrying a U.S. passport. His crime seemed to have been getting involved in a financial dispute with a company that has ties to a senior member of the Communist Party. We picked him up and sent him over the border anyway. It was a signal to Beijing that we would honour our agreement, no matter what. Two days later they told us in which four cities we could start operating, and gave us the names of the local officials who would work with us. From our side, figuring out which gang gets to operate in which city is going to be tricky. I'm going to be doing a lot of consulting before I make a decision . . . Did you notice that I said I'll be making the decision? That's the other thing that's happened, Gui-San."

Uncle stood up and moved closer to the niche so her face was directly in front of his. "The gangs formed the alliance I wanted and then went a step further. The Communists wanted me to be the contact they deal with in Hong Kong. I thought that would be an issue with my colleagues, but my friend Fong had been lobbying for days for the creation of an

Executive Council with certain limited powers. The gangs not only agreed to it, they elected me chairman and gave me sole authority to make some decisions. I'm honoured and flattered, but it does pose a few challenging questions. One I've been asking myself is, can I continue to function as Mountain Master in Fanling and also adequately perform the role of chairman of the triad societies? Maybe I can delegate some of my day-to-day duties in Fanling to my deputy or the White Paper Fan, but that still leaves open the potential for conflict of interest. The chairman can't be biased; he can't play favourites. And in both those cases, perception is as important as the reality. I have to be *seen* as impartial, as making decisions that are based on facts and are in the best interests of the entire triad community."

Uncle looked into Gui-San's eyes and began to feel calmer. He stood there quietly as the questions in his head began to sort themselves out. After a few minutes he kissed the tips of his fingers, pressed them against her lips, and said, "There, you've helped me again. I knew you would. The next time I visit, it will be as Chairman of the Hong Kong Triad Societies."

Uncle moved the urn into the middle of the niche, picked up the stool and bag, and left the worship hall feeling completely at peace. His life was about to change again, but as long as he had Gui-San and his brothers, there was nothing to fear.

ACKNOWLEDGEMENTS

When I first presented my storylines for the Uncle trilogy, this particular plot was one of them. At the time, the idea that the Hong Kong triads and the Chinese Communist Government were or would become partners was — I thought — a bit far-fetched, but current events and the history I came across overtook what had started out as a fictional what-if.

History took the form of Tao Siju, who was the Minister of Public Security for the People's Republic of China between 1990 and 1998. As I researched possible ties between the Hong Kong triads and the government in Beijing, his name appeared in a surprising way. During a trip to Hong Kong in 1993, Tao Siju held a news conference during which he spoke openly about Hong Kong's triads. He admitted, among other things, that the government in Beijing had and maintained links to the triads. The quote on page 287 of this book states his actual words, which were spoken at that conference. In my opinion, it seems obvious the People's Republic of China and the Heaven and Earth Society in Hong Kong did strike a deal and became partners.

That partnership became evident during the recent pro-democracy demonstrations in Hong Kong. Given the conditions of the handover agreement, the Chinese could not intervene militarily and left it to the Hong Kong police to manage the protests. But as the police struggled to contain them, it was reported that groups of "citizens" had taken it upon themselves to attack the protesters. Several media outlets suggested that the "citizens" were triads acting on behalf of Beijing as a paramilitary force. What Uncle sensed might happen, had come to pass.

Plots in several previous Ava Lee and Uncle books mixed fact and fiction, and sometimes foreshadowed real events, but never in a way that caused me distress. This plot was different. Given the empathy I have for the current situation of the citizenry of Hong Kong, I actually struggled to continue with it. Whenever I did, I asked myself this question: Would Uncle have gone ahead with the deal he negotiated if he had known the consequences twenty-five years later? I believed the answer was no, and pressed ahead. Still, the story may not be finished. I was supposed to write only three novels in the Uncle series, but now I feel compelled to continue. I am anxious to discover, for example, the actual state of Uncle's life when he first encountered Ava, and to learn what emotions she unleashed in him. Equally, I am drawn to the final months of his life. We have seen them through Ava's eyes, but I want to see them through Uncle's. What did he take pride in accomplishing? What did he regret? Did he rue his agreement with Tao Siju? So there could be a fourth book, and maybe even a fifth. Stay tuned.

Now to my thanks.

My editor, Doug Richmond, once again did a masterful

job. Doug is precise, not heavy-handed, and he has excellent instincts. As always, he made this a better book. What more can you ask of an editor?

And once that work has been improved, who better to see it through to completion than Maria Golikova, the managing editor at House of Anansi? Thank you, Maria.

In addition to my wife, Lorraine, I am blessed with a team of first readers who generously give me their time and their expertise. I have met only some of them personally, but feel I know them all. Many thanks to Catherine Rosebrugh, Kristine Wookey, Carol Shetler, John Kruithof, Lam Lau, and Ashok Ramchandani.

Lastly, I want to say thank you to the many readers who reach out to me via email and other ways. Your messages have brightened some dreary days, and they have often encouraged me to keep writing. So please don't hesitate to let me know what you think of this book or any of the others. You can reach me through my web site, www.ianhamiltonbooks.com.

IAN HAMILTON is the author of thirteen novels in the Ava Lee series and three in the Lost Decades of Uncle Chow Tung series. His books have been shortlisted for numerous prizes, including the Arthur Ellis Award, the Barry Award, and the Lambda Literary Prize, and are national bestsellers. BBC Culture named Hamilton one of the ten mystery/crime writers from the last thirty years that should be on your bookshelf. The Ava Lee series is being adapted for television.

NOW AVAILABLE
from House of Anansi Press

The Ava Lee series

Prequel and Book 1 — THE WATER RAT OF WANCHAI — AN AVA LEE NOVEL — IAN HAMILTON

Book 2 — AN AVA LEE NOVEL — THE DISCIPLE OF LAS VEGAS — IAN HAMILTON

Book 3 — AN AVA LEE NOVEL — THE WILD BEASTS OF WUHAN — IAN HAMILTON

Book 4 — AN AVA LEE NOVEL — THE RED POLE OF MACAU — IAN HAMILTON

Book 5 — THE SCOTTISH BANKER OF SURABAYA — AN AVA LEE NOVEL — IAN HAMILTON

Book 6 — THE TWO SISTERS OF BORNEO — AN AVA LEE NOVEL — IAN HAMILTON

Book 7 — THE KING OF SHANGHAI — AN AVA LEE NOVEL — THE TRIAD YEARS — IAN HAMILTON

Book 8 — THE PRINCELING OF NANJING — AN AVA LEE NOVEL — THE TRIAD YEARS — IAN HAMILTON

Book 9 — IAN HAMILTON — THE COUTURIER OF MILAN

Book 10 — THE IMAM OF TAWI-TAWI — AN AVA LEE NOVEL — THE TRIAD YEARS — IAN HAMILTON

Book 11 — THE GODDESS OF YANTAI — AN AVA LEE NOVEL — THE TRIAD YEARS — IAN HAMILTON

Book 12 — IAN HAMILTON — THE MOUNTAIN MASTER OF SHA TIN

Book 13 — THE DIAMOND QUEEN OF SINGAPORE — AN AVA LEE NOVEL — THE TRIAD YEARS — IAN HAMILTON

www.houseofanansi.com • www.facebook.com/avaleenovels
www.ianhamiltonbooks.com • www.twitter.com/avaleebooks

ALSO AVAILABLE
from House of Anansi Press

Uncle returns in...
The Lost Decades of Uncle Chow Tung

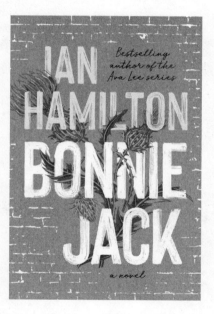